HE HAD IT COMING!

BRIAN LYNCH

*Who helped her murder and why
did an innocent man confess to it?*

For

Ellis Lynch

CONTENTS

INTRODUCTION

'May you rot in hell'

It was already light as the man made his way slowly and uneasily along the corridor. The morning sun was still low in the Eastern sky but shining strongly enough through the windows to make him shade his eyes with his hand.

Outside the windows, the wakening birds flitted about in the trees and on rooftops announcing the arrival of a new day - their combined chatter the summertime choral symphony of nature that always greets the dawn. On the dew-wet grass beneath them families of rabbits were emerging warily from their beds for an early breakfast, their mothers nibbling cautiously as they kept watch for foxes and other dangers while the younger members of their brood played.

It was the same level of uncertainty that was making the man in the corridor, worried whether leaving his post was the right thing to do, hesitant. He'd experienced the wrath of his superior for that before, but the silence and the lack of any signs of activity along that long passage was not normal and was making him a little bolder. As he moved slowly towards it the door at the far end he was staring at remained tightly and reassuringly shut.

At this time on a Sunday morning that was definitely not normal and that emboldened him the close he got to it. Yet even as he did get closer he still half expected it to be thrown open and for its occupant to emerge, angrily demanding to know why he was there instead on his ward.

But as he reached it still nothing stirred and there was no sound, apart from the din in the trees outside, but even that seemed to fade into the background as his mind played tricks with his imagination. It was forgotten as the heavy silence that seemed to get more menacing by the second took control of his mind. Nervously and still worried about getting a bad tempered reaction, he tapped nervously on the door There was still no sound from inside so, taking a deep breath, he gripped the handle and turned it pushing the door open just far enough for him to peer inside.

Seated at the table in the centre of the room, head cradled on his arms as though sound asleep, was the man he'd been so worried about. He coughed, loudly to waken him and attract his attention but the man never moved and for a second or two he stared at the scene before moving into the room. Even then the figure at the desk never stirred – something was clearly wrong and that set his visitor's nerves jangling even more.

Coughing even louder in a ridiculously needless final attempt to make his presence known he entered the room, but there was still no reaction from the apparently sleeping man at the desk. No movement - just an ominous silence along with a slightly chemical odour he couldn't identify hanging in the air of the windowless room.

Suddenly the instincts and experiences of a man who had seen so much death and horror in the trenches of the Great War kicked in. Now suddenly more confident he moved to the table and lifted the man's head up by the hair. He jerked it violently upwards so he could see the expressionless face and what he saw told him everything.

Dropping it deliberately heavily back down into the man's arms, he stood and thought for a moment before picking up the telephone on the desk. Still staring down at the dead man he rattled the cradle up and down to alert the night operator. A bleary voice finally responded, and he told the operator there was an emergency and to wake up the Hospital Director and get him down to the night superintendent's office fast.

Then, braver now as he waited for Dr Byron to arrive, he stared down at the dead man and suddenly his face twisted into a satisfied, almost triumphal grin.

'Johnson, you lying vicious bastard, you had it coming. May you sodding rot in hell' he jeered

HE'S DEAD

'I'm afraid we have some bad news'

Fred Johnson looked up from his evening paper and grunted his thanks as his wife came into the tiny kitchen to lay the greaseproof paper wrapped packet on the table by his hand.

'Yeah, thanks Em, - they should get me through the night. What's in em?' he asked as he drained his big china mug, knowing full well that they would be cheese and pickle with a piece of her apple pie thrown in for good measure. He stared briefly at the arrangement of tea leaves in the bottom before standing up and stretching his legs to relieve them of the twinges of cramp brought on by sitting down for too long.

There are those who claim to be able to tell the future by examining tea dregs but, perhaps sadly as things would turn out that night, the burly ex-soldier was not so gifted. It was just an old habit picked up during his days in the trenches when almost any hint of coming good fortune was eagerly sought by desperate men.

'D'ya know what Em, I think I'm getting too old for this lark' he growled, as she helped him on with his jacket before he went through his regular 'Daddies off to work' routine. After passing his fingers through her long black hair he gave her a quick and meaningless kiss on the lips before cuddling both children and offering his own cheek to them for a wet slobbery return kiss. Then, thrusting the sandwiches into his coat pocket and with them all following him down the passage to the front door, he left the house and walked away.

Emma, her tired face showing no signs of emotion at her husband's departure, stood at the door with little Freddie in her arms and Sarah gripping her skirt with one hand as she waved her daddy goodbye with the other. They watched him stride away up the hill past the railway station towards the 'asylum' and his night shift. She knew he'd be calling into the Essex Arms first but she didn't mind that. In fact she rather welcomed the fact that he'd be having a few pints before going to work, rather than on his way home as he'd done when he'd been working days.

She had what he'd always told her was an irritating habit of rubbing her tongue against the inside of her cheek when she was thinking. As she watched Johnson disappearing up the road on that warm July evening, the vigorous movement inside her mouth showed that at that moment she was clearly thinking very hard indeed. She didn't actually hate Fred, but it was always a relief when he left the house to go to work and she certainly never begrudged him a couple of beers before work.

Johnson was a 'man's man', very much of his time with very firm ideas on a woman's place in the home and in society generally, so there was never very much real passion in the marriage. But he'd given Emma and their children stability - providing them with a home and the cloak of 'poor but honest' dignified working class respectability. There were many a great deal worse off in those days and she was suitably grateful for that at least.

In 1934 the hungry years of unemployment and the depression were still very fresh in people's minds so that level of modest comfort and security meant a great deal and particularly in a world where women were still struggling to achieve social equality. Emma had actually met her husband in the Essex Arms, where she'd been serving behind the bar and had been flattered by his attention. A former soldier who liked to show off his military bearing, he was a handsome thick-set man with a bushy moustache and self-confidence that seemed to attract women. More importantly he had a steady job at the asylum so Emma had been only too happy to marry him and bear his children, but it had not been an easy relationship.

His petulant fits of temper had shown him to be a bully, not shy of using his fists even on her. Even sober he was often short-tempered and demanding, but when he lurched out of the pub with a belly full of best bitter inside him he could be a very violent husband too. To be fair he was never brutal with the children, who in his way he genuinely loved, but Fred Johnson never left anyone and Emma in particular in any doubt about who was head of the family.

Married or not he had retained his eye for the ladies and whenever an extra-marital opportunity presented itself would never hesitate - a freedom of course that he would never allow Emma. Just as he knew, and enforced, his dominance in the home she knew her place there too and was suitably submissive.

As far as the sexes were concerned the Great War had emasculated Europe. On both sides men who had survived its horrors had emerged to find a world full of women desperate to find a man. England had been no different and there has probably never been a period when so many single women were searching for prospective husbands. All too often, when the opportunities arose neither gender had many scruples about respecting the sanctity of marriage, and Fred Johnson was no exception.

As a young soldier he'd sowed many a wild oat and in civilian life having a wife and family had not changed him as far as his own promiscuity was concerned. He was a serial seducer who once his interest, and lust, was aroused could be very charming and who regarded any woman, married or single, as fair game. In the then attractive little raven-haired barmaid, prepared to put up with his lifestyle and bear his children, he guessed he'd found a woman to give him all the comforts of home without too many restraints on that lifestyle so he'd married her.

Domestically things had improved a little for Emma after Fred had been promoted to be the hospital's head night superintendent, but only because he was now working most nights instead of spending his evenings in the 'Essex Arms'. He was earning a few pounds a week more of course, but the pub's landlord and his frequent girl friends had seen more of that than Emma and the children had. Despite keeping her short of cash for housekeeping, he still expected the lion's share of whatever happened to be in their tiny larder and often complained, blaming her, about the meagre lack of choice.

That evening, as she watched him vanish from sight in the gathering gloom, so many thoughts were ploughing through Emma's mind; but they were quickly brushed away as her maternal role took over. It was time to get little Freddie and Sarah bathed and ready for bed, so she closed the door and began to be a mum again.

· · · · · ·

Early the following morning Emma was wakened from what had been a fitful night's sleep by a frantic banging downstairs on the front door. She yawned blearily and stretched before reaching for her dressing gown, glancing at the bedside clock as she started to put it on. It showed that it was almost eight-o-clock and as if to confirm that, she could hear the 7.58 non-stop to Liverpool Street puffing through the station, a few hundred yards away.

Quickly she checked the children to make sure they were still sleeping soundly before, still half asleep, making her way down the stairs to the door. On the step outside were two tall men – one of them being vaguely familiar, though for the moment she couldn't place him.

'Good morning, Mrs Johnson – sorry to wake you so early but may we come in?' he asked. As he spoke she remembered who he was and, nodding her recognition, opened the door wider to let them in. Automatically adjusting her dressing gown to ensure modesty, she led them into the kitchen before turning to face them and waiting for them to speak.

'Ma'am would you like to sit down? I'm afraid we have some bad news,' the first man said. Almost instinctively she obeyed the invitation and sat down at the table before looking up at him.

'You're Dr Byron, aren't you? She queried.

'Er yes that's right Mrs Johnson, Dr Richard Byron and I'm the Director of the Mental Hospital. This is Detective Sergeant Wilkins of Brentwood Police' he added indicating his companion. 'Look ma'am, I am afraid what we have to tell you is the worst possible news and there is no easy way to say it'.

He paused to stare closely at her before continuing, almost stumbling over his words as he spoke. 'The fact is, well I'm very sorry to have to tell you that early this morning your husband, Mr Frederick Johnson, was found in his office in the hospital by other members of the night-staff. I'm afraid he was dead,' he added sympathetically.

Byron put his hand out to steady Emma as she moved to stand up to react to the shock of what he'd told her. At the last moment she seemed to remember that the children were still asleep upstairs and with her right hand she muffled the scream that had been gathering in her throat.

'Dead? What do you mean dead? How? He can't be. Who found him? What happened? Are you sure?' In her shock a thousand pointless questions formed in her mouth but she could only stammer out a disjointed and panicky few, in tones that bordered on hysteria. Now for the first time the policeman spoke, gently, his voice equally as full of sympathy for the distraught young woman as his companion's had been.

'Mrs Johnson. I am very sorry but what Dr Byron said is true. Your husband was found dead at his desk shortly after 6-o-clock this morning. We can't say too much at the moment about how he died, but can you think of any reason as to whether or not your husband might want to take his own life?' Emma's eyes widened in shock at the idea and the policeman put his hand on hers and moved quickly on to reassure her.

'Nothing is certain yet of course and a lot of tests and enquiries are already being made, but there has been a suggestion that he might have killed himself,' he told her.

'What? Fred kill himself? Don't be ridiculous! He would never leave me and the children like that. How did he die?' Still visibly shocked she scoffed at the idea that her husband would take his own life. The policeman patted her shoulder comfortingly.

'Well, as I said, a lot of tests are still being made but it does look as if he may have swallowed a very strong and powerful disinfectant,' he said. Emma's eyes widened even more and the policeman paused to let the thought sink in before continuing.

'If he did that willingly it could suggest that he would have been an extremely desperate man because there are less painful ways of killing yourself. At this stage we are simply looking for possible reasons to establish how desperate he could have been and if so why', Wilkins explained.

While Wilkins had been speaking Dr Byron had been watching Emma closely with a great deal of concern evident on his face. Now he intervened to spare her further distress.

'I think that's enough for now, Sergeant. I don't think we need to go further at this time. Mrs Johnson, is there anyone we can call to be with you? A neighbour perhaps or a relative? Is there anything we can do - anyone we can contact for you? Needless to say if the hospital can help with money or anything, all you have to do is ask,' he added gently.

Emma, still evidently in shock, shook her head. 'No, no thank you, sir! You're both being very kind, but I think I need to be alone for a while to get myself together before I get my children up and dressed. I have to find a way of telling them their daddy won't be coming home, but thank you so much for your kindness' she replied

Now seeming to be more in control of herself, she stood to show her visitors out assuring them she would be fine, though understandably her mind did seem to be elsewhere. As she closed the door behind them she stood with her back to it for a moment, reflecting on what she'd just been told, and wondering what the future would now hold for her and the children.

Then, as the full import of what she'd been told began to sink in, the merest hint of a grin started to flicker around her mouth. Gaining in strength and mobility it began to spread across her face, her lips widening into a huge smile that lit up her face and gave an added sparkle to her eyes.

A movement from upstairs told her that young Freddie was awake and it brought her back to reality. Reminded of her responsibility to her baby, she began to run up the stairs to quieten him before he woke his sister too.

• • • • • •

John Hamilton looked up from his desk as a wet and soggy figure pushed its way into his newsroom. Sourly he peered at it from beneath the green eyeshade (the editor's traditional 'badge of office' in those days), clamped across his forehead and scowled in the direction of the newcomer. Outside the window the rain was still beating heavily on the glass and there had been more than a hint of thunder in the air that morning, none of which had done a lot to improve his temper.

'Morning, Hart. Nice of you to look in' he sneered unkindly, as the reporter took off his hat and tossed it onto his desk before starting to take his coat off.

'Yes, sorry about that sir. That bike is always pretty

hard going in this sort of weather and to make things worse the chain came off in the High Street this morning. Can I make you a cup of tea?' Cyril Hart offered apologetically as he moved towards the kettle in the corner of the room.

Hamilton shook his head impatiently and held up his hand to stop him. 'No, no and you haven't got time for that either. You've got a story to follow up, so keep your bike-clips on and put your coat back on'.

Hart stopped in his tracks and, inwardly furious, turned back reluctantly towards his desk. He'd been looking forward to a few quiet moments to dry off and enjoy a quick cuppa before settling down to start writing that week's issue. His shoulders sagged in muted frustration and weary resignation as he waited for his boss to explain.

'Right, I want you to get down to the asylum and find out who died there over the weekend. I was tipped off in church yesterday that someone had popped his clogs, so go down there and find out more'.

'Yes sir. Probably one of the loonies I suppose. They're always chucking themselves onto the railway line, or hanging around swinging from a rafter in the hospital somewhere' Hart joked, cynicism getting the better of compassion. He was resigned to going back out into rain and was clearly unhappy at the prospect.

Hamilton was unimpressed. 'Do you think I'd send you out just for that kind of story? It may not have been an inmate and let's not forget what happened down there a few years back when the hospitals director topped himself. That dear boy is why you are going down there to get the story. You might as well check it out with the rozzers at the same time,' the editor said. Then he looked up and glared at the reporter even harder.

'Look, this might be a good front lead so if you can beef it up a bit all the better. All I know is that after the service in church last night the vicar tipped me off that he'd heard something had happened to a member of staff in the asylum, though he wasn't certain who it was or what had happened. So get down there and see if it stands up and if it does get the bloody story' he added impatiently.

Hart glanced across the newsroom towards the window to see what was happening outside. The rain was still beating a vicious staccato rhythm on the glass before running down the panes in rivulets to drip off the wooden frame to make their way down to the drenched pavement.

There had been many times since coming to Brentwood's Time when he'd felt like chucking the whole thing in and this was very clearly one of those moments. The problem was that, even by the post depression mid-thirties, jobs on local newspapers were not always easy to come by. Even more, working with the 'three P's' – pad, pencil and pushbike – was better than the dole queue, getting dirty hands digging ditches for the local council, or slaving away on the car assembly lines a few miles away in Dagenham. There was another thing in its favour too.

Although he would never admit it, there was the buzz any journalist gets from seeing a story he wrote, actually in print. It gets to be an even bigger one when it's under his by-line as well, though in Brentwood's Time editor Hamilton was never over generous with them it if wasn't his own.

Hart suddenly became aware that the editor was staring at him, clearly waiting for him to move so, shrugging his shoulders in resignation, he picked up his soggy and bedraggled hat. Ostentatiously giving it a vigorous shake he put it back on his head, picked up his note pad and managed to waste a few more moments sharpening his pencil. He felt, rather than saw, Hamilton's steely eyes boring into his back as he left the newsroom to make his way slowly back down the stairs and out into the street again. There, the leather of its saddle gleaming wet in the rain, his padlocked bicycle still leaned against the wall where he'd left it only minutes earlier.

Thankfully, as he prepared to get back onto it, the intensity of the rain seemed to ease off a little. Then as he pedalled back out into the High Street it had stopped completely and the clouds began to clear. There was even a hint of sunshine appearing to be trying to break through. By the time he'd struggled up the hill towards the asylum he was even beginning to feel warm and even the road was starting to dry out in the very welcome warmth of the morning sun.

Locally it was still called the 'asylum' even though, after the war its name had been changed from the Essex County Lunatic Asylum to the more appropriate title of the Brentwood Mental Hospital. A massive Victorian Gothic building standing in five acres of sprawling countryside, when it was first opened in 1850 it had been regarded, even up to the early part of the 20th century, as little better than 'the workhouse'. It was typical of its times – an institution where apart from those with genuine mental problems, people whose abilities or position did not allow them to cope with society's demands were often confined, sometimes for life and not always legally.

During and after the war it had been one of the hospitals up and down the land where 'shell shocked' soldiers – the ones who had survived the allegations of cowardice and the firing squad – were sent to try to rebuild shattered minds. Under its more enlightened status as a Mental Hospital, it still held hundreds of patients who were spoken of as 'inmates'. An official change of name does not necessarily change the way such grim places were perceived locally, where they were still invariably seen and disparagingly spoken of as 'the asylum'.

As Hart pedalled his bike through the big iron gates on Warley Hill and up to the huge main door of the hospital, the warmth of the mid-morning sun was making things feel much more pleasant, though his clothes were still very damp. Padlocking the bike to the cycle rack by the main door he was certainly feeling a great deal better and more comfortable than he had been when he'd left the office ten minutes earlier.

He pushed through the heavy doors to find himself in the big high-ceilinged raftered hall that served as the main reception area. 'Can I help you?' the lady polishing her nails at the reception desk asked as he approached, banging his still sodden hat against his side to try and knock the rain out of it.

'Yes – I'd like to talk to Dr Byron please. My name is Cyril Hart and I am a reporter with Brentwood's Time. Dr Byron does know me,' he lied.

'Well, I'm afraid Dr Byron is very busy right now. Can anyone else help?' she asked without stopping work on her nails.

'Well, yes – perhaps the Deputy Director, Dr Abbott?'

'Sorry, I'm afraid he's tied up too.'

'Well, just who can I talk to? You had someone die in this place over the weekend and I just need to speak to someone about it for the newspaper.' Hart, still a little annoyed at even having to be there anyway, was fishing for reaction. To his joy the receptionist's face broke into a smile.

'Well, why didn't you say so? That's why they are all so busy this morning. They're with the police about it at the moment. Really sad about old Fred though and poor Mrs Johnson - they had two kiddies, you know.'

'Mrs Johnson?' Hart didn't know the person but he now knew a name and his instincts told him that such a casual reference to tragedy and the police was relevant. It indicated that Hamilton had been right and that there could be more to this story than the untimely death of an inmate. This was clearly the sudden death of a member of staff, and the police were involved, so he continued to listen without interrupting her flow of information.

'Yes, Fred's wife. They lived down near the station.' His garrulous informant was chatting away now, gossiping about things she should never have been. Without fully realising it she'd told him the dead person's name, marital and parental status and even where he'd lived. Hart began to realise his instincts had been right and that he needed to be careful in phrasing his questions now for fear of her realising she shouldn't be talking to him.

'Yes, it must have hit her very hard. What was old Fred's job these days?' he asked, suggesting a familiarity with the deceased man that didn't actually exist of course.

'Oh, he was the Head Night Superintendent. I know some people never liked him much but I always got on well with him – well, he was a bit of a charmer, you know. In any case nobody deserves to die like that, do they?' she said tantalisingly.

'No you're right, nobody does. Have they established what killed him yet then? I know they were investigating but I don't know how far they've got', the reporter continued to fish for information by setting out his bait of familiarity again.

'Well, all I know is that he is supposed to have drunk some bleach or something, but I thought Fred only ever drank best bitter,' she giggled at her sick joke. Suddenly she realised that she'd probably said too much.

'Look Mr Hart, that's all I can tell you. I will let Dr Byron know you are asking for him but I'm sure it won't be for a while yet. Look, please don't tell them I've been talking to you about this. I could get the sack if they find out,' she pleaded.

Hart grinned reassuringly. He knew exactly how to treat people who could well be useful in the future.

'No, no, of course I won't, love. Don't worry. I won't say a word to cause you any problem,' he reassured her. 'I will just sit down over there and wait for Dr Byron. Incidentally, where did you say Mrs Johnson lives?' He added.

'Gresham Road, and please don't ask me any more' she muttered, waving him away towards a chair on the opposite wall. Hart smiled his thanks and went over to it where he sat down on it. Pulling out his notepad he scribbled a few hasty notes on what he'd already learned before settling down to wait for the asylum's boss to turn up. There was no way he was leaving now until he'd spoken with Byron.

Opening the Daily Sketch he'd shoved into his jacket pocket before leaving the office that morning, he appeared to be engrossed in it. On the surface he appeared to be reading about Fred Perry performing miracles at Wimbledon over the weekend. In fact although he was looking at the newspaper he wasn't reading it, because he was busy trying to collect and control the thoughts whirling around in his brain.

Cyril Hart had been in newspapers long enough to know a good story when he saw one. This one suddenly held a lot of promise and he needed to work out how he was going to handle it so, while he appeared to be calmly reading the paper, he was actually deciding his tactics.

Most reporters worth their salt will acknowledge that they always approach a story with Kipling's 'six faithful serving men' in mind. The established principles of '*what, why, when, how, where* and *who*' that the great journalist had defined, form the basic skeleton of any newspaper story; but there is an even more important element to be achieved before they are even asked. Before you ask the questions, they need to be designed and asked in order to guarantee the right answers for the story. For any journalist it's crucial to get the answers that make sense of the story he wants to write.

As far as Cyril Hart was concerned a routine story that morning about the death of what he'd cynically assumed had been an inmate, had become a major one as soon as it had been confirmed that the victim had been a senior member of staff. As his editor had reminded him, a few years earlier Dr Byron, who'd been the Deputy Director at the time, had been appointed as the hospital's Director after his predecessor had allegedly turned a shotgun on himself following an apparent mental breakdown. Dr Harold Gillespie's death had led to a great deal of speculation at the time, but nothing more than suicide had ever been established so gradually the story had faded into the archives.

Hart had not been around at that time but now another staff member, albeit this time not as senior in the hospital, was dead. As he sat there mentally planning and writing his story, he knew what answers he needed to provoke and the kind of story he wanted to write; suddenly a voice broke into his thoughts.

'Cyril, good morning, fancy seeing you here today. I understand you want to see me.'

A slightly built man in his thirties, with a wispy 'Douglas Fairbanks' moustache quivering on his upper lip, was calling over to him from the receptionist's desk. Behind the Deputy Director, Hart could see her clearly pleading with him not to let her down and he smiled reassuringly. Outside the hospital he really did have a long friendship with Tom Abbott, so in a way he was pleased to see him rather than the Director.

'Hello Tom, yes please; either you or your boss. I would like a word if that's possible.'

'Mary can you get me a couple of cups of tea? I'm sure Cyril could use one and I certainly could' Abbott asked the receptionist, gesturing his visitor to walk with him along a corridor towards his office. The reporter nodded his thanks and, thrusting the newspaper into his pocket, joined his friend.

The two men walked side by side along the well scrubbed but grubby corridor towards Abbott's office. 'How's Jane?' Abbott asked conversationally as he opened the door to let Hart in.

'Yes, she's fine thanks Tom. Still working in the library - how about Susan and your youngster? Are they well?' The reporter was quite happy to make polite conversation. He and Abbott were both members of a local debating society called the Warley Parliament, and their families had socialised with each other on many occasions.

'Yes, they're both well. The school holidays start soon

and I am hoping we can get away for a week,' the Deputy Director responded, gesturing his friend to take a chair by his desk. He looked up as Mary came into the room carrying a tray with the two cups of tea and a plate with a few biscuits on it. One last pleading look as she put them down towards the reporter, who winked back reassuringly, and she was gone leaving the two men sipping their tea. Abbott spoke again.

'Ok Cyril, why have you really come here this morning?'

Hart smiled back across the desk at him. 'Oh, come on, Tom. You know very well why I'm here. You had a murder here over the weekend!' He had decided it was time to speculate really outrageously and was rewarded with a look of genuine shock passed across Abbott's face at the word.

'Murder? Whoever told you that? Yes it is true we've had an incident here over the weekend that the police are looking into and someone has died; but for God's sake, wherever did you get the idea it was murder?' he gasped.

Inwardly, the reporter smiled. Up to now his information had been largely based on hearsay and gossip – now for the first time, by tossing in the murder suggestion, he'd got an official admission that something out of the ordinary had indeed happened. He had an answer he could start to build his story on, but there was clearly more to come so he decided to stand his ground.

'Well, to be honest Tom, it was a tip-off my editor picked up in church yesterday. The way he heard it your Night Superintendent, a guy called Frederick Johnson, was murdered on Sunday morning' he lied, partly to protect his informant at the front desk but mainly to maintain his bluff about how much he really knew.

Abbott sat silently for a moment, clearly thinking about how to respond to a situation now clearly spiralling out of his control. Finally he made up his mind. He rose from his chair and, indicating for Hart to stay where he was, left the room.

The reporter listened to his friend's footsteps echoing up the corridor outside, and heard another door further along opening. A few minutes passed before he heard the footsteps coming back, but now there were more of them. The door swung open again and Abbott came back in, now accompanied by a tall well built man in his fifties with a distinct air of authority about him. Tom Abbott made the introductions.

'Cyril this is Dr Byron, the Director of the hospital. Doctor, this is Cyril Hart who works for the local paper. I've known him as a friend for a few years and I'm sure we can rely on him.'

Hart got to his feet to shake hands with the newcomer. He had seen him before but they'd never actually met although, because of the council meetings he had to write about from time to time, he did know his wife as a local councillor.

'Good morning doctor. Nice to meet you,' he exclaimed.

Byron gestured for him to sit and drew up another chair for himself to sit down with Abbott on the other side of the desk. 'I understand you want to know what happened here over the weekend', he smiled. Hart nodded, but waited for the Hospital Director to speak again before replying.

'Well let me get one thing straight right now, Mr Hart. Yes we did have a sudden death over the weekend and as you would expect the police are investigating the circumstances; but this was not murder. The man's name was Frederick Johnson, he was the senior member of my night staff and he may have committed suicide,' Byron paused, as if to emphasise the point, before continuing.

'This was not murder, I can assure you of that, but more than that at this stage I cannot say. As we have already pointed out, the matter is in the hands of the police. They are still investigating, so we would not like the wrong or any misleading information to get out before they have finished their enquiries.' As he finished, a new thought seemed to occur to him.

'Tell me Mr Hart. Do you have anything to do with the national newspapers? I mean do you have you any contacts or the like in Fleet Street?'

It was an odd question that seemed to imply that Byron was already more than a little concerned about the possibility of hordes of national newspaper journalists descending on the hospital, and not without reason.

A few months earlier Brentwood had been at the centre of a major national news 'scandal' when a local vicar had mysteriously vanished from a village along with his housekeeper. His butler, who it turned out later had been a fraudster with a police record, had also disappeared and there had been dark mutterings along with many rumours circulating in the town about the whole thing.

That mystery had been solved when it emerged that the almost bankrupt cleric in fact had had a nervous breakdown and had fled to Canada one step ahead of his creditors. The story had died a natural death, but it was clear that Byron was dreading the possibility that Fleet Street might come back in big numbers again if it sensed another story. His obvious unease actually strengthened Hart's growing belief that there was more to this story than he was being told and it would be prudent to hold out the possibility.

'Well it's true that they do rely on local newspapers to tip them off about stories, but a lot depends on their sensation value. Obviously 'murder in the asylum' is a much more emotive headline to sell newspapers than one of 'hospital suicide', he grinned teasingly before asking his next question. 'Why do you ask, sir?'

Byron, who'd flinched at the word 'asylum', thought for a moment before replying. 'Well, Mr Hart the answer to that lies in that very perception of what we do here and in the use of words like the one you have just used. Despite all our efforts to dispel the old image by changing names and modernising this kind of hospital and treatments for mental illness we are still seen locally as asylums; even worse, some people still even see them as being lunatic asylums.

'The truth is that these days we are becoming more and more recognised for what we really are - hospitals for people in need of psychiatric care and treatment for mental illness. We've made great strides in the diagnosis and treatment of it since the war, and here in Brentwood we've been at the forefront of that progress,' he paused for a moment to let the thought sink in before continuing.

'If a hospital like ours makes national headlines for the wrong reasons, headlines that that include the word 'asylum', it would put the public perception of our work back by years. For that reason alone we must do everything we can to play down any lurid aspects of this story and I am wondering whether you can help us do that,' he added.

Hart could hardly believe what he was hearing. Even as they had been speaking he'd been writing potentially one of the biggest stories that a local newspaper, or he as a journalist, might ever have in his mind. Yet here was an acknowledged pillar of the local community, married to an equally well respected local councillor, hinting that he should bury it - or at least the 'juicier' and more emotive bits of it.

Of course what Byron was telling him may well have been valid and well intentioned, but did that justify him suggesting a cover-up? The reporter stared back at him, trying to decipher what was going on behind the Director's equally impassive face. 'God, I'd hate to play poker with you mate' he thought to himself before replying.

'Well, to be honest doctor, it's not up to me? I am just the reporter and the best I can do is write the story up as factually as I am able to with the information I have. What happens to it after that and how he handles it, is really up to my editor. I know he values the freedom and integrity of the press a great deal and I don't really know how he would react to any suggestions of a cover up, but I have my doubts'.

Byron, having realised the implications of what he'd said, straightened up in his chair and flapped his hand. 'No, no, Mr Hart. Please don't get me wrong, I'm not asking you to cover anything up. I just want you to recognise that this does seem to be nothing more than the suicide of a good man who happened to work in a mental hospital although we don't yet know why. Mr Johnson had a nice family with young children too so, if only for their sake, I don't think making a big fuss before we know all the facts would help.'

Hart stood up, slipped his notepad into his jacket pocket and held out his hand to say goodbye. 'Dr Byron, of course I will respect that and I will pass your concerns on to my editor. Thank you for taking me into your confidence, and let me assure you that I will not be tipping Fleet Street off myself. However, I can't guarantee that in due course they won't pick up from our story' he assured the two men.

Not that he had the slightest intention of honouring that particular pledge - the dailies always paid good money for tip-offs, and sometimes bought the whole story. As he stood up to leave the room, Tom Abbott stood as well. 'I'll walk you out, Cyril,' he said

Silently the two men walked back along the corridor, both deep in thought and uncomfortable for different reasons - one worried, the other trying to conceal his excitement. They reached the main door and Abbott came out of the building with his friend and walked the few steps with him to the cycle rack. It was midday and the sunshine was now very warm - the storm of earlier that day a distant memory. Suddenly Abbott broke the silence between them.

'Tell me, Cyril. What do you really think?

'Well Tom, clearly it's a great story but like your boss just said, at the end of the day it's probably just a suicide - albeit a gruesome and pretty painful one by the sound of it,' Hart replied. He put the cycle clips around the bottom of his trousers again and unlocked the padlock holding his bike to the rack, as his friend stood silent.

Suddenly the hospital's Deputy Director took a deep breath, clearly trying to make up his mind about something. As his friend prepared to mount the cycle he put a restraining hand onto the journalist's arm. It had been very clear that he had something more on his mind and now he appeared to have come to a decision.

'Cyril look, we've been friends for a long time now and I trust you. I will deny this conversation ever took place if I am ever asked and nor would I want to be quoted on it. Whatever you may have heard here today, personally I think Fred Johnson was murdered,' he said.

HE WAS NOT A NICE MAN

'You knew him in the army, didn't you?'

Before the astonished journalist could react to Abbott's words, his friend spun on his heel and vanished swiftly through the big door back into the hospital. Hart, stunned for the moment, stood there his mind racing as he tried to put them into context.

Earlier that morning, when he'd tossed him the speculative line about Johnson having been murdered, Abbott's face had registered shock. Hart had assumed that had simply been a reaction to his 'fishing trip' but now he was really confused. A few minutes earlier the hospital's top man had been very clear, almost insistent, that Johnson had committed suicide. Now his deputy was confidentially suggesting that the Night Superintendent had indeed been murdered.

Suddenly the question of a potential 'asylum versus mental hospital' element of the story seemed almost irrelevant. The issue now was 'murder or suicide' and the big question was why the two top men in the hospital apparently had different views on the matter.

Deep in thought Hart unlocked the bike and, throwing his leg over it to sit on the saddle, he began to pedal slowly away down the long drive out of the hospital.

He was actually pretty unsure about where he was going at that moment. Hamilton had told him to check the story with the police before going back to the office, but things had changed. Now he felt it had to be the office to tell the editor what he'd learned before going down to the nick.

As he thrust down heavily on the pedals the bike chain came off its cog again, almost throwing him out of the saddle and onto the road. At least this time it wasn't raining and the delay as he up-ended the bike to push it back into position even gave him more time to think.

Pushing and sweating with the effort of pedalling up the long hill, he was breathless by the time he reached the High Street. Now he had to make the choice of going left for the police station or turning right for the office. He hesitated for only a second or two before swinging his handlebars right.

Hamilton, who was editing one of the regular weekly newspaper columns when he arrived, looked up as Hart came back into the newsroom. Thankfully he did seem to be in a better mood and even the hint of a smile crossed his face, though it did not linger. Hamilton was not a relaxed and happy man at the best of times and Monday, with the pressure of starting to put a new newspaper together, was never his best day.

'How did you get on? Is there a story there?' he snapped.

'Well you could say that sir, and yes I think there is which is why I felt I needed to talk to you before I go down to the cop shop', Hart replied.

Suddenly intrigued, Hamilton put his pencil down. 'Talk? What about?', he asked.

Hart smiled at having got his editor's full attention. 'It's curious, boss. As your tip-off said, a senior member of the night staff did pop his clogs over the weekend and you were right that it wasn't natural causes. The thing is there does seem to be a difference of opinion in the hospital on whether it was suicide or murder'.

Now he had Hamilton's undivided attention so, taking a deep breath, he launched into what he'd learned that morning.

'It seems that early on Sunday morning a man called Fred Johnson was found dead in his office. He was the head of night staff and the cause of death appears to have been that somehow he drank some bleach or disinfectant of some sort. Whether or not it was self-administered though seems to be pretty vague and depends on who you speak to. Dr Byron, the hospital's Director, seemed to be quite insistent that it was suicide but, speaking to me strictly off the record afterwards his deputy, who is a personal friend of mine, reckoned the geyser might have been murdered.'

'Bloody hell's bells!' The expletive was all that Hamilton could stutter for the moment. Like Hart he'd immediately spotted the story potential and he sat for a moment or two taking in what the reporter had told him. 'What do the police say about it?' he asked thoughtfully.

Hart shook his head. 'I haven't asked them yet sir. As I said I thought I'd better come back and talk to you about it first. Oh, there is one other thing - Dr Byron wants it kept as quiet as possible and local; he doesn't want Fleet Street nosing around'.

Hamilton grinned. 'I bet he doesn't - and neither do we until we've run our own story. These people don't like any hint of scandal at the best of times but until we've gone to press on Wednesday with our own story we keep it to ourselves, understand? You were right to come back here before going down to the police station. We need to think about this', he confirmed.

Hart had picked up the implied warning about him not tipping off the nationals. 'Yes sir, I appreciate that and there's one other thing. Byron doesn't want the word 'asylum' used in our story either. He kept reminding me that it was a mental hospital these days and they are trying to leave the old lunatic asylum image behind. He was quite insistent on the point actually.'

Hamilton grinned again. 'Yeah, well you just let me worry about that. You go out and talk to the coppers and then write up what you've got. While you're at it see if you can get anything from the widow as well' he added.

That was the intrusive part of the job that, like most journalists, Hart never relished. Clearly at some stage it had to be done but interrogating recently bereaved family members was never easy and talking to a grieving widow was really difficult at any time. In these circumstances it would be even more difficult.

'Yes sir, I will try and talk to her, but she only lost her husband yesterday and she may not welcome me just yet', Hart said. Hamilton waved his protests away

'Look I know that man, but try anyway and if you do get to talk with her, be gentle and sympathetic. I don't want the Time to be seen as insensitive – we are a family newspaper don't forget. If we upset her this early it could cause problems for us later so lets keep her on side - see if we can help etc,' he added, bringing a touch of hard-nosed newspaper realism to his instructions.

Hart knew there was no point in delaying things further so, picking up his notepad again, he got up to walk out of the newsroom and back downstairs to his waiting bicycle. At least it wasn't raining now and perhaps the police would put a more official slant to the story. It was just the thought of talking to the widow afterwards that was depressing him.

. . . . . .

Mary Olson looked up, straightened her back and wiped her brow as she heard her husband coming down the stairs. His appearance in their tiny kitchen so soon after going to bed, gave her the excuse she needed to stop rubbing the shirt she was cleaning on the washboard. Monday was washday and normally she was able to do all the boiling, scrubbing, wringing, mangling and pegging the clothes out on the washing line in their cramped garden, before he got up in the late afternoon.

He'd only been in bed a few hours after coming off his night shift that morning so his appearance gave her cause for concern. 'You alright, love? Can't you sleep? You haven't been in bed long and you're back on duty tonight. Whatever happened yesterday, you do still need your sleep. Can I get you a cuppa tea, or anything?' she offered.

Fred Olson nodded his thanks as he flopped down heavily onto the chair by the kitchen table. 'Aye thanks lass, that might help. To tell the truth, after what happened yesterday I haven't really been able to get any proper sleep. You'd think that after what I went through during the war I'd be used to the sight of death, but finding Johnson like that really hit me hard, Mary', he said gloomily. Despite having lived in Essex for almost fifteen years, whenever he got emotional his voice and accent still betrayed his northern roots. At that moment he was giving every indication of being close to the edge.

The woman's face softened as her eyes welled up a little. She put the soggy shirt down and came over to where her husband was slumped to put her arms around him. As she embraced him his own huge arms responded to her touch and stretched out to almost encircle her ample figure to hold her close. Her clothes were damp with the steam and she smelt strongly of soap flakes, but at that moment her touch and that perfume of domesticity was exactly the trigger he needed to unleash his emotions.

Her own eyes filled with tears of compassion as she hugged the big man she loved so much close to her. Physically he was so strong and masculine yet at that moment she could feel him sobbing silently in her arms. She held him close until she sensed his tears had subsided and that he was back in control of himself again. Mary Olson was a shrewd wife and would certainly not have embarrassed her man by letting him know he was crying like a woman.

As his arms loosened their grip around her waist, she drew back and kissed him affectionately. 'Let me put the kettle on love and I'll make you that cup of tea. Can I make you a sandwich as well?'

He smiled at her. 'Thanks sweetheart, yes that might help. Have you got any of that boiled ham we had for tea yesterday left?'

She got up, kissed him again and nodded that she had. Laundry forgotten for the moment, she began to bustle around her tiny domain, putting the kettle on and pulling the loaf from the breadbin and breadknife from its drawer.

'Fred, would it help to talk about it some more?' She asked, as she began to slice the bread.

'What more is there to say, love? I walked into his office because he hadn't been round to check up on us that morning, and there he was. His head was cushioned on his arms on the desk and at first I thought he was just having a nap. To be honest Mary it did cross my mind to leave him like that, so the day staff would come in and report him for sleeping on duty, but decided to wake him.

'But as soon as I shook him I realised it was more serious than a man just having a kip. I just couldn't wake him and his head started to flop around all kind of loose. I tell you Mary I saw many dead men during the war, especially on the Somme, but finding Fred Johnson like that was probably the biggest shock I ever had. God knows, he was not a nice man and we were never exactly the best of mates, but just the same...'

His voice tailed off as his mind revisited the scene that had faced him early that Sunday morning. It was one he'd been unable to purge from his mind, despite it having to compete with another vivid memory - of another morning long ago where Fred Johnson was also present.

'You knew him in the army, didn't you?' she said, handing him his ham sandwich as she tried to keep him talking while pouring the hot water into the kettle. Mary Olson had once been a psychiatric nurse at the hospital herself – it was where she and her husband had met – and she knew that getting patients to talk about their problems was a technique used by doctors dealing with mental illness.

He grimaced a little. 'Yes. Well vaguely. We were never drinking buddies or anything like that, but at one stage we were in the same unit and we did see some action on the Somme then but that's about all. He was a sergeant then so he was used to throwing his weight about and when I joined the night staff at the hospital he was still doing so. For some reason and I have no idea why, he seemed to resent me and took every opportunity he could to try to embarrass me. Perhaps he thought I knew something about his time in the army that he wished I didn't, but I can't think what that could have been,' he lied.

His wife was a little relieved to hear him unburdening himself because, just as she had hoped it might, it did seem to relax him a little. She smiled as she put his mug of tea on the table in front of him as he finished his sandwich.

'I never knew him when I worked in the hospital because I was always on days, but I met him and his wife in Brentwood High Street a few weeks ago,' she said. 'I think her name's Emma and she seemed quite nice, though a bit shy. He struck me as being a bit of a bully and I had the feeling she was a bit scared of him. I got the impression that he knocked her about and I didn't like him much. You're right, he was not a nice man, but don't they have a child as well?'

He nodded. 'Yes, they've got two actually. I seem to remember they had a little girl of about four or five, and a baby son too'.

'Poor little mites,' Mary said with concern. 'They will never know their father now. Fred, do you think I should go and see her, to see if there is anything we can do to help? I think they lived somewhere down by the railway station.'

He shook his head. 'No, best not, love! Not at this time at least. There will be enough people - family, neighbours, friends and the like - around her at this time. The last thing she might need is a visit from the wife of the man who actually found his body. There's also the point that now he's gone they might offer me his job and that could make things embarrassing as well,' he pointed out.

'Yes, perhaps you're right. I daresay they'll have a whip round for her at the hospital and you can put something into that for us. When the dust has settled after the funeral, perhaps then we can both go to see her,' she said, turning to plunge her hands and arms back into the steaming copper again.

Fred smiled. 'Aye, that's a better idea, Mary. That's what we'll do'. He gulped down the rest of his tea and stood up. 'I'll try and get some sleep for a few hours. Thanks lass!'

He leaned over to kiss her before turning to walk back to the foot of the stairs. As he slowly climbed them on his way back to the bedroom, he thought again how much he loved this woman he'd met and married at the hospital. She was so strong, so loving and full of life and, as she had just shown yet again, was always there for him when he needed her. She was as much in love with him as he was with her and she was the best reason he'd had since leaving the army for not going back to Yorkshire. He really hated himself for having to lie to her.

· · · · · ·

Olson tossed and turned as he tried desperately to get back to sleep again. He could hear Mary downstairs as she carried on with her wash-day routines, but memories of hell were still piercing through his fevered brain upstairs.

He remembered a bleak autumn morning in France, a firing squad and the terrified face of a childhood friend he'd had to tie to a post and blindfold. He saw again the impassive face of the sergeant who had organised the line of riflemen and, despite knowing of his relationship with the man about to be executed had insisted on his personal involvement. After all those years he could still feel the thud of the bullets as they found their target and tore poor Kenny's heart to shreds.

It had been almost twenty years since the slaughter on the Somme, but his memory of the events of that day were still as fresh as they had been every day since. His discovery of Johnson's body had stirred everything up in his mind about that morning again. He had never forgotten the explosions as firing pins hit cartridges, and could still see the image of their target slumping to one side while still held tightly to the post with the bonds he'd knotted.

The Great War went down in history as one of the biggest bloodbaths in military history, with thousands of men on both sides dying in the mud and confusion that the war came to represent. In one of them, the Somme offensive conjured up by General Haig in July 1916 went on over five months and a million British, French and German young men were killed or wounded - some crippled for life. History has it that they were sacrificed on an alter of military incompetence and tactics so outdated that even a horse-mounted cavalry regiment was put on standby, in the expectation it would be used once the advance had begun to succeed.

The irony of the Somme offensive was that it had been conceived simply as a diversionary attack, aimed at relieving the pressure on the French army at Verdun, close to Paris itself. Yet, on the first day of that battle alone, over 20,000 men perished while another 40,000 were wounded.

Many units, including those such as the 'Bradford Pals', were decimated and in some cases wiped out completely by the German machine gunners. They were cut down mercilessly as they carried out a suicidal 'fixed bayonets' advance over open ground along a 25-mile front. In the chaos and confusion caused by the pounding of the guns, followed by the whining and exploding of their shells, the shouting, screaming and the pall of smoke and smell of death that hung over everything, it was small wonder that so many men cracked.

Most of them were volunteers anyway, not professional soldiers. Young men who had been enthused and excited by Kitchener's famous call to arms, with its expectation of great adventure. By the time reality set in they were either dead or screaming in pain by the thousand on the killing fields of the Somme.

It took longer before it was generally accepted but even by 1914 the symptoms of what had been dismissed as 'shell shock' or cowardice were beginning to be recognised in medical circles as genuine psychiatric illnesses. Not, however, in some military minds where it was much simpler and politically expedient to call it cowardice and desertion. That brought the risk of a court martial with an almost inevitable 'shot at dawn' sentence – one intended more to discourage desertion than to treat mental illness.

The 'Great War' would see over 300 British soldiers facing the firing squad before its end and not until the start of the 21st century would such men be posthumously pardoned and forgiven.

It was just such a dreadful situation that had led to the execution of Kenny Thomas, the young foundry worker who had joined the Bradford Pals with his mate Fred Olson back in 1915. They weren't alone – over twenty other young men in their village had joined up that February - all keen to play their part in the great adventure. That was why the 'Pals battalions' had been formed in the first place. It seemed like a great idea on someone's part to make it easy for volunteers to feel they were among friends, rather than with strangers, when they joined up to fight for their country. They would fight, and often die, for their country together as comrades in arms.

The idea may have been well intentioned, but its results were catastrophic for so many small communities up and down the land. Huge casualty lists showed that many of them had lost the flower of their young men as a result of the concentration of 'Pals'. Fred Olson, Kenny Thomas, and so many of their friends and neighbours in their village just outside Bradford, had experienced the brutal realities of life in the trenches even before the Somme.

What happened during that action however had really brought home the full horrors of the Great War to these once enthusiastic young men. This was not the great adventure they had so patriotically signed up for; it was an unspeakable hell that their worse nightmares could never have imagined in their pre-war mundane peaceful lives.

The Bradford Pals had been among the early units to go 'over the top' on that dreadful first day of the Somme offensive. A heavy artillery attack had been designed to 'soften up' the Germans, but they had simply taken cover in well protected holes in the ground, emerging when the big guns had stopped to inflict mass slaughter. The advancing allied troops had been mown down by the field of withering and unforgiving fire the enemy machine gunners laid down to greet them. Fred and Kenny, with their friends and colleagues already collapsing around them, had been advancing with fixed bayonets when they each took their bullets.

Both had fallen - Kenny had been hit in the upper arm, while Fred had taken his in a leg. Neither wound was fatal but they'd had to lie where they'd fallen for hours before being carried back to a field station for first aid treatment, then being taken to hospital. After a couple of weeks of treatment, the hard pressed hospital doctors had passed both friends as fit and almost ready to back to the trenches again, well physically ready at least. Fred's leg wound had been a little more immobilising and he'd been held back in hospital for a further week. When he did finally rejoin his unit, he was horrified to find that Kenny was under arrest.

Broken by what he'd already suffered, his friend had refused go back into the line again and had been charged with cowardice. By the time Fred was back with his unit his friend had already been charged, convicted and sentenced to death. The military authorities, always determined to make a quick example to deter other possible deserters, ordered returnee Fred Olson to be one of the firing party.

The officer commanding the firing party had at least shown some compassion when he'd learned of Fred's relationship with the condemned man, but told him he still had to do his duty. While he'd relieved him of the responsibility of actually firing one of the rifles he ordered him to escort Kenny to the stake, tie him to it and blindfold him.

The terrified look on the face of his mate as he'd reluctantly and tearfully carried out his orders, had stayed with him ever since. So had the face of the sergeant in charge of the firing squad. Fred had not wanted his face to be the last one his poor terrified friend would ever see and he'd appealed to the sergeant organising the execution to let him off that duty too. He had been coldly reminded that he'd already had one concession by not being part of the firing party.

'Look Private, you've already got away with being one of the triggers because we've got a soft officer. If I had my way you would shoot the cowardly bastard yourself and be happy to do it, because he let you and your mates down, so just get on with it,' he told the distraught soldier.

That sergeant whose face, like that of Kenny's, he'd never been able to expunge from his mind, had been Sergeant Fred Johnson of the Essex Regiment.

· · · · · ·

The 'bobby' looked up as Hart came into the police station and walked up his desk.

'Hello Cyril! What are you doing here this morning?' He was well used to seeing the reporter on regular police calls and probably knew exactly why he was there, but felt he had to ask anyway.

'Hiya, Tom. How are you doing?' He let the policeman nod his satisfaction about his personal well-being before continuing. 'Look, who is looking into the suspicious death over the weekend in the asylum?'

PC Tom Harris grinned. 'Suspicious death? What are you talking about Cyril?'

'Oh, come off it Tom.' Hart snapped. 'We've known each other too long for silly games. We both know someone got topped down the loony bin over the weekend, so just tell me whose handling it and whether I can see him?'

The policeman relented.

'Detective Sergeant Wilkins is the man you want Cyril. Hang about a bit and I'll see if I can find him,' he said. Even as he spoke a tall rangy red-faced figure, a large bushy moustache overlapping his mouth, appeared out of one of the doors behind him, and Harris called him over.

'Sergeant, this is Cyril Hart. He works for the local rag Brentwood's Time, and he wants a word.'

The detective smiled and came over holding out his hand for Hart to take.

'Nice to meet you, Mr Hart. I was only transferred here from Chelmsford a few weeks ago, so I'm still getting to know people in and around the town. Tell me, what can I do for you?'

Cyril took the proffered hand and shook it warmly. 'Welcome to Brentwood Mr Wilkins, I think you'll find it a nice friendly little town. Now, I understand you are looking into the death over the weekend of Fred Johnson down at the mental hospital and I'd like to talk to you about that if I may.'

Wilkins stared hard and thoughtfully at the journalist for a moment, then smiled and gestured for him to follow him back into the room he'd just come out of and what was clearly the CID office. Pointing to a chair for his visitor Wilkins went behind the desk and sat down. He leaned forward to offer the reporter a cigarette from a packet that lay on the desk and, after Hart refused saying he didn't smoke, took one himself and lit up before speaking.

'Look Mr Hart, can I call you Cyril by the way? I have been a copper now for over ten years in Chelmsford and I have always valued the co-operation we get from the local press. I always do my best to return that in good measure, because I believe working together helps both of us do our jobs properly. My first name is Albert by the way. That said, tell me what you know so far about Mr Johnson and what happened to him'.

It was clear that the policeman wasn't going to reveal more than he had to so Hart realised he had to play a similar game, using his own cards just as sparingly.

'Well to start with, I could not agree more about our being able to help each other and I look forward to working with you. I'm sure I speak for my editor as well when I wish you well here in Brentwood. Now as I understand it, early yesterday morning Fred Johnson, who was the Night Superintendent down at the hospital, was found dead in suspicious circumstances. I suppose you can confirm that. I have spoken to Dr Byron and his deputy by the way and they did give me some details. In fact Byron was hinting about suicide,' he said reassuringly before sitting back to wait for a reply.

The policeman thought for a moment, drawing heavily on the cigarette and staring at Hart through narrowing eyes. He was clearly summing the journalist up before replying and suddenly came to a decision.

'Yes. I can confirm that Fred Johnson, a 45-year old senior staff member at the Brentwood Mental Hospital, was found dead in his office early on Sunday morning by another member of the night staff. At the moment investigations are at an early stage with forensic examinations and an autopsy being carried out. Much more than that at this stage, I cannot really tell you', he said.

'Well, do you know yet what it was that actually killed him? I was told that he swallowed some hydrochloric acid, which I suppose is fairly easy to find in a hospital', Hart lied about the acid and got exactly the reaction he'd been hoping for with the bait.

'Hydrochloric acid? Good God, no! What he apparently did drink was bad enough, but it certainly wasn't that. No, we think he drank some Lysol which is a strong disinfectant hospitals use quite a lot for cleaning purposes. Although it is being analysed as we speak, I am pretty sure it's that what killed him.'

Hart looked startled. 'Lysol? That's acid as well, isn't it?'

'Well, no. Not exactly, and certainly not the same kind of acid you mentioned.' Wilkins was quickly very keen to set that particular record straight. 'Lysol is a mix of a disinfectant with creosote. Pretty powerful stuff in its own right, but definitely not hydrochloric acid which, to be honest I don't think it would be possible for anyone to drink. It wouldn't get past their lips without burning them to hell and you're right - that would be pretty painful, though I think a mouthful of Lysol would have stung a bit as well' he grinned, more sardonically than humorously.

Hart grinned too, and inwardly celebrated - he'd already got something new and, now the two men were on first name terms, it was time to dig deeper. He was already beginning to like this man.

'In any case Albert whatever it was, surely there is no way this could be accidental? I mean, if you even sipped a cup of that stuff you would know pretty quickly without actually swallowing it all, right?'

The detective nodded. 'Yes, I think that could be a pretty fair assumption', he said thoughtfully.

'So that just leaves us with murder or suicide.'

Wilkins shrugged his shoulders. 'I guess that too would be a pretty fair guess for any journalist to make, but I am a policeman and not a journalist. I can't speculate, so if you don't mind Cyril I would prefer to wait and see what the pathologists come up with. Lets not forget that, whatever happened, it was a pretty horrendous act and difficult to achieve. I mean, how do you force a man to drink that sort of stuff?' he pointed out.

Hart, busy scribbling into his notebook as Wilkins spoke, looked up.

'So can I quote you as saying you are investigating both possibilities?'

'You can quote me as saying that for the moment I am keeping an open mind until my investigations are complete, but that's all I can say for now. Cyril, can we talk off the record for a minute or two?'

The journalist looked up – this was something he certainly hadn't expected. Ostentatiously he deliberately laid his pencil and notebook onto the desk to give the impression he was going along with the policeman's wishes. 'Yes, of course we can Albert' he said, curious at this latest turn of events and carefully maintaining the first-name relationship he was already developing with Wilkins.

The detective drew heavily on his cigarette to finish it before plunging the dog-end into the ashtray on his desk. Leaning forward he lowered his voice as though to take Hart into his confidence.

'The truth is Cyril, I think this is going to be a bit of a hard nut to crack and I would like to think that the story that you write might help lift a lid here and there to help me find some answers. Tell me, do you think it possible that we could work together, unofficially of course, comparing notes on a strictly private basis and trusting each other?'

Hart had been a working journalist on Brentwood's Time for over two years, often talking to local policemen about routine crime stories in the district, but he'd never before had such a proposal as this put to him. Clearly it was a very attractive proposition for any journalist to get an inside track with the local rozzers, but there may well be some drawbacks about sharing his information with Wilkins. He needed to think about it, so he played for time.

'Albert I take it that this would be strictly between the two of us and would not involve our immediate bosses? To be honest I'm not sure how my editor would react to my passing on any exclusive information I get through my sources, even to the police.'

Wilkins nodded vigorously. 'Absolutely! I don't think my

own guvnor would be too happy about me giving you the sort of stuff that we get and that I am proposing to share either. The point is that as a journalist you can talk to people without putting them on guard, as they would be if they were talking to me while I can get more official information. No, this must be a strictly personal and private relationship with just the two of us involved', he said softly.

'Well ok,' Hart hesitated for only a fraction of a second. 'But I've already told you as much as I know, so where do we start? You must have something else for me,' he queried.

'Yes, but not here!' The policeman put a finger to his lips to emphasise the private nature of the conversation before continuing. 'Tell me Cyril, is there someone quiet in this town where we can have a discreet chat, a good pub for instance?'

'Well, I often have lunch in the Grey Goose in the High Street. They do a good pork pie, sell an excellent pint and the saloon bar is usually quiet at lunchtimes. It's as good a place as anywhere', Hart told him.

'That sounds perfect. I know where that pub is, so suppose we meet there in say, half an hour?'

Hart nodded and stood, picking up his notebook as he prepared to leave, but then paused. 'Look Albert, I do like the idea of our working on this story, well to you it's a case, but can you at least tell me why you think its necessary,' he said.

Wilkins sat for a moment, pursing his lips as he thought about the question, before responding.

'Yes, that seems fair enough. The fact is I think the geezer was murdered, but apart from proving that, I want to find out why the boss down at the hospital is so keen to make me believe it was suicide,' he said.

HE HAD HIS ENEMIES

If he'd been confused when he'd left the hospital earlier that day, by the time Cyril Hart left the police station on his way to his pub lunch rendezvous with Detective Sergeant Wilkins, his mind was in turmoil.

He could not get the policeman's words out of his mind. Not only had he expressed the same off-the-record opinion as Tom Abbott, but had added a new element entirely. Was the hospital's Director really trying to cover up a murder simply to protect its reputation or for another reason completely - if indeed he was? As he tried to put things into perspective, Hart even began to fantasise about Byron being more deeply implicated – perhaps even a killer. What a story that would make he thought before dismissing it from his mind as being a little too fantastic.

Reaching the Grey Goose, he locked the bike up on the rack outside and went into the saloon bar to wait for his new friend. Harry Ross, the publican, was wiping glasses up behind the bar and looked up to greet the reporter.

'Morning, Cyril, you're a bit late today. Usual?'

Hart nodded. 'Please Harry, and I am expecting company in a minute so make it two pints and if you've got anything behind the bar you shouldn't have, keep it out of sight because he's a copper,' Hart laughed at his own joke and watched as the landlord pulled the foaming bitter from one of the bar pumps into two pint jugs.

As he finished filling the second pint the door swung open and Wilkins walked in. Cyril introduced him to the landlord.

'Harry, this is DS Wilkins who's just been posted to Brentwood and who's been looking forward all morning to one of your famous pork pies', he smiled.

Publican and policeman leaned over the bar to shake each other's hand before Harry bustled away to get the pies. Wilkins and Hart picked up their jugs of ale and took them to a table in far corner of the bar, well away from any prying eyes or flapping ears. In fact, although they could hear plenty of dartboard activity going on in the public bar on the other side of the pub, the saloon bar was empty.

Wilkins took a long pull from his pint before putting it down to wipe his lips of the beer with an appreciative hand. 'God, I needed that,' he said. 'Yes, Cyril you're right, he does a pretty good pint here' he said, glancing at the publican who was approaching the table with their food. Ross nodded his thanks at the compliment, put the pies down onto the table and went back to his bar.

The two men began to tuck into their lunch, both clearly thinking hard and waiting for the other to speak. Hart broke the silence first.

'Have you seen the widow yet, Albert?'

Wilkins nodded and cleared his mouth of the food before replying. 'Yes, I actually went with Dr Byron to break the news to her early on Sunday morning.' He anticipated Hart's next question. 'To be honest, considering the time of the morning and what we had to tell her, I think she took it surprisingly well. She was obviously very shocked, but she does seem like a nice and very capable woman who was more concerned about her children than anything else,' he told the reporter.

He took another long swig of the beer before putting it down and lowered his voice to the more conspiratorial level he'd used earlier. 'In fact, Cyril, it was that visit that got me wondering about Dr Byron's insistence on it being suicide. Perhaps it's just the copper in me but we'd only found the body a couple of hours earlier and it was as if he'd already made up his mind that Johnson had killed himself and needed to plant the idea in my mind. To be honest that worries me a great deal,' he confided.

'You see, over the years I have had to deal with a number of suicides and in every case they left a note. Usually they need to explain and apologise to their nearest and dearest about why they'd done it. I was in the hospital by 7-o-clock that morning and I searched that office thoroughly – but there was no note. For God's sake Johnson was a family man who is said to have worshipped his kids. If he really has topped himself, surely at the very least he would have wanted to give his wife and kids some kind of explanation but there was nothing and I find that very odd.'

Wilkins sat back, picked up his beer again and took another mouthful while he waited for his words to sink before continuing.

'All we found was a bottle containing some dregs of what I presume was Lysol on the floor close to a man sitting apparently peacefully at his desk, with his head on his arms at a table as though he was just having a nap. Think about it Cyril. It may not have been the hydrochloric acid you thought it was, but how do you think you would have reacted if you'd swallowed even a mouthful of Lysol, or come to that any disinfectant?

'Somehow I can't see a person who's swallowed that kind of substance being able to quietly put his head down and wait to die. He would have been screaming in agony and threshing about like mad in that office making a hell of a noise – he wouldn't have been able to help himself. Yet in the middle of the night no one even heard so much as a whimper, let alone a scream or any banging, from an office just yards away the end of the corridor. The only reason he was discovered was because he hadn't turned up on the wards to do his rounds and check on his staff before end of shift. That worries me a great deal too, Cyril.'

Hart was stunned at the suggestion. 'Christ, Albert! I think you've got a point. In any case this is a hospital we're talking about and as a supervisor surely he would have had keys to the drugs cupboard for emergencies. I would have thought a lot less painful ways of committing suicide would be stored in that cupboard.'

It was the policeman's turn to sit bolt upright up in his chair. 'Good thinking Cyril, you're right. Why didn't I think of that? I need to check on whether he had those keys. Look, this is exactly why I have suggested we work together on this. We're both investigators, I know police work and you know this town, the hospital, the people and how to dig out your story.'

Wilkins grinned as he spoke. In fact he'd known about the keys early on and had found that Johnson did indeed keep them in his desk, but he needed Hart to believe he was playing an important role in their new relationship so he was quite happy to let the journalist think he'd thought of it first. The detective was a pretty good psychologist who many times during his career had shown himself to be very good at weighing people up and getting them to do what he wanted. *So why is he not Inspector yet?*

He also sensed that something else was troubling Hart, and it wasn't long before the journalist unburdened himself. 'Look Albert, we don't go to press for a couple of days yet but my editor will be demanding a story of some sort. He knows it was murder or suicide - it was he who got the original tip-off - so what do I tell him?'

'Of course he needs to know something,' Wilkins reassured him, 'but at this stage he doesn't need to know it all, does he? If your paper blows this up into a big story before we have all the facts ourselves, you are going to have Fleet Street down here in droves. If that happens they will shove you out of the way won't they?' He paused to take another swallow of the beer before continuing.

'So why not tell him that for now we are investigating an unexplained death and that if he doesn't reveal too much about it at this stage, I have told you the paper will get a real exclusive out of it.'

Wilkins may have been new in town, but he'd been a copper for a long time and he knew exactly what effect that particular carrot would have on a local newspaper editor. But he had another, even juicier, one to offer, so before Hart could say more he carried on.

'Look Cyril, don't tell him that you and I are actually working on the case together – only that I have promised to keep you up-to-date exclusively on my progress. Let him think you have me in your pocket and he'll be happy', he smiled as he stood up to go.

The two men shook hands and Wilkins made his way out of the pub to return to the police station. He was confident that, far from being in Hart's pocket, he now had a measure of control of the local press. He already liked his new pal, but had had no scruples about leading him on a bit. Anyway he genuinely did think that the new press/policeman arrangement could work very well for both sides, provided he was pulling the strings.

For his part Hart sat quietly finishing his own beer, deep in thought and more than a little excited at the turn of events. He'd started that morning half drowned and morose at being sent out into the rain to follow up what should have been a routine 'small-town' sudden death story. Now, providing he handled it right and kept both Wilkins and Hamilton sweet, he could well be on the verge of a career-making exclusive – possibly even a book.

He stood up and prepared to leave the pub, content until the thought of his next visit struck him. Now he had to find and talk to the widow.

• • • • • •

As he walked back through the High Street Albert Wilkins was also was going over the whole case in his mind. He'd still been in bed that Sunday morning when he'd been woken up by the duty constable's telephone call from the nick, telling him he needed to check out a sudden death in the local mental hospital.

Marie had still been sound asleep as he'd dressed and slipped quietly out of the police house they'd been allocated. A police car had been waiting outside and within minutes he'd been introduced to Dr Byron, the hospital's Director. Byron had briefly explained what had happened before taking him to the tiny office where the seated body of Frederick Johnson was still slumped over the desk.

'One of our night staff was worried because he hadn't done his rounds, and came in just before six this morning to find him like this. His name is Johnson and he was our night staff superintendent', Byron had told him.

It wasn't much of an office – more like a cubicle with a desk and chair in the centre. Against the opposite wall stood a cupboard above which was pinned a chart that appeared to detail the names and duties of the night staff. A largish bottle, without a cork, lay on the floor by the desk. Wilkins had picked it up and smelt it, to find it still contained some kind of cleaning fluid. He could smell the same pungent odour around Johnson's head and face and he'd looked quizzically at the hospital director.

'It's Lysol, a very powerful disinfectant. We use it a lot throughout the hospital, mainly to clean and disinfect drains,' Byron had explained.

The only other furniture in the room had been a small cane waste paper basket which contained some crumpled up greaseproof paper, an apple core and a cork that probably could have come from the bottle on the floor. Apart from some official forms and blank sheets of paper, the desk drawer had proved to be empty. The policeman guessed that the greaseproof paper had probably contained Johnson's sandwiches.

'Who found him?' he asked.

'As I said, it was another member of the night staff. His name is Olson, Fred Olson, and I've asked him to wait and talk to you before going home this morning,' the Director had explained.

'Right, yes – thank you, I will do that now but first tell me, doctor, what do you think happened here?' Wilkins asked.

'Well, we will have to carry out an autopsy of course

and have an inquest, but at first sight it looks like another suicide. It wouldn't be the first we've had here. Admittedly most of them were patients, but Mr Johnson wouldn't be the first member of staff to kill himself here either.

In fact I was appointed to my job after my predecessor had some sort of mental breakdown and blew his brains out with a shotgun. Life in hospitals like these, even for staff, can be very stressful and he left a note talking about "this awful place". I think that shows that, whatever level you are working at in mental hospitals, stress can get to you', Byron explained.

Wilkins had nodded his thanks. 'Well there are no obvious signs of violence so you could be right, doctor. I'll get our fingerprint team down here but, given the amount of people presumably in and out of here every day and night that will be a formality and probably a complete waste of time. What about the autopsy? Who will do that?' The detective glanced at Byron as he asked the question.

'I will do that myself tomorrow. It's alright Sergeant, it's legal. I am a qualified pathologist and have to carry out autopsies on patients in the event of sudden death. Its part of my job, so that the coroner can hold an inquest with the full facts at his disposal' Byron told him.

'OK, let's go and talk to Mr Olson. By the way do you know whether Johnson drank tea at night?'

The hospital director looked a bit puzzled by the question. 'Well, yes I suppose he did. It would be difficult to go through the night without a drink of some sort and most of them use the kitchen at the other end of the hospital to make it. Why do you ask?'

'Well, if he did I am wondering what he drank it out of, because there's no cup here,' Wilkins pointed out.

Byron shrugged his shoulders. 'Perhaps he left it in the kitchen, or on one of the wards, during the night,' he said.

They found Olson sitting in Byron's office. He'd been up all night but the events of the last couple of hours had left him wide awake and visibly shaken. He told the detective how he'd gone to Johnson's office early that morning because the night supervisor hadn't done his ward rounds for hours.

'At first I thought he was just having a kip, but when I couldn't wake him I called Dr Byron on the internal telephone,' he told Wilkins.

'Did you touch him, or move him in any way?'

'Well, yes. As I said, I tried to shake him awake but once I realised it was serious I put him back as I found him.'

'Did you move, touch or remove anything at all from the office?'

'No nothing.'

'And you left him exactly how you found him?'

'Yes sir,' Olson replied.

'What time did you actually last see Mr Johnson alive?' Wilkins asked him.

Olson thought for a moment before replying. 'Well, I guess it wasn't long after midnight, when he did his early evening rounds. He used to pop in to the wards for a few minutes to check up that everything was ok, so he could write up in his overnight log. Normally then he would come back around 5-o-clock in the morning, but today he didn't and that is why I got curious.'

'Thank you Mr Olsen. Tell me; was Mr Johnson popular among the night staff?'

'Well, he had his enemies because some people can't take discipline, but I don't think he was particularly unpopular, though he was respected. He could be a bit hard sometimes but he was ex-army and I guess that was part of his job anyway.'

Wilkins smiled his appreciation. 'OK, Mr Olson, thank you. That will be enough for the moment, but I may need to talk to you again.' He paused as an afterthought seemed to strike him. 'Oh, just one other thing. Did Mr Johnson have his own teacup?'

'Yes, as a matter of fact we all do, well his is a mug actually. I know because I've got one exactly the same. It's a big china regimental mug and I noticed it because of its similarity with mine. It's white with an Essex Regiment crest on the side. There's a lot of them on sale in this town, because the regiment is stationed across the road in Warley Barracks', Olson replied.

'Of course, thanks. Do you remember seeing it in the office this morning?'

Olson seemed to be trying to remember, but finally said, 'No I don't, and now you mention it that's a bit odd because it was always on top of the cupboard in his office.'

'You say you've got one the same? Were you and he in the same regiment then?'

Olson shook his head. 'No sir! I think he was in the Essex during the war, but my wife bought my mug just because it had an army crest on it. Women don't know one regiment from another, do they? I was on the Somme in a Bradford Pals unit with the Yorkshire Light Infantry.'

Wilkins smiled his thanks, said he would probably need to talk to him again and gestured that the man could leave. Dr Byron broke into his thoughts.

'Look, Sergeant. I have a very unpleasant job to do now, and I wonder if you would care to come with me. I have to break the news to his wife and it might help to have the two of us there.'

The policeman smiled his agreement. 'Yes, of course I will. Sooner or later I will need to talk to her anyway so it will be a good opportunity to meet her. Does she live far from here?' he said, picking up his hat and walking out of the hospital with Byron. Within a few minutes they were banging on Emma Johnson's door.

• • • • • •

Anyone might have thought Emma Johnson's seeming lack of grief on hearing the news of her husband's death, was simply down to shock. She seemed almost cheerful as she ran up the stairs to sort out the children and prepare them for the day.

Sarah was old enough to be despatched to the bathroom to turn on the Ascot gas water heater and put enough hot water into the chipped enamel bowl to wash her hands and face. Emma picked Freddie up and carried him downstairs to the kitchen sink where she washed and dressed him. Then, with both kiddies tidied up, she sat Freddie in his high chair and told Sarah to sit at the table while she ladled out plates of porridge for their breakfast.

'Is daddy home yet, mummy?' Her daughter's sudden question broke into her thoughts. She took a deep breath, before deciding how to respond to it.

'No, sweetheart. He's not! Look, you're a big girl now and I know I can rely on you to be brave, because daddy will not be coming home at all. He had a heart attack when he was at work last night and died in the hospital.'

If she had expected a floor of tears from the child, she was disappointed. Sarah simply looked down at her porridge and was quiet for a few moments before speaking again.

'Mummy - does that mean I can sleep in your bed now?'

The unexpected question made Emma half smile, and she hugged her daughter tightly. Sarah loved getting into bed with her mother but finding her there when he'd come home in the mornings had always angered her father. Fred Johnson liked to find his wife still in bed when he came off shift, but he did not like sharing it with his children as well.

'Course you can, love. Well, for the moment at least, but do you understand what I've just told you?'

The little girl nodded gravely. 'Yes, daddy's gone to heaven. That's where Red Riding Hood's grandmother went after the wolf ate up her you know. Then he pretended to be her because he wanted to eat Red Riding Hood up as well. We learned about her in school last week,' she confided. Then she paused, as another thought struck her. 'Mummy, if daddy is not coming home any more he won't be able to shout at us so much, will he?'

For the first time that morning Emma was close to genuine emotion at Sarah's mix of childhood innocence with the memory of the brutal reality of their father. She hugged her daughter even closer and kissed her on the cheek. Meanwhile, oblivious to everything except the splashes of porridge on and around him, little Freddie was showing signs of boredom. His mother straightened up from cuddling his sister and went over to the high chair to rescue the floor from more of her son's breakfast.

'Come on, you two. I think we should go to church today and pray for daddy,' she laughed, picking the boy up.

Three hours later Emma and the children arrived at St Thomas's church. The town's 100-year old church, in a side road a hundred yards from the High Street, was where she usually went on Sundays. There she would hand Sarah and Freddie over to Mrs Harris, the vicar's wife who ran a crèche during services so that parents and her husband could concentrate on their devotions.

When the little family arrived that day she eyed Emma, who was wearing a white blouse with a long black skirt and jacket topped with a small black hat on her head, curiously for she could sense something was amiss. The young mother seemed to be a little emotional but she decided not to ask and as she handed the children over Emma smiled her appreciation before going into the church where she was greeted by the Rev. John Harris. Like his wife he too immediately noticed her oddly sombre mood for a usually quite cheerful parishioner who he knew and liked.

'Good morning, Emma', he said. 'Are you alright, my dear?' As she shook her head he was not expecting what she was about to tell him.

'No Reverend, not exactly. We had some terrible news this morning and I am still a little upset by it,' she was clearly very close to tears and he was immediately concerned.

'Look my dear, we've got a few minutes before the service starts. Come into the vestry where we can talk in private' he said, ushering her into the tiny room where the church's vestments and spare hymnbooks were kept. He'd barely closed the door behind them before Emma had turned and thrown herself into his arms, bursting into floods of tears.

'Come on. Whatever is it, my dear?' he said holding her close and gently patting her head.

Sobbing her heart out, the woman could not speak at first but gradually she began to take control. Between the tears she was able to tell him the tragic news she'd been told just a few hours before and even of the suggestion that Fred may have committed suicide. He was visibly shocked, especially by the idea of suicide – not just a mortal sin of course, but in an age when even attempted suicide was a criminal offence – bad enough. He comforted the weeping woman in his arms for a few moments before speaking again.

'Look, Emma, should you be here today? Would you not be better off grieving at home with your children? Let me ask Mrs Harris to take you and the children home and stay with you, at least for a few hours'.

Emma shook her head and wiped her eyes with her hands. 'No thank you Reverend. I had to come to church today to pray for Fred's soul. I think we owed him that. Somehow it felt right, both for me and for the children, even though they wouldn't understand and won't be in church for the actual service. I'm alright now, I promise.'

She smiled reassuringly at him through eyes still glistening with the dampness of her tears as she spoke. Harris was a man who spent a great deal of his life comforting people in trouble and he understood that people reacted to grief in many ways. He was particularly pleased to hear her reasons for coming to church that morning of course.

'Alright my dear if that's what you want, then of course that's what you must do. I will include him in our prayers and, if Mr Johnson did commit suicide we will ask for His forgiveness,' he told her, gently shepherding her back out into the church where the congregation was already gathered and curious about the little scene unfolding before them.

Wiping her eyes dry though clearly still in great distress Emma made her way to her usual pew close to the altar and already occupied by a tall, young man. He moved slightly to one side to give her room to take the seat next to his. As they all settled down Harris began to lead his choir and other church officials, in procession behind him, through the congregation towards the altar.

The vicar began the service by announcing the sad news Emma had just given him before his usual introductory 'Let us pray'. Everyone, after glancing towards Emma to sympathise leaned forward to begin their prayers. At that moment of pious solicitude nobody one else in the church would have noticed Emma's hand briefly brushing and pausing momentarily to touch, the hand of her neighbour in the pew.

After the opening prayers Harris announced a hymn number and everyone leafed through their hymnbooks to find the words as they stood up to join the choir in song. Only at that moment did Emma, pretending to sing the words of the hymn, make vocal contact with the young man standing alongside her.

'They came to tell me early this morning darling' she sang quietly, mouthing the words as though she was singing the hymn.

In response he replied the same way, like her as though he was singing the hymn. 'Well he had it coming, but we must be careful Em. After today we must not make any contact with each other, at least until after the post mortem and the dust has settled.' He sang just loud enough for her to hear and, equally surreptitiously, she nodded her agreement.

'I love you'. She mouthed the words in time to the music, glancing up at him as the hymn reached its final verse.

He smiled back. 'I love you too sweetheart, and I can't wait until all this is over and we can be together properly at last... Amen' he sang as everyone began to sit down again.

For the rest of the service, even while the vicar was telling the congregation about the tragedy and - as he'd promised - leading the prayers for her dead husband, Emma and the man by her side avoided any further verbal, eye or any other kind of physical contact. When the service ended he left the church without a backward glance, as other members of the congregation moved towards her to hug her and express their condolences. Eventually, after she was able to respond graciously to all the offers of help from shocked and sympathetic worshippers, she collected the children to take them home for their lunch.

She never went to the evening service in the church – she never did - but another regular churchgoer did. He was John Hamilton the editor of the local newspaper and what the vicar told him after evensong had led him to order Cyril Hart the next day to follow the story up.

HE WAS A BASTARD

'My name is Tilly and I'm having Fred's baby'

It wasn't hard to pick the Johnson house out from the others in Gresham Road, despite all of them being the typical 'two up – two down' identical terraced houses built at the turn of the century with working class tenants in mind. In keeping with the convention of the day all its curtains were closed - signalling that those inside it were in mourning. Cyril Hart hesitated for a moment before knocking on the door.

As he waited for a response, he glanced up and down the street. It seemed to be hushed and respectful, with just a light breeze cooling the warmth of the afternoon sun. It was a school day so no children would have been playing outside anyway and the only real sign of life came from the front-gate housewives, clearly gossiping to each other about the news in suitably hushed tones. They looked curiously towards the visitor as he knocked on Emma's door, but they only served to emphasise the atmosphere that hung like a dark shroud over the whole street.

When the door was opened it was to reveal a relatively young woman in her middle thirties, but with a pale expressionless face that had all the signs of a hard life on it. Apart from the floral pinafore, she was dressed head to foot in black – even her hair, tightly screwed up in a bun at the back of her head, was jet black. Hart had not really thought about what he'd expected, but probably it would not have been the quietly calm figure that now stood in the doorway waiting for him to speak.

'Mrs Johnson'? He touched the brim of his hat and she nodded that she was, the barest hint of a smile crossing her face. Inside the house behind her the reporter could hear the sounds of small children laughing and playing, while his nose detected the warm and inviting smell of baking coming from the kitchen. He hated this part of the job but somehow the sounds and smells of normality lifted his spirit a little and made him feel less intrusive.

'I am so sorry to disturb you at this time ma-am; my name is Cyril Hart and I'm from the local newspaper, Brentwood's Time. I know this is a difficult time for you, but we were told about the tragic death of your husband and wondered if you were up to talking to us and also to see whether we could help in any way.'

For a brief second or two, as Emma Johnson considered what he'd said, Hart thought she was going to slam the door in his face, but she seemed to relax a little. She moved back slightly to open the door wider, gesturing for him to come in and swiftly closing it once he was inside. Politely he stood to one side so she could pass and she led him through to the kitchen, where she gestured him to sit on a chair at the table. Through the open back door he could see little Sarah and Freddie laughing and playing in the afternoon sun in the tiny backyard. Emma read his thoughts.

'They are too young to realise what's happened,' she explained, staring out at the toddler and the baby enjoying themselves. 'Right, Mr Hart, now what can I do for you? Can I offer you a cup of tea?'

'Thank you Mrs Johnson, I'd like that. Look we do realise that this must be a very difficult time for you to say the least and if you would rather I left I would understand and will do so. We are a local newspaper, not one of the national dailies who trample over people's emotions to get a story. Brentwood's Time is your local paper and we would like to offer you our sympathy for your loss and offer you any help we can give.' She waved a hand asking him to stop there.

'No, no Mr Hart. It's alright; I knew that sooner or later the papers would want to talk to me about Fred and what happened. I would much rather it was our local rag. It's all been a great shock of course and thank you for your sympathy and your offer of help, but tell me what you want to know.'

At that moment, though he had winced at the term 'local rag', the reporter's heart went out to her in genuine sympathy. Relieved at the way she had taken his turning up on her doorstep, he smiled his thanks and reached into his jacket for his notebook and pencil as she turned to put the kettle on.

'OK, first tell me how you heard the news?' he asked.

'First thing on Sunday morning when the hospital's director Dr Byron and a policeman knocked at the door and woke me up to tell me what had happened. They were very kind and sympathetic because of course it came as a great shock.' Emma wiped her eyes as the memory of that early morning visit came back and Hart hurried on with his questions.

'Yes, I can imagine how that must have been a terrible moment. I understand he was found in the early hours of the morning and that he may have drunk some poison or something. Did they say why or where he got it from?'

She shook her head in bewilderment. 'No, well they said it might have been suicide but to be honest I find that hard to believe,' she said. 'I just can't think of any reason why Fred would want to do such a thing. He was devoted to the children and had a good job which paid enough money to provide for us and pay the bills. We were happy, so why would he want to kill himself?' she asked, putting the cup of tea she'd made as she was talking down onto the table.

Hart picked up the cup and, smiling his thanks, took a sip before speaking. 'He said nothing before he went to work that night? Or even recently, to suggest he might have been unhappy or worried about anything at all?' He asked.

She shook her head as she moved over to the oven to take the cake she'd been baking from it. For a few seconds she busied herself checking it with a kitchen knife see if it was done, before replying. 'No absolutely nothing. He'd been in bed all day after doing his Friday night shift. When he got up he read the evening paper, had his tea and went off to work after kissing me and the children goodnight just as he always did. In fact the only odd thing he said was that he was getting too old for the job, but that was just a casual jokey comment, not a serious complaint'.

Hart scribbled a few notes before looking up again.

'I see. So how was your life with Mr Johnson? I take it you got on well, so what sort of man was he?'

Emma smiled. 'We've been married for six years and yes, we've had our ups and downs, but generally speaking I have no complaints,' she lied, thinking back to her husband's drunken brutality and known infidelities. 'Look out there - we have two wonderful children to show for it,' she added.

'Yes, they do look like great kids,' he'd meant it as a compliment, so was a bit taken aback by her sudden reaction.

'They're children, not baby goats,' she snapped.

Hart was swift to apologise for his remark. 'Oh, yes, I'm sorry about that. Force of habit among us blokes, I'm afraid Mrs Johnson. How old are they?'

'Well, Sarah is nearly five, and Freddie will be two in November', she told him.

'Right. How about you, Mrs Johnson? How old are you, or shouldn't I ask?' He grinned, relieved that he appeared to be back on track with her.

She smiled coyly. 'Why, Mr Hart, you know you should never ask a lady her age. Actually I was born on the day the old queen died – in January 1901 – so you work it out.'

The reporter now feeling he was really getting on the right terms with her, took some more mouthfuls of the tea. He was now confident enough to push his questions to a new level.

'Tell me, Mrs Johnson, if you don't believe your husband committed suicide as they suggested, what do you think happened? Do you think it was an accident or was he murdered? If so, why and how?'

He was careful to watch her face as he asked, but found he wasn't getting any answers there. Despite being so recently and tragically bereaved Emma Johnson seemed to be very much in control of herself, even when faced with questions deliberately designed to provoke an emotional response. She shook her head almost wearily.

'To be honest Mr Hart, I just don't know. I really

cannot imagine Fred being desperate enough to kill himself, and he was a big strong powerful man well able to look after himself. In the war he fought on the Somme you know. I find it difficult to believe that anyone could kill him by forcing something down his throat against his will. Perhaps it was an accident of some sort. To be honest I just don't know what to think,' she said desperately.

Hart, realising he'd got all he was going to get at that stage but satisfied he'd struck up a working relationship with the bereaved woman, finished scribbling his notes. He put the notebook back into his jacket but before preparing to leave, had one final question. 'Perhaps you're right and it is a real mystery but tell me Mrs Johnson, are you and the children going to manage alright now he's gone? Was he insured? Did he have an army pension?' It was a loaded question because if Johnson had been insured, suicide would almost certainly have invalidated it.

She shrugged her shoulders. 'To be honest Mr Hart I haven't had time to really think much about it. He did have a small army pension but I'm not sure it will come to me as his widow now he's gone. We did have life policies for a hundred pounds each, for which Fred paid sixpence each week when the man from the Pru came round. Whatever the case I will manage somehow and my children will not suffer, even if I have to take in washing. Why do you ask?'

Hart stood up to go. 'No reason Mrs Johnson'. Somehow it didn't seem the right moment to remind her of the suicide risk to that life insurance policy. 'Other than to say that if there is anything we can do at Brentwood's Time to help you and the children in that sense, perhaps with an appeal, please let us know.'

'Thank you Mr Hart and I do appreciate your kindness

and understanding. I know you have a job to do and I will bear what you say in mind. All I ask is that when you do write your story you do not sensationalise it and are kind to us. I have my children to think about,' she said, leading the reporter back towards the front door.

As she opened it, they were taken by surprise to find another figure on the doorstep, just about to lift the knocker. She was a young and quite attractive, if slightly plump, girl who was clearly very nervous. She was as startled as they were to find the door opening before she'd actually knocked.

'Oh!' she said.

Hart, who had been standing back a little to let Emma open the door for him, watched silently as the new arrival stammered.

'Is it true? Is he dead? Please tell me it's not true'. She was clearly a very agitated young woman.

'Who? Is who dead?' Emma asked, straightening her back.

'Fred. Fred Johnson. He lives here, doesn't he? Where is he? For God's sake please tell me he's alright', the girl begged, holding out her hands as though she was trying to make contact.

Emma's patience was being stretched to the limit and she ignored the outstretched hands. 'Look miss – just who are you, and why are you so interested in my husband?' She snapped.

The young woman's eyes filled with tears and there was panic in her voice as she answered.

'My name is Tilly. Tilly Masters, and I'm having Fred's baby', she said.

Brian Lynch

· · · · · ·

After leaving Hart to finish his lunch in the Grey Goose that afternoon Det. Sergeant Wilkins, deep in thought and confident that he now had some measure of control over the local press, walked the few hundred yards through the High Street back to the police station. He found a note on his desk, asking him to telephone Dr Byron at the hospital.

He sat and thought for a moment before reaching for his phone and asking the station's switchboard operator to find the number and get the hospital's director for him. After a minute or so the phone rang and he picked it up to be told that Byron was on the other end of the line.

'Hello, good afternoon doctor, how's things? What can I do for you?' He asked.

Byron's voice sounded a little tinny, indicating that the connection was not of the best quality, but the tones still came through firm and clear.

'Well Sergeant, I thought I ought to warn you that we have had the press up here this morning. He was asking about Fred Johnson's death and trying to make it sound worse than it is.'

'Really?' Wilkins, who already knew about Hart's visit of course, made the word sound like a question. 'What do you mean sir, tried to make it sound worse than it is?' he asked.

'Well, he'd obviously picked up some vague information about a sudden death here over the weekend and I got the impression he was trying to sensationalise it like these scandalmongers do. I did tell him that all the indications were that Mr Johnson had committed suicide,

- 82 -

but I don't think he wanted to believe that. I suspect he will soon be coming up to see you so I thought I'd better warn you.'

'Thank you doctor, I really do appreciate that and I expect you're right that he will be making his way here. As they say, forewarned is forearmed and now I will be ready for him', Wilkins told him glibly. At no stage in the conversation had he felt it necessary to tell Byron that he and Hart had spent the lunchtime together in a High Street pub, or what they'd discussed.

'Tell me, doctor. Is there anything new at your end since we spoke yesterday?' He asked.

'Yes, I have had a call from the Coroner, Dr John Martin. I had to inform him of course because there will need to be an inquest and he has asked me to carry out a post mortem to establish the cause of death. I will probably do that later on today. If you want to come and observe, you are quite welcome to do so,' Byron invited.

'Er, no, no thanks' Wilkins said hurriedly, 'But I would of course appreciate a full report on your findings as soon as you can let me have one,' he added.

'Certainly! I'll send a copy over to you by hand once I have completed it, but I fully expect it will show that he died after ingesting the cleaning fluid Lysol,' Byron assured him.

'I'm sure you're right doctor, but I would also value your opinion on whether there were any indications about how he came to drink the stuff. Check for any cuts or bruises for example and whether or not his fingers and hands showed any signs of handling it – were they stained etc. It's all routine stuff of course and I don't want it to sound like I am trying to teach you your job. By the way, did his tea mug turn up?' The last question was Wilkins way of moving on from any suggestion he was questioning Byron's expertise.

'No, not as far as I know, though to be honest I hadn't realised it was so important to your investigation. As far as the post mortem is concerned I can assure you that, as a qualified pathologist I have performed autopsies on patients here many times over the years and I do know what to look for.'

'Of course and I never meant to question your competence sir, but don't forget I am new here myself and still learning the local ropes so to speak. I apologise if that came over wrong. As far as the tea mug is concerned I simply felt it was an odd thing to be missing from his office especially since he obviously drank what killed him, so I need to find it to see if the Lysol was in that,' Wilkins reassured him.

'Oh, one other thing,' he added. 'Can you draw up a list of the names and addresses of those members of staff who worked with Johnson? I will need to speak with them, so if you can give me their names I would be grateful.'

'Of course. I will include it with my autopsy report,' Byron promised before hanging up the phone.

Wilkins sat for a while, collecting his thoughts. Again he'd got the impression that the hospital director was trying to guide the investigation in the direction of suicide and that worried him. Without having anything specific in mind to go on he had a gut feeling, a copper's instinct perhaps, that there was more to it and suddenly he had a thought.

Getting up from his chair he made his way back out into the office where all the station's filing cabinets were kept. He flicked through them until he came to the file he was looking for - the one marked 'Brentwood Mental Hospital'. Removing it, he took it back to his desk where he sat down and began leafing through it.

He still wasn't sure exactly what he was looking for, only that he needed to take in as much information about the hospital as he could, but there was one thing in particular he needed to know more about. On Sunday Byron had made a passing reference to his predecessor's suicide and that seemed like a good place to start. It wasn't long before he found it.

It was short two-page report on Dr Harold Gillespie, who had been appointed to the position of Director of the hospital in November 1927. A highly qualified former army psychiatrist who'd studied the effects of battle on soldiers during the war, Gillespie had arrived at the hospital with his new bride, Marion. An extremely compassionate man he'd begun to make an impact, particularly in the treatment of the many 'shell shocked' ex-soldiers who were still in mental hospitals and 'asylums' nearly ten years after the armistice.

In fact he'd developed a reputation in the field of mental health and under his leadership the Brentwood Mental Hospital began to make great strides in psychiatric treatment. Rumoured to be on the verge of a knighthood for his work in the field, he was frequently invited to lecture on the subject at medical conferences. He had also campaigned hard to change the military thinking about 'shell shock', by proving it was the result of a genuine medical condition and not the simple cowardice it had often been dismissed as during the Great War.

Yet, on the morning of Christmas Day 1930, barely three years after he'd arrived at the hospital, he'd left his wife downstairs still eating breakfast and making plans for their day. Three minutes later she'd heard a bang and had raced upstairs to find her husband sprawled across the floor with his head covered in blood. Lying next to him was the shotgun he'd apparently used on himself. She'd screamed for help and in seconds the hospital's deputy director Richard Byron, who had a room on the same floor, was with her.

During the inquest which had been held into his death the jury had been shown a letter in which he'd apologised to Marion for what he was going to do and explained he could carry on no longer. Its whole tone seemed to indicate that the psychiatrist was himself close to a mental breakdown, exacerbated by an almost paranoid belief that some people in the hospital were plotting against him. In despair he'd even described the hospital he'd done so much to improve as '*this awful place*'. A deeply distressed Marion had confirmed that her husband had seemed a little odd of late, though she hadn't thought too much about it and certainly hadn't thought him suicidal.

The inquest had decided that Gillespie had killed himself while the balance of his mind had been disturbed and the coroner had offered his condolences to Marion Gillespie. Suddenly Wilkins sat bolt upright as the names of the two people present at the time of death and on the scene that morning leapt off the page to swim into his focus.

One was that of Gillespie's deputy director, Dr Richard Byron, the other was that of a member of the night staff - Mr Frederick Johnson.

• • • • • •

'What!' Emma's shriek had been instinctive, loud and almost deranged.

For a moment she forgot the journalist who was standing right behind her as the mask of serenity she'd carefully maintained slipped a little. Just briefly another woman – entirely different from the self-controlled bereaved widow – emerged from beneath that veil. The new arrival blanched and swayed back a little, as if to avoid the ferocity her words had triggered.

'I'm sorry, I really am, but.....' she stammered. She got no further before the raging storm that a few minutes earlier had been a grieving widow quietly talking to a local journalist, blew up again. Gripping the doorframe to lend extra support, Emma Johnson launched a vicious tongue-lashing onto the frightened young girl standing on her doorstep.

'How dare you? Who do you think you are, coming round here defiling the memory of a good and decent man who only passed away a day ago? Get away from here, you filthy little bitch. Bugger off you bloody whore. There's nothing here for you, so go away and take your nasty insinuations with you' she screeched, her high-pitched voice carrying along the street to where the gossips were curious at the sudden intensity of noise that had interrupted their chat.

Even Hart had been surprised at the tirade the older woman had levelled at the trembling youngster on her doorstep, but he stood there saying nothing. There are times when a good journalist needs to just listen and this was clearly one such moment.

Emma, furious at the unwelcome surprise intrusion on her doorstep, wasn't going to give Tilly any more time and, stepping back into the hall she slammed the door shut leaving the weeping girl outside. It was only then that, still shaking with anger, she remembered the reporter was still there. As quickly as the storm had erupted, she calmed down, regained her composure and began apologising.

'Oh, Mr Hart. I forgot you were still here. Look I'm so sorry about that but have you ever heard the like? I have no idea who that woman was, but I am not going to let anyone talk about my dead husband like that. The very idea – coming here at a time like this to make such wicked allegations' she said, reopening the door again a little.

She glanced outside to make sure the girl had gone before fully opening it wide to let him out. As he left the house he did his best to reassure her.

'Mrs Johnson, please don't apologise. At times like this you will get all sorts of cranks turning up. Don't worry about her, she's gone now. Thanks again for talking to me. Goodbye and don't forget, please let us know if we can be of any help.' Now he was in a hurry to leave but didn't want to make it too obvious.

He walked away slowly until he heard the door close noisily behind him, when he increased his pace to a brisk walk. The reporter in him needed to catch up with Tilly Masters before she got out of sight and he was sure she would be heading for the railway station. As he turned out of Gresham Road into Kings Road, he saw that he'd guessed right. She was fifty yards in front of him, almost running now with her head down, and even from that distance he could see her shoulders were shaking with emotion.

'Tilly!' The girl stopped, turning to see who had called her name and he could see she was still sobbing uncontrollably. She waited as he approached and as he reached her a protective masculine instinct made him put his arms out. Despite the fact that he was a total stranger, she welcomed the comfort his arms offered and wept on his chest. He let her cry herself out before easing his grip around her to introduce himself.

'Look, Tilly. My name is Cyril Hart and I am a journalist with the local newspaper, Brentwood's Time. I was in Mrs Johnson's just now and I saw what happened but you must understand that she is very distressed. I'm afraid that it's true that Mr Johnson died over the weekend and of course she's still in shock as a result.'

As he spoke the words he looked closely at her face and saw the panic beneath the tears streaming down her cheeks. 'Look, there's a teashop near the station - let me buy you a cup of tea. It will give you a chance to settle down and compose yourself.'

She looked back at him through swollen eyes and, her body still shaking from the shock of what had happened on that doorstep, nodded her gratitude. 'Thank you sir,' she sobbed, taking his proffered arm and allowing him to shepherd her towards the Two Trees Teashop. There was no other customer there so he led her over to a table by the window, where they sat down and waited to be served. He ordered tea and buns and waited patiently while she wiped her eyes and composed herself before speaking again.

'Tilly, who are you, and why did you tell Mrs Johnson you were expecting a baby by her husband?' he asked gently.

'Because it's true, I am having his baby'. She pointed towards her stomach and, for the first time, Hart realised that his initial view about her being plump had been right but for a different reason than he'd first thought.

'Tell me about it,' he invited as the tea arrived. She

waited until the waitress had put the tray on the table and Cyril had done the honours by pouring their tea before launching into her story.

'I didn't know Fred was married when we first started going out, honest. He didn't actually tell me he wasn't single, but I just assumed he was because he acted as if he was. When he did admit it he told me it was a marriage in name only and that they were only still together for the sake of the children. He said that it was me he loved and I still believe that.

'I know that he was a lot older than me but he was my first real boy friend - a very attentive and wonderful man who treated me like a real woman. I had no reason not to believe him and by the time I did find out he was married I was deeply in love and I trusted him completely,' she explained. Hart, who was suddenly getting a very different mind image about Fred Johnson to what he'd been told, let her open her heart to him.

She told him how Johnson, even though she only been seventeen when they'd first started going out together, had courted her. Once or twice a week he'd pick her up from a High Street bus stop, or the railway station, before starting his night shift. At time when Emma thought he'd left home early so he could go to the pub for a few hours before work he was actually taking Tilly dancing or to the cinema. Then he'd see her safely on a bus to go home before going to the hospital to start his shift.

'Sometimes he'd smuggle me into the hospital and we'd spend an hour or two cuddling in his office, before I had to catch the night bus home', she smiled at what was clearly still a pleasant memory.

'Is that when that happened?' the reporter asked, nodding significantly towards her swollen stomach.

'Yes, but sometimes we even did it in his house'.

'What, in his own home?' Cyril really was shocked this time, as Tilly continued.

'Even in his own bed. His wife has family in Southend and she would often take the children there to spend the day with them and Fred would take me home while she was out. That's how I knew where they lived,' she explained quite shamelessly.

'What happened when he found you were pregnant?' Hart asked.

'Well, at first he was pretty angry and wanted me to have an abortion but there was no way I was going to do that,' she said. 'Then he seemed to get used to the idea and promised to look after us both. Once the baby had arrived we'd planned to run away to Canada and be a proper family – it's a big country and we could start again there with a new life, you see.' Once again tears began to fill her eyes and Hart waited for her to get herself under control again, before continuing.

'Tilly love, how did you first meet Fred? He asked.

Despite her distress, her eyes brightened at the memory. 'I actually met him at the hospital when my dad worked there. Dad works in Fords foundry in Dagenham now, which is why we moved to the Becontree estate over there so he could be near his work, but before that he was one of the night staff at the mental hospital. One night last year he took me and Mum to a stage show put on by the staff and patients. I met Fred by chance at the tea bar during the interval. We started chatting, well flirting really, and that's where it all started,' she explained.

'So your father knows Fred Johnson - well knew him, that is?'

'Yes he worked for him, but he never knew I was going

out with him. Fred suggested it was probably a good idea to keep it to ourselves for a while and I thought so too. Dad is often on a short fuse and can get pretty angry sometimes. I knew he wouldn't like me going out with a man so much older than me, especially Fred, and I was afraid of what he'd do.'

'Does he know now, then?' Hart asked. Tilly nodded, a grimace at the memory of when her father found out briefly passing across her face.

'Yes. It was after Mum guessed I was having a baby and made me tell her who the father was. She told Dad and he went mad – shouting that Fred was a bastard who was already married with kids. He wanted to go and knock Fred's block off there and then, but Mum managed to calm him down. She suggested they ought to wait and see what Fred had to say first. To be honest I think that at moment Dad would have killed Fred with his bare hands.'

'When was that, Tilly?' the reporter asked thoughtfully.

'A week ago,' she said.

'And did your father ever have that meeting with Fred?' This time the girl shook her head.

'No. I told Fred about what dad had said and how he wanted to meet with him to discuss the baby and he said he would. That was last Friday, then this morning Dad told me he'd heard that Fred had killed himself. I didn't believe that, so decided to come to Brentwood to find out for myself. Honestly Mr Hart, I never meant to upset Mrs Johnson but I just had to find out if it was true.'

Again she burst into tears, raising the curiosity of the waitress sitting quietly in the corner pretending not to listen. In despair the distraught girl looked up at her table companion again.

'Oh, Mr Hart – what am I going to do now? And what is going to happen to me and my baby?'

Cyril put out a comforting hand to rest on her arm as she worked her way through this latest wave of emotion.

'Tilly love, I think you need to be brave, both for yourself and your baby. Sweetheart your Mum sounds like a sensible person to me and I'm sure she'll want to help, so go home and tell her everything' he told her. The truth was that Hart was now anxious to see her on a train and on the way home, because he had a lot of thinking to do now.

The girl wiped her eyes yet again, blew her nose into her now soggy handkerchief and nodded. 'Thank you Mr Hart. I am sure you're right and I am very grateful for you helping me like this, for listening and for your advice. Thank you for the tea as well.' As she stood up to leave, the journalist smiled and took her hand.

'Good luck, Tilly. Do you have far to go?'

'We live in Becontree Avenue. It's on the big LCC estate and they're all new big houses with three bedrooms, two rooms and a scullery downstairs and big gardens at the back and the front. We've even got inside toilets,' she added almost proudly, her own predicament forgotten for the moment.

He made a mental note of the name of the street but decided not to pursue the question of the house number in case it raised her guard. He guessed it wouldn't be hard to find it out anyway when he needed it. What he didn't know was that Becontree Avenue was over three miles long with over a thousand houses in it, but as he watched the girl making her way across the road to vanish into the station, he was thinking hard.

He'd noted that she had not once asked exactly how

x where Bryan Lynch grew up.

Fred had died, but he put that down to her distress and worry about her own future. It was time to go back to the office to collect his thoughts and write up his notes. It had been a busy day but this new development had been totally unexpected and was one that he also needed to talk to his so recently acquired 'detective partner' about.

He'd realised that he'd not only had a genuine motive for suicide handed to him on a plate – but one for murder too. He even had a possible murder suspect.

HE WAS A BLACKMAILER

'but I do know of him and that Susan was afraid of him,'

Richard Byron looked up and smiled as his wife came into the room, a cup of tea in one hand and a plate with a sandwich on it in the other. She smiled as she put them down on his desk and ruffled his hair playfully.

'Here you are, darling. You must eat something, especially if you are going to do that post mortem on poor Mr Johnson this afternoon. I thought I'd go and see Mrs Johnson to see if there is anything she needs or if we can do anything to help. Apart from being from the hospital in a sense, I'm also her local councillor, and I remember how helpful he was when Harold died' she pointed out.

He smiled, grateful both for the sandwich and for her display of affection. He loved this woman as much now as he had when they'd first been introduced, perhaps even more so. At that time she'd been married to his boss, Dr Harold Gillespie, but the attraction had been immediate and mutual. Within months they'd become lovers and after her husband's death, and a suitable period of mourning had elapsed, they had made their relationship both legal and respectable.

'Thanks Marion. As usual you're right, sweetheart. Yes

I think it might be a good idea for someone from the hospital to go and see Mrs Johnson. See if there is anything we can do for her and the children or help in any way,' he added as she bustled out with a cheerful wave of her hand, closing the door behind her.

As he listened to her heels clattering down the hallway, his mind drifted back over the years to that fateful morning she'd been widowed and wondered if she'd ever guessed the truth. History has shown that the power of love can make anyone, man or woman, act out of character but it would still take an extreme passion to turn a young, recently qualified psychiatrist, into the murderer he'd become that day. However the depth of feeling he had for Marion still truly ran that deep, and his mind wandered off to those early days.

From the moment the hospital director Harold Gillespie had introduced his wife to his new deputy, Byron had been smitten. His new quarters had been two rooms – a bedroom and sitting room - in the director's house in the grounds of the hospital. It hadn't been long before such close proximity to each other had begun to turn friendly familiarity into love on both sides.

Marion really did love her husband, but within weeks she'd fallen as much in love with his deputy as he had with her. They had given themselves to each other, secretly but passionately, ignoring the feelings of guilt over their affair that each had.

Over the months that followed Byron had realised that for him an affair wasn't enough. He'd begun to envy Gillespie, not just as Marion's husband, but for his job too and he coveted both. Increasingly he'd begun to feel that his boss was living in the past. Having initiated, pioneered and developed many advances in the treatment of mental health, he seemed to be reluctant to go further. As his impatient deputy, Richard Byron became increasingly resentful and more convinced that it was time for the 'old fashioned' Director to retire so he could take over and run the hospital his way. He began to dream of doing that with Marion at his side.

He'd never been quite sure when, or how, he came up with the idea of murder as a solution. It could have been the growing realisation that without the Director's removal his dreams could not be fulfilled. Gradually frustration with the older man, and his desperate lust over Marion, began to dominate his thoughts. He would lie awake in bed, knowing the love of his life was only a few yards along the corridor in her husband's bed and the thought drove him crazy.

Then one day he saw Gillespie return home, after a day's shooting with some of the local landed gentry, with his shotgun casually hanging over his arm. It was at that moment that the idea of how to kill him really began to solidify in his mind, but the problem was how and when to do it without ending up on the gallows.

It had actually been the death of one of the hospital patients, who'd hung himself in the hospital gardens – not an unusual event in such a place - that led him to the idea that Gillespie had to 'commit suicide'. He knew Marion loved her husband as deeply as she did him and would not have stood for such a thing so he had to keep her in the dark about his plan. In any case her genuine distress when it happened would strengthen the assumption of suicide.

Christmas morning may seem an odd day to commit murder, but Byron had estimated that for his purposes it was perfect. Everyone would be relaxed and in festive mood, so the hospital would be quiet. Even the police would be difficult to get hold of on that particular morning, so he began to formulate his plans based on that day.

Assiduously he'd studied Gillespie's handwriting over and over again until he felt that he could do a reasonable copy. He was confident that it would be assumed to have been written by a man no longer in full control of his emotions or senses. Indeed it would appear to be an example of extreme paranoia, clearly showing the writer to be desperate and convinced that all those around him were plotting against him. As a psychiatrist he knew exactly how to write a note conveying the paranoid desperation of a man in mental torment.

In it he described the hospital as 'this awful place', and begged his wife's forgiveness for what he was about to do. Byron signed it using Gillespie's name, rightly guessing that his forgery would be near enough to the director's own signature for it to be accepted as genuine. He had even been amused at one suggestion he'd implanted, allegedly in Gillespie's mind that everyone had been plotting against him, since of course that was exactly what he had been doing.

The real master stroke was starting the note with the phrase 'My sweetness' – words that only Marion would recognise as her husband's particular form of personal endearment towards her. Without realising how he would use it, Marion had once told Byron of it during one of their bouts of passion.

The note was ready in his room that Christmas morning when he'd heard Gillespie coming up the stairs. A creature of habit the Director's timing had been as perfect as ever and in fact he'd relied on it. After enjoying breakfast with his wife, Gillespie would always go back upstairs to their bedroom to get dressed, leaving her to finish her coffee and organise her housekeeper's day. While they'd been at breakfast Byron had *quietly taken the Director's shotgun from his room and loaded it in his. Hearing the door close after Gillespie had climbed the stairs Byron had walked quietly along the corridor and, without knocking, had walked into the bedroom.*

Startled by the unexpected intrusion Gillespie had spun round. The last thing he'd seen in this world was that of his deputy holding a shotgun pointed straight at him. Byron, tense and quivering with excitement and knowing he'd now gone too far to change his mind, let him have both barrels. The Director had been thrown back against the far wall of the room - dead before he hit it with his chest all but destroyed. Byron, stunned by what he'd done even though it had gone to plan, had tossed the gun onto the bed and rushed out - anxious to get back to his own room before Marion made it to the top of the stairs.

He'd listened as the frightened woman had run up the stairs, perfectly timing his emergence from his own room so that as she opened her bedroom door and screamed, he was there by her side. He grabbed her to stop her rushing into the room towards the still figure of her husband who was lying, sprawled against the far wall facing the door his face and chest a bloody mess.

'Marion, Marion. Stop! Look, let me go in there to see what's happened', he'd almost shouted at her, in an effort to calm her hysterics. Finally she obeyed and stood silently trembling in his arms, trying to take in the full horror of what she'd just seen.

As he let her go Byron had heard more feet running up the stair. He turned to see a man he vaguely recognised coming up them towards him. 'What's happened?' the newcomer asked.

'It looks as though Dr Gillespie has shot himself,' Byron

told him. 'Look, can you look after Mrs Gillespie for a few minutes while I go back into the room to see if I can do anything? Take her downstairs and call for an ambulance and the police', he asked.

The man nodded. 'Yes sir, I'll do that,' he said, putting his arm protectively around the stricken woman's shoulders to shepherd her gently away from the door and back towards the stairs.

Byron thanked him and as the newcomer took the still shaking and sobbing woman down the stairs, he went back into the bedroom. The truth was he'd needed to get in there to make sure Gillespie really was dead and to put the suicide note in a place where it could be easily found. Once he'd done both he'd closed the door behind him and gone back downstairs. Marion, who was standing by the breakfast table with the stranger, looked up as he came into the room and he nodded to her.

I'm so sorry Mrs Gillespie, but your husband's dead and it looks as though he shot himself'.

She began to shriek and scream anew. 'No no, please God no!' He moved towards her, taking over the responsibility of looking after her.

'Thanks for that,' he smiled at the man. 'Who are you and what are you doing here anyway?'

'My name's Johnson, sir and I am one of the night staff. Mr Hicks, our supervisor asked me to drop the night's report sheets over to Dr Gillespie on my way home. It's something we do every morning,' he explained.

Byron nodded. 'Oh, yes, of course. Thank you! Look Johnson, can you hang on a little bit longer before going home. I know its Christmas Day and obviously you will want to get home to your family, but I have to wait with Mrs Gillespie for the ambulance and the police of course. In the *meantime the police will want us to stop the maid or anyone else going into that room until they arrive. Would you mind popping upstairs and waiting outside the door for me until they do, to stop anyone trying to go in?' Johnson stopped him.*

'Yes sir, of course sir. I'll be happy to help out in any way I can. I've already called the police and for an ambulance and they'll be here shortly. Don't worry, leave it to me,' he'd assured Byron before leaving the room to go upstairs. Byron had turned his attention to comforting Marion's very genuine shock and grief.

After that   it had all gone even better than he'd hoped. Neither the police nor anyone else had voiced any suspicions and, while there were a couple of things even Byron did not understand, the subsequent inquest accepted the facts. Just as he had hoped it had concluded that Gillespie had committed suicide while the balance of his mind was disturbed.

Within a few weeks he'd been appointed to Gillespie's job and, after a suitably respectable period of mourning, the grieving widow had agreed to become his wife. One day after their wedding Johnson had knocked on his office door. He'd explained that Charlie Hicks the night supervisor, was retiring and that he wanted his job.

'Well, of course Johnson. You will be considered like any applicant will be. I still remember how helpful you were on the day Dr Gillespie died however and my wife and I are eternally grateful for that,' he'd begun.

Johnson held up his hand to stop him in mid-sentence. 'I'm glad you brought that up sir because now it really is time for you to thank me properly because you and I both know you murdered him.'

'What?' Byron was stunned but before he could demonstrate his outrage further, Johnson had stopped him again.

'Look doctor. I spent a lot of time in the army and if it taught me anything, it was about guns and about the effects of recoil when they're fired. As soon as I went into that room I knew Dr Gillespie hadn't shot himself. He was lying up against the far wall while the gun was lying on the bed eight or nine feet away. That's much too far away for the recoil if he'd done it himself. No sir, there was no way that gun would have been thrown that far from the body naturally.' Johnson had paused for a moment to let the full implication of what he'd said sink in before continuing.

'Who do you think took it off the bed and put it closer to the body in the position it would have been in if the gaffer had done it himself? Who do you think wiped any fingerprints from it and put Gillespie's onto it using his dead hands, because I am fairly sure you never thought of that? In any case I was upstairs so quickly nobody would have had the time to do what the killer should   have done,' he point out, grinning mirthlessly.

Byron was having difficulty believing his ears by that time. His mind was in turmoil as he'd tried to come to terms with what Johnson had said. Quite suddenly his nice comfortable little world was in jeopardy and he knew he was cornered, but he had one more try.

'The inquest was months ago, and it brought in a suicide verdict. Why would anyone believe you if you told them what you say you'd found?' he spluttered.

'I notice you didn't deny it sir and you could be right' Johnson had sneered. 'But the fact is the last thing you need is to risk that inquest being reopened, right? If that suicide note was a forgery, as I think it probably was, then a proper murder investigation will certainly discover that and how would your new wife take that? Look doctor, I am not an unreasonable or a greedy man – all I want is a quiet life, *security with a comfortable job and a few quid now and again for me and my family to be able to enjoy life a little more. I promise you that will be all.'*

Byron had made one last desperate attempt to salvage something. 'If you tell the police you interfered with the evidence, you will go to prison as well as me.'

Johnson smiled again. 'Yes doctor – that's very true. We could both go inside, but they will hang you'.

From that moment the Director of the hospital had been Johnson's prisoner, though in fairness the blackmailer had been true to his word and hadn't been too greedy. He'd been clever enough to moderate his demands, but he did like a drink and he did seem to have a great many women friends other than his wife, whom he liked to entertain – very often on Byron's cash. On a more positive note he'd also proved to be an efficient night staff superintendent.....His train of thought was interrupted as Marion put her head around the door again.

'Bye love – I'm just off to see Mrs Johnson, then I have to go to the council offices for a meeting but I will be back by teatime' she promised as she waved goodbye.

He smiled and waved back without speaking as she disappeared back down the corridor. He really did love this woman and dreaded what she might do if she knew the deadly secret that had haunted him ever since they'd married. He'd never been totally sure of Johnson's silence but now the blackmailer was dead it would be a fear he could put behind him for ever. At last he could enjoy both his wife and his job again.

• • • • • •

It was getting late in the day when Cyril Hart got back to

the Brentwood's Time office, his mind a carousel of thoughts and emotions trying to determine what to do next. He had a lot of notes to write up a story now that would be good enough to satisfy the demands of his editor, but he also needed to talk to Wilkins again fairly urgently. He was still trying to decide on priorities as he walked back into the newsroom.

His problem was solved when Hamilton looked up as he came in. 'Well, have you spoken to the coppers?' he barked.

'Er, yes sir – and I've also been down to see Mrs Johnson'.

'Good, well what's the story then?'

'It does seem to be the general opinion that he topped himself, especially down at the hospital, but no one appears to know why. To be honest no one is sure about anything. There's going to be a post mortem and an inquest but no date has been set for that yet', Hart, still unsure about revealing too much of the day's events, decided not to tell him about the spat between the widow and Tilly Masters.

'What about the suggestion that he was murdered, then? Will that stand up?' Hamilton was no fool and he could clearly smell a good story turning into a routine one if it wasn't handled properly.

'I did ask the detective in charge of the case, Detective Sergeant Wilkins, about that but he didn't seem to keen on giving me a straight answer either, saying he preferred to wait for the inquest. I did get the impression though that he would be very helpful if we didn't go overboard yet' the reporter lied, having decided to hold back on the deal he'd actually struck with Wilkins.

Hamilton grunted. 'Ok, just do a low-key piece on the

death that will not attract a lot of notice for now and concentrate on the widow's reaction. What was that, by the way?'

'Much as you would expect really sir. Actually she seems to be a nice lady, keeping calm for the sake of the kids and not really sure of what the future holds. I told her we would be as helpful as we could and she appreciated that,' Hart didn't feel it was necessary, or the right moment, to mention Tilly's unexpected arrival on Emma's doorstep and what had happened after that.

'Fair enough, pending further developments we'll keep it on ice for the moment, so get it written up for Wednesday as an inside page lead. With any luck, tomorrow we'll get a different big story for the front but it could still be a good back-up if we don't,' Hamilton growled.

Hart, relieved that the editorial inquisition was over for the moment, nodded and sat down in front of his typewriter. Taking the cover off it and putting some paper and a sheet of carbon into it he opened his notebook and settled down to write a carefully phrased story. Heading it *'Shocking tragedy in mental hospital - was it suicide?'* he began to write.

A Brentwood family was left grieving after father-of-two Frederick Johnson was found dead in the Brentwood Mental Hospital early on Sunday morning.

Mr Johnson, (50) head night superintendent at the hospital, was discovered by colleagues after he failed to do his rounds and early suggestions were that he may have taken his own life. A hospital spokesman said a post mortem was being carried out and an inquest would be held at a later date but early indications could suggest that Mr Johnson had committed suicide by taking poison.

Brentwood Police however, say they are keeping an open mind and would continue with their enquiries before making any statement.

Mrs Emma Johnson (35) was given the news of her husband's death early on Sunday morning by the hospital's Director Dr Richard Byron. This week she told Brentwood's Time that she had no idea why her husband would have taken his own life. She is being cared for by neighbours and friends and says she is grateful for the help and consideration she had been shown by everyone.

'My children, Sarah and little Freddie, are too young to fully understand what's happened and my duty now is to remain strong for them', she told us.

No date has yet been set for the inquest but three years ago the previous director of the hospital, Dr Harold Gillespie, committed suicide by shooting himself. He left a note expressing his dismay at what he called 'this awful place', showing that the pressures of working in a mental hospital were too much even for the professional people there.

Hart sat back and went over what he'd written. It was exactly what Hamilton had demanded, just the basic facts and leaving room for more to come, while leaving him free to work quietly with Wilkins. He grinned and nodded in satisfaction. 'That will do for now,' he muttered as he walked across the newsroom to drop it into the basket on Hamilton's desk.

Hamilton read through the copy and grunted his satisfaction before rising from his chair and walking over to the coat stand, clearly deciding he'd done enough for the day. 'Right, goodnight Hart – try and not be late tomorrow, you've got the magistrates court to cover in the morning. Keep an eye on this story as well' he growled as he went through the door.

'Yes of course, goodnight sir', Hart replied to the departing figure, muttering 'good riddance' under his breath. He waited until he heard Hamilton close the office door downstairs before reaching for the telephone and asking the operator for the police station.

Wilkins was deep in thought when the phone on his desk rang and, after he picked it up and grunted his response, heard the operator put Cyril Hart through.

'Hello Cyril – that was quick. What can I do for you?' he asked.

'Albert, we need to talk again as soon as possible', the reporter told him. 'I think I might have a new lead.' He could not see the satisfied smile spread across the policeman's face of course. Wilkins knew now that he'd been right to take Hart into his confidence in order to widen the potential of his investigation. Here was the proof of the pudding.

'Yes, Cyril, I think you're right because I've had some thoughts too, but it's getting late now. Let's sleep on them and meet up in the pub again for lunch tomorrow'.

'That sounds like a good idea, Albert. See you tomorrow', Hart agreed, hanging up the receiver. In truth he was a little relieved, because he was just beginning to realise what a long, though satisfying, day it had been. It was time to get on the pushbike again to go home to Jane who would have their dinner in the oven by then.

His wife looked up from her pots and pans to smile when he arrived home and walked into the kitchen. 'Hello darling. Had a good day?' she asked. 'Dinner will be in about ten minutes,' she added as he leaned over to kiss her cheek.

'Well yes, very busy day as it happens.' He said, hanging his hat up in the hall and taking his jacket off before continuing. 'Someone in the mental hospital died over the weekend and there seems to be a mystery over how and why he did. I saw Tom Abbott there this morning and he sends you his regards by the way'.

'Oh that's nice, how is he? And how is Susan and their little boy? Haven't seen them for weeks,' she smiled, her mind still on the bubbling saucepan she was stirring on the gas stove. She and Cyril had been married for over three years, but she still loved playing the housewife and was particularly proud of her cooking skills.

'Who died?' she asked casually, as she fiddled with her pots.

'The night staff superintendent...' Hart got no further before Jane spoke again.

'What? You don't mean Fred Johnson?' She seemed incredulous and so was her husband, having been startled at her reaction to what he'd just told her.

'Yes, Fred Johnson! Why? Don't tell me you knew him', he blurted out.

She shook her head. 'Well, no. I didn't know him myself, but I do know of him and that Susan was afraid of him,' she said.

'Susan? Who Susan Abbott? Why would she be afraid of him? He asked.

'Because he kept trying to get her into bed, that's why', his wife replied. She saw the puzzled look on his face and laughed. 'Look love, it's well known around here that Fred Johnson really fancied himself as a ladies' man and was always trying it on with the charm and flattery. I never met him myself but I'm told he was very good at it too. Susan told me she met him at a hospital function and he started chasing her, even though he knew she was Tom's wife,' she paused, clearly amused at the look on Cyril's face.

'Oh, I don't think he got anywhere, well actually I know he didn't; but for some reason, though I have no idea why, she was too frightened to tell Tom about it. She only told me because she needed to talk to someone about it, but she swore me to secrecy, so darling, please don't tell her I've told you. For Pete's sake don't put it in the paper either' she pleaded.

He smiled reassuringly. 'Course not, but now I am wondering whether Tom actually knew about it,' he said, thinking back to his own strange conversation with the hospital's Deputy Director earlier that day. If Abbott had known about his wife and Johnson, it could put yet another whole new light on the victim's mysterious death. On the other hand if he had known, why had he insisted it had been a murder in which he might well have been a prime suspect?

'I'm pretty sure he didn't know. Now go and get washed up for supper darling while I lay the table' Jane said, as she began getting plates out of the cupboard.

• • • • • •

It was dark when Emma opened the door, but there was no mistaking the figure on the doorstep. In a sense it was one she wasn't completely happy to see, yet a little relieved and excited that he had come.

'Darling, I thought we'd agreed no contact for a while' she said, hurriedly pulling him into the house so she could close the door behind them and falling into his arms.

'Yes I know Em, but I just had to see you to make sure that you were alright. Anyway I'm on my way into work and what's more natural than seeing how the wife of a colleague who has just died is coping? Just another member of Fred's team popping in to offer his condolences, that's all I am' he grinned, pulling her towards him.

She melted into his arms, and relaxed as he gripped her body and held it to him so they could kiss passionately.

'I can't pretend I'm not happy to see you darling, but I can't help worrying. If people see us together they might start putting two and two together. That's what we agreed from the start, remember,' she whispered.

'Emma, so far the word in the hospital is that Fred committed suicide. Nothing's happened to change that so far and it won't,' he comforted her. He led her back into the kitchen where he took off his hat and jacket to make himself at home on what had been Fred's chair. She filled the kettle and put it onto the stove, took the teapot down from its shelf and reached for the tea-caddy before replying.

'I had the local paper round this morning,' she told him as she bustled round the tiny kitchen getting the cups and saucers ready as she waited for the kettle to boil. He glanced up at her as he sat down at the table – the same table where a few nights earlier Fred Johnson had eaten his last supper.

'I suppose that was inevitable. They were bound to poke their nose in sooner or later because it's a good local story. Did they say anything much?' He queried.

She shook her head. 'No – just asked about me and Fred. He said he'd been told at the hospital that it was suicide and that his paper would help us in any way they could. In fact he was very sympathetic and seemed to be a very nice man, but just as he was leaving I had another visitor.'

She told him about Tilly and the scene that had taken place on her doorstep. For the first time since his arrival he was shaken.

'Yes, I remember seeing him with a young girl leaving the hospital a few times. That must have been her, and you say she was pregnant?'

'Oh yes darling that much was pretty clear, believe me'.

His face furrowed a little as he thought about this new and unexpected twist. 'Em, do you think there is any way she could cause us any trouble?'

She thought for a moment or two before answering.

'Well, I don't see how. There is no way she can prove Fred was the father of her baby is there but on the other hand if it was true it could be a good reason for him to have committed suicide, isn't it? That kind of pressure might well have caused him to take an easy way out,' she pointed out.

'Yes, I suppose it could have', he nodded. 'But the reason we didn't organise a suicide note was to encourage the possibility of Fred dying because of an accident. I suppose we could write one now that someone like a pregnant girl friend has just turned up at home, but that might complicate things. No I think we'll leave well alone,' he added thoughtfully.

She finished making the tea and poured it into the cups. He was still deep in thought as he stirred it and lifted the cup to his lips. She sat on the other side of the table, watching his face and trying to determine what was in his mind. He finished drinking his tea before speaking again.

'Sweetheart, I think you're right. I suppose in a way it is a bit of a bonus. If it was true and it did come out it would put you into the position of a betrayed wife and that would bring you even more sympathy rather than suspicion. Nobody would ever seriously consider you as being guilty of anything other than bitterness at being betrayed by Fred. You weren't even in the hospital that night anyway and nobody has ever seen us together. Tell me, did this girl leave any address or anything to say where she came from?'

Emma shook her head and almost giggled. 'No, to be honest I never really gave her much of a chance before slamming the door in her face. Why?'

'Well, if you can find out where she lives it might be useful for you to get in touch with her to express your apologies for your outburst and invite her here. It could be a way to use this development in your favour. Invite her here, and get that press chap back so you can get the story about you being the forgiving wife into the paper. After all, she'll have no rights to Fred's estate, if there is any that is, but it would give the coppers another reason to assume he did himself in.'

He sat back and thought for a moment. 'Look Em, I will make enquiries at work because I'm sure I have seen Fred with a young girl in the hospital and someone might know about her, but I will have to be discreet. We don't want to draw attention to the fact of you and me being together.'

She smiled, happy now that the Tilly problem had been resolved. 'That sounds good to me darling. Now, what time are you on duty tonight? Have you got some real time to spend with me?' She murmured, stroking his cheeks seductively as she draped her body across his.

He grinned and kissed her full on the lips, before trying to stand up to go. 'No my love, I'm sorry but I have to clock in in about twenty minutes. Anyway I need to start making casual enquiries about your husband's mysterious girl friend?'

She was saddened by his departure, but she knew that it made sense. 'You're right darling. Hang on while I go out to make sure the coast is clear,' she smiled, getting off his lap and straightening her dress.

Holding a milk bottle in one hand she walked to the front door. Opening it, she made a noisy show of putting the bottle out on the step for the milkman to collect as usual in the morning. What she was really did was check up and down the street to make sure none of her nosey neighbours was watching.

He looked up as she came back into the room. 'It's all quiet out there darling. There's nobody about' she assured him. He stood up and put his hat and coat back on.

One last embrace and he was out of the door, walking briskly up the dark road towards the hospital less than a mile away. A few nights earlier, Fred Johnson had left the same house by that same door and had walked up Gresham Road for the last time. Now the wife he'd kissed goodbye then was his widow and this time she had a genuine tear in her eye as she watched the man she really loved disappear into the darkness. She was remembering what had been and what now could be.

Even now she could hardly believe that she had finally found real love, and in the most unexpected place – in the hospital. It had been one of the few occasions when Fred had taken her out and then only because it was a Christmas party for the children of the staff and he wanted her to take Sarah.

On that occasion Freddie was too young to go and had been left with a neighbour for an hour or two while they took their daughter. Then, so predictably, he'd left Emma to keep an eye on Sarah while, with an eye on seduction he trawled the other young mums to see what he could pick up. Emma never knew it, but that had been the evening he'd tried his best to add Susan Abbott to his list of conquests, unsuccessfully.

Emma had been sitting quietly on her own watching the children play when she had felt, rather than saw, the man approach. He asked politely if he could sit with her and for a moment or two she just thought he was another young father watching his child. They had spoken for a few minutes before he confessed that in fact he'd actually come over because she looked so lonely.

He'd introduced himself and once she had told him who she was, he'd revealed that he was actually a member of her husband's night staff team. He seemed to be such a nice person and it all seemed so very innocent, but before either of them became aware of it a mutual attraction began to germinate and take root. It was a few precious minutes in which Emma found herself happily discussing all manner of things with this attractive young man.

All too soon the moment ended as an excited Sarah rushed up to her mother to show her the little parcel that Father Christmas had just given her. Her new companion smiled as he shared in the child's excitement before, having spotted Fred coming back to his wife and daughter, standing up to leave. Emma thanked him for his company and wished him a happy Christmas as he left.

It should have stayed at that but by pure chance Emma and he had met again the very next morning. He wasn't a regular worshipper at St Thomas's because he lived in another town but he was a religious man and because he'd been staying in Brentwood that weekend he'd gone to its church.

So it seemed almost ordained by God that the two should get closer. He was single and a very vulnerable normally shy young man, while she was the classic brutalised wife desperate for affection. Together they found that and contentment in each other and began to find reasons to meet more often. Over the following weeks and months that innocent friendship gradually ripened into deeper feelings and then into a real and passionate love of the kind she'd never felt with her husband.

It had all seemed so impossible but the further they fell in love, the deeper their desperation became. He had few career prospects outside the hospital while she was a prisoner of a brutal marriage but, apart from their feelings for each other, the one thing they had in common was a deep hatred of Fred Johnson. Each of the lovers had their personal reasons to hate - she because of her domestic ties and he because of the contemptuous way Johnson regarded him at work. It wasn't long before their attachment to each other had combined to create a third and very powerful joint one.

It had been a combination of all those reasons that had led them into the plot to kill him. As Christians they knew it was wrong to even think about an act that went totally against their beliefs, but they reached a point where there seemed to be little choice than murder.

Now it was done and the man they both had cause to hate really was dead and the world seemed to be a much brighter place for each of the lovers. Provided they both held their nerve, a new and brighter future beckoned not just for them but for Sarah and Freddie too.

HE DIED PAINFULLY

'Didn't anyone tell you?' They're poofs.'

As Tilly pushed open the front gate in the Avenue she was still trembling over what had happened in Brentwood, and the thought of now having to tell her parents about it was making her more scared. Jessie Masters was in the scullery preparing the vegetables for the family's evening meal when she heard her daughter come into the house.

'Is that you Tilly? She looked up from the potatoes she was peeling in the sink to smile a welcome. 'Where have you been, love?'

The girl swallowed hard before answering – on the way home she had decided to follow Cyril Hart's advice and tell her mother the truth. 'Mum, I've been to Brentwood to see Fred's wife. I had to find out for myself if it was true about him being dead and it was...' The confession proved too much and she burst into tears without finishing the sentence, before throwing herself into Jessie's arms and burying her face in her mother's shoulder.

'What! Good grief girl, whatever did you do that for?' She hugged her daughter tightly as she asked the question.

'I had to Mummy. I just had to go there and find out for myself, but I wish to God I hadn't. She was so cruel –

she shouted at me and then slammed the door in my face,' Tilly sobbed.

'Well for goodness sake, Tilly. What did you expect? The woman has just lost her husband and then a pregnant teenager turns up on her doorstep saying he responsible. That must have been a terrible shock to the poor woman.' There was a tinge of realism mixed with compassion, for both Tilly and Emma Johnson, in Jessie's voice as she tried to comfort the weeping girl. 'Look love, put yourself in her place and think how you would have reacted to such a visit,' she scolded.

Gently she led her daughter into the 'back room' where the family spent most of its time (keeping the front one as the 'best room' one for Sunday tea and visitors) and sat her down at the dining table. Giving her a handkerchief to mop up the tears Jessie waited patiently for her to regain control before speaking again.

'Now, tell me what actually happened?' she asked as Tilly stopped weeping to wipe her swollen eyes dry.

Still visibly upset the girl told her word for word what had happened on Emma Johnson's doorstep. Then she mentioned Cyril Hart and the way he had comforted her and taken her for tea to calm down after the confrontation. 'He was very kind and told me I should come home and tell you everything,' she sobbed.

Suddenly she remembered that Hart had also told her he was a journalist. 'Mummy, Mr Hart was a newspaper reporter and he was talking to Mrs Johnson when I arrived.' A new thought suddenly struck her. 'Oh, no – do you think he will write about me and my baby in his newspaper?' She looked up at her mother, desperation and fear clouding her tear-stained face even further.

Like so many women of her time, Jessie Masters was no

fool and from the moment Tilly mentioned that Hart was a newspaper reporter, her mind had been spinning but not necessarily about her daughter's fear of publicity. Perhaps it was female intuition kicking in, but instinctively she guessed that if the newspapers were involved there might be something unusual about Johnson's death. Among the thoughts scrambling around in her worried mind at that moment was whether or not her husband was also involved somehow.

'Tilly, sweetheart – how did Fred Johnson actually die? Did anyone tell you that while you were there?'

The girl shook her head. 'No Mum. I never really thought to ask, I was that upset. Why?' she asked.

Her mother smiled, and stood up. She patted her daughter on the shoulder. 'No matter - no matter, love. Stay there and I'll make you a cuppa', she muttered as she left the room to go back into the scullery. Her husband would be home in an hour and she remembered how angry he'd been about Fred Johnson getting his daughter into trouble. Now she had questions to ask him.

• • • • • •

Hart was already well into his pint in the Grey Goose when Wilkins arrived, nodding to publican Harry Ross as he came through the door. The reporter lifted his glass in welcome and gestured to the other pint on the table clearly meant for the policeman.

'Morning Cyril,' the detective said as he pulled up a chair and sat down. Picking up the beer, he took a deep draught from the glass before putting it down and smacking his lips in satisfaction. 'God, I needed that,' he grinned.

'Yes, the first is always the best' Hart agreed. 'So what sort of day have you had so far?' he asked.

'Well, not a bad one actually,' Wilkins grinned, before taking another mouthful of the beer. 'I've got a list of the night staff on duty that night, but I've also found something a bit unusual about a previous death at the hospital. What about you? What have you got for me?' he asked.

Hart took a deep breath. 'Well, I think I might well have found another murder suspect or at least another reason why Johnson might have topped himself,' he announced, relishing the look on the policeman's face. He told Wilkins about his visit to Emma Johnson and about Tilly arriving with her startling news. He explained how he'd caught up with the distraught girl and had taken her to the tearooms.

'From what Tilly told me in the teashop her father, who used to work at the hospital by the way, is a man prone to violence and he was furious to hear about the baby. She said that she thought he'd kill Johnson if he'd got his hands on him. I know he no longer works there but he obviously knows its routines and how to get into the place at night,' he said.

Wilkins nodded his agreement. 'You're right Cyril, it is certainly a lead worth exploring and I will. Well done. I also agree that the pressure of a pregnant girl friend and the fear of exposure could well be another reason for Johnson to have committed suicide. Now, do you have any files in your office that could give us any information on how the previous hospital director died?'

The question puzzled Hart for a moment. 'What, you mean Dr Gillespie? I wasn't here then, but as far as I know he shot himself. Why do you ask?'

'Well, I do have copies of the formal inquest and investigation report that says that too but I suspect that the press coverage of a case like that might be much more informative. Police reports are simply factual and are not intended to be anything else whereas newspapers stories give more background. If you do have such a file I would like to get hold of a copy of it to look at,' Wilkins said.

Hart nodded that he would help and then another thought struck him. 'Yes by the way you did know that Gillespie's widow married the present director and is Councillor Mrs Byron these days didn't you,' he said. Wilkins eyes widened at the news.

'Hmmn, so she's got local influence too. No, I didn't know that - it's not the kind of thing that would appear in the official file anyway. When did she marry Byron, then?'

'I'm not sure but I will check it out,' the reporter assured him. 'Why are you interested in that old story, anyway?' he asked. Wilkins looked at his new friend quizzically and took another sip of his beer before answering. He'd wanted to drop a bombshell and now he decided was the time.

'Well Cyril, as I told you yesterday I am not altogether sure about Dr Byron. I was very suspicious about his eagerness to get me believing Johnson committed suicide. It nagged at me even more when I found from the official report in our files that, apart from the widow and Dr Byron, Fred Johnson was the only witness who gave evidence at the Gillespie inquest.

'Yes, by coincidence he just happened to be there on that Christmas morning and I am not comfortable with coincidences. Think about it mate. Under Gillespie he was just a member of night staff, but he was there that morning and when Byron gets appointed as the new

Director, Johnson gets promoted to Night Superintendent. I have to ask myself whether that was a natural and earned promotion, or did he have any kind of hold over Byron?'

Hart had been listening open-mouthed as Wilkins expounded his theory.

'Jesus Christ, Albert!' He sat for a moment or two trying to take in the full import of what Wilkins had outlined, with the policeman closely watching his face and trying to read his mind. 'Are you suggesting that Dr Gillespie might have been murdered and that Byron and possibly Johnson knew something about it?' He was speaking in hushed tones now, clearly astonished by what he'd heard.

Wilkins nodded his head and held up a cautionary hand to restrain his friend's excitement and quieten him down a little. 'Hang on Cyril, let's not get carried away here. We know very little so far and what I am suspecting may well be totally wrong, but the fact is that we have two men in the same workplace who both met their end, albeit some years apart, under suspicious circumstances.

'I've been a copper for years now and coincidences like that worry me. We need to know much more about both of these men before we can even start to draw any real conclusions. Your newspaper files may well contain the sort of information we need, the kind that would not appear in an official police report. Tell you what, you check them out and I will interview Johnson's workmates to see what sort of person he was,' he told the reporter.

Hart sat there, still toying with his beer but now with his mind filled with a whole notebook of potential 'exclusive' story lines. His brain was visualising a jumbled mass of emotive headlines, all with his by-line on them.

Wilkins picked up his beer and emptied the glass before rising to go. 'Cyril, I will also check out the Tilly Masters angle because you're right, she could be a reason for either suicide or murder and I need to see if her father fits into this story now,' he said.

Putting the glass down on the table he said goodbye and walked out of the pub, leaving Hart still stunned. The journalist knew now that he could be on the verge of a major career move, but would have to be even more careful in the office now. He certainly did not want John Hamilton to get any hint of what was really going on now but he still had to satisfy him to a degree.

In something of a daze he rose from the table and, hardly acknowledging Harry's friendly goodbye, left the pub to emerge into a High Street still bathed in early afternoon sunshine. There was no sign of the policeman who was well on his way back to the police station by then, so Hart turned up into St Thomas' Road to walk briskly, even a touch excitedly, back to the office.

When he got back to the newsroom he was relieved to find it empty with Hamilton clearly at lunch, so he took the opportunity to go straight to the filing cabinet. Within minutes he found what he was looking for and, still wary of the editor's return, swiftly shoved it into his desk drawer. He'd barely closed the filing cabinet before Hamilton walked back into the room.

That afternoon proved to be a fairly routine one for any journalist, writing up the usual sort of mundane stories and flower show reports that fill most of any local paper's pages every week. It seemed an age before Hamilton looked up at the clock and, announcing that he was off, put on his hat and coat before vanishing out of the door. The moment he'd gone Hart took the file from his desk and began to read it. As he read the first story, the hairs on the back of his neck began to tingle for he was now seeing it in the light of Wilkins' suggestion of possible murder.

It was headlined **'Christmas Day tragedy at mental hospital'** and had been written by John Hamilton, presumably when he'd been just a Brentwood's Time reporter.

In a shocking tragedy at the Brentwood Mental Hospital on Christmas Day its top man shot himself following what has been described as a mental breakdown.

After having breakfast with his wife Dr Harold Gillespie, the hospital's Director, went back to his bedroom. Shortly afterwards Mrs Gillespie heard a gunshot and dashed upstairs to find her husband sprawled against a wall with massive wounds to his head and chest.

Another resident in the house, the hospital's Deputy Director Dr Richard Byron, was actually the first on the scene to discover the body. He said it was clear from the moment he'd entered the room that Dr Gillespie, one of the country's foremost psychiatrists, was dead. He'd managed to prevent Mrs Gillespie from going further into the room to see the dreadful scene for herself and sent her downstairs to call the police.

This week Dr Byron spoke to Brentwood's Time about what happened, saying it had been a great shock to everyone in the hospital.

'I think it is pretty clear that death was self-inflicted, and I believe the police did find a suicide note. At this time I think all our sympathies are with Mrs Gillespie', he said.

Another witness to the event was Mr Frederick Johnson, a member of the hospital's night staff who happened to be in the house to hand over night reports before going off duty. An ex soldier who saw action on the Somme during the war, Mr Johnson said he had seen a lot of death there but seeing it this close to home had been a shock.

'Dr Byron asked me to look after Mrs Gillespie and, when he came down then asked me to go back upstairs and stand guard outside the room to stop anyone else entering it until the police arrived. The door was still open when I got up the stairs, so I closed it but could not help seeing what had happened before I did and it was a dreadful sight,' he said.

A police spokesman said a post mortem had established that Gillespie had died as a result of a gunshot wound to the chest. An inquest will be held next week.

Hart sat and thought for a moment or two as he took in what he'd read. Just as he'd with done with Johnson's death a few days earlier, Byron had apparently rapidly come to the conclusion at the time of Gillespie's that he had killed himself too, although perhaps on that occasion he had good cause. Or was he trying to persuade a coroner of it by going public with his view both then and now?

The other story in the file was a brief report about the subsequent inquest which seemed to have been very quick and almost routine. Without too much evidence being produced it had reached a verdict of suicide while the balance of the mind was disturbed. That was exactly what Byron had said it was and while it would have raised no suspicion at the time, in retrospect and in view of what the policeman had suggested, it now began to take on a whole new and perhaps more sinister dimension.

There had been a suicide note in Gillespie's handwriting, confirmed by his widow, in which he had seemed more than a little paranoid alleging that people had been plotting against him. Surely if he had been that close to a breakdown someone would have noticed, especially in that particular environment, yet that, along with the evidence of Byron and Johnson, had seemed to make it an open and shut case.

The reporter in him now realised why Wilkins had been so interested in Johnson's relationship with the hospital's Director. Not only had he been in the house on the day of Gillespie's death but had been left on his own to guard the Director's bedroom door until the police had arrived that morning. So as Byron comforted the shocked widow downstairs, Johnson could have easily gone into the room and tampered with any evidence. Obviously that was why Wilkins had told him they needed to find out more about Johnson's character.

It also raised another question in Hart's mind, now he'd told him about Byron's wife, one he felt sure was also now in Wilkins'. If Byron and Johnson had really both been involved in the death of Harold Gillespie was his widow, the now Councillor Mrs Byron, part of it too?

· · · · · ·

Detective Sergeant Wilkins was still deep in thought as he drove to the hospital that evening, on his way to talk to the members of the night staff who had been on duty the night Johnson died. Always a great believer in doing the unexpected he'd guessed that they would not be expecting to be interviewed during their shift.

Before leaving the police station he'd been phoned by Richard Byron who had confirmed that the autopsy had confirmed that the ingestion of Lysol had been the probable cause of death. The doctor had also told him that the acidic effects of the disinfectant on the stomach and other organs in the body had made it difficult to detect anything, other than that Johnson had probably eaten some cheese sandwiches before he'd swallowed the Lysol.

'I suppose the only thing we can be certain of is that he died painfully', Byron had told him. The detective had realised that from the moment he'd seen the body and it was why he'd been so puzzled about the body being found in such a relatively peaceful and relaxed condition.

As he sat outside the hospital in his car he looked again over the list of night staff he was planning to talk to. Obviously first on the list had to be the man who had discovered Johnson's body in the night superintendent's office that Sunday morning. According to the list he had in front of him the man, acting as temporary night supervisor, would be found in that same office.

Getting out of his car and walking into the building the policeman found a sign in the reception area pointing towards the room he was looking for and made his way towards it. Coming to it, he knocked quietly on it, opening it to see Fred Olson sitting at the desk sipping tea from an Essex Regiment mug, presumably of the same kind Johnson had drunk from and which was missing.

'Mr Olson?' The policeman asked before, without waiting for a response, walking into the office. He closed the door behind him and sat down in the proffered chair before speaking again.

'I don't know if you remember me but we met early on Sunday morning. My name is Detective Sergeant Wilkins from Brentwood Police and I am looking into the death of Mr Frederick Johnson here early on Sunday morning. Of course it was you who discovered the body and we did speak briefly, but I am here tonight to talk to any members of the night staff who might know anything at all about what happened that night. I am also keen to know a little more about Mr Johnson himself,' he explained.

Olson smiled. 'Yes, of course I remember you Mr Wilkins – it wasn't the sort of morning anyone would forget easily and of course anything I can do to help I will be glad to do. Can I offer you a cuppa?' he asked, gesturing towards his own mug.

'Thank you sir, but I'm fine and I had some tea before I left the station. Are you doing the night superintendent's job now then?'

'Only on a temporary basis until a permanent appointment is made. I am the senior night staff member here and used to stand in for old Fred whenever he was sick or off duty for some reason'. Olson explained.

'Right, I see. Was that very often then – I mean did he miss many of his shifts?'

Olsen paused and thought for a moment before answering. 'Well, one doesn't like to speak ill of the dead but the man did like his booze and sometimes that did interfere with his duty nights,' he grinned confidentially.

Wilkins nodded his thanks for the information and made a note or two in his notebook before looking up again. 'Did that happen a lot then? If so did the management not take note of his absenteeism?'

'They never appeared to. To be absolutely honest Fred was one of the worst and most persistent absentees on the night shift, usually because he was drunk. I never remember him getting hauled over the coals about it though', Olson replied.

Again the policeman nodded thoughtfully. 'Usually?' he queried.

'It was usually because he was drunk but he was also a

bit of a lad with the girls and sometimes that was the reason, but I will deny ever telling you that if I'm asked. It was none of my business and if that came out it would only hurt his missus and she's a nice lady who has enough on her plate at the moment,' Olsen added.

Again the detective nodded his thanks and added some more words to his notebook, before looking up. 'Thank you for that Mr Olson and don't worry, that will remain our secret. I'm simply trying to build up a picture of the man. Now can you run through the events of that night for me again,' Wilkins asked.

'Yes, well it was a pretty quiet night all round really, though they are not always that way. I was on Ward 3 and at first Fred made his regular ward visits to check things were ok for his duty log. But after midnight he never came again and that was pretty unusual, though not completely so. As I said before, if he came in full of beer he'd often fall asleep after doing his pre-midnight rounds.' Olson paused to take another swig of tea from his mug before continuing.

'But even on the nights he did that he never failed to make his early morning round around 5a.m., I'll give him that. But that morning he didn't come and by six o-clock I was getting a bit concerned because that really was out of character. I popped out to ask other night staff if they'd seen him but none of them had since his midnight visit. I thought he might be oversleeping because of the booze again so decided to pop down the corridor to wake him and you know the rest. Tell me Mr Wilkins, why are you asking about this? Wasn't this was a simple case of a bloke committing suicide? That's what we've been told' he said.

Wilkins, who had been taking copious notes as Olson spoke, looked up and turned the question around. 'Yes, it must have been a shock to find him like that. Tell me, do you think it was suicide? Did Mr Johnson ever give any indication that he was thinking about taking his own life?'

A look of surprise flashed across Olson's face. 'Well, no, not exactly, it's just the rumour going around the hospital. I was a bit doubtful because he was always full of himself especially when he'd had a few and he was certainly not the sort of bloke easily depressed. No it's what Dr Byron said that morning after I raised the alarm.'

'What exactly did he say?' The policeman asked.

Olson thought back for a moment before replying. 'Well he walked in here, took Fred's pulse to make sure he was dead and said that it looked as if he'd killed himself, though he never said why he thought so.'

'And you say this office was clean and tidy with nothing untoward or out of place, other than that the dead man was sitting at the desk with his head on his arms when you came in? Must have been a bit of a shock,' Wilkins said.

'Well yeah, that's right. I must admit I was a bit shaken up by the whole business. With the kind of patients we get in here you do see a lot of death here of course and I saw a lot of it in the war as well, but this took me totally by surprise. Well, all of us really,' he added.

Wilkins stood up to go. 'Thank you Mr Olson, you have been very helpful. By the way is that your mug, because I understand Mr Johnson had one just like it?' he asked, nodding towards the tea.

'Yes I believe he did, but we all bring our own mugs to work and this is mine. You can buy them by the crate in the High Street – this is a military town, don't forget, though to be honest I wasn't in the Essex Regiment. Women don't know much about the army, do they, and my wife bought me this one.' Olson replied, as he walked the policeman to the door.

'Thanks again, I am off to Ward 3 now. Who is on duty there tonight?' Wilkins asked as they parted company.

'It should be Silly Billy. Sorry, Billy Taylor. He's a nice guy but not always the sharpest tool in the box. He suffers with his nerves a bit and some of the blokes here think he should be a patient, but like I say he is a nice bloke. He does his job well and he is very popular with the patients', the supervisor said before his visitor, waving a hand of appreciation for the information, began to walk down the corridor.

It had been Ward 3 where Fred Olson had been doing the night shift on the morning of his grim discovery and Wilkins wasn't quite sure what to expect when he got there. It was still early in the evening and by the general clatter it was clear that the hospital hadn't fully settled down for the night, so there was a little trepidation in his step as well as he went in.

In fact the ward was fairly quiet. Most of the thirty or so patients were already asleep while a few others were sitting up in bed reading. Seated at the desk and apparently in charge of things, was a dark haired youngish looking man who glanced up sharply as the policeman entered the room and came towards him.

'Mr Taylor, my name is Detective Sergeant Wilkins from Brentwood police...' he'd barely got the introduction out of his mouth before he realised that the man was almost trembling. It was a reaction he was well used to – even totally innocent people sometimes get nervous when a policeman speaks to them.

Taylor pulled a nearby chair over to the desk for

Wilkins to sit on before managing to get any coherent words out of his mouth. 'You're a policeman?' My brother is a policeman in Southend,' he said.

Wilkins nodded. 'Yes I'm a policeman and I'm investigating the death of Mr Johnson. I've come here tonight to talk to all the members of the night staff who were on duty on the night he died and I believe you were one of them,' he said pointedly. He'd been a copper long enough now to see in Taylor all the signs of a very nervous man, but whether it was based on guilt or not was not so easy to figure out. He decided to phrase his questions based on the need to find out more about the man himself.

'First of all tell me a little about yourself, Mr Taylor. How long have you worked here and what were you doing before? That sort of thing,' he asked gently, and anxious not to sound too inquisitorial.

Taylor's hands trembled slightly as he fiddled with the pencil he'd been writing his log-sheet up with when Wilkins had arrived. He was clearly trying to formulate his answers.

'Well, I've been here about eighteen months. To be honest, it's the first real job I've had since the war. Although I never saw active service, because I worked in an army hospital, what I saw in that place did leave me with some terrible memories and if I am to be honest a bit high strung. In fact I was a patient in a hospital like this for a while myself. I tell you Mr Wilkins, you don't have to be physically injured to be scarred by war. Like so many of the patients here I needed a lot of psychiatric help after it was all over.

'I couldn't hold down a steady job at first after I left hospital. If it hadn't been for my brother and his wife letting me live in their house I don't think I would have ever recovered. It was only coming here and working with people even worse than I was that I was able to cope, perhaps because I felt I was able to help them because of my own problem,' he added, almost as an afterthought.

'Oh, right - well thanks for that. Now can you tell me how you got on with Mr Johnson?' Even as he asked the question, Wilkins was asking himself why he'd even bothered to ask it, but just as he had with Fred Olson, he got a very specific answer to his questions about Johnson's character.

'He was a bully and I hated every bone in his body', Taylor said firmly, staring him directly in the face.

A little surprised at the venom and ferocity with which Taylor had suddenly spat out the words, the policeman raised his eyebrows. He waited silently for the ward supervisor's obvious bitterness to subside and let him continue.

'Oh don't get me wrong, he knew his job alright but he was always picking on me. He found out that I'd never actually seen active service in the trenches during the war and after that never stopped reminding me what it had been like for those who had. Honest Mr Wilkins, that man took every opportunity he could to mock me in front of people and I hated him for it, but I never killed him.'

Wilkins looked up sharply. 'Why did you say that? I never said anything about Mr Johnson being killed. Do you think he was?'

Taylor blushed, almost guiltily. 'Well, my brother is a policeman and when I told him what had happened he asked me whether it was possible someone had done him in. It was just a remark but it stuck in my mind for some reason because, believe me, there's plenty of other people here who wished him dead.'

'Like who?' Wilkins asked.

'Well, it's not for me to say, but he had his enemies.'

'Tell me more,' the policeman pressed.

'Look, for a start, there are a lot of angry husbands and fathers around this town. Johnson was a married man, but he liked to chase other women around as well and he was pretty noisy at boasting about it afterwards,' Taylor said.

'I see. Well, thank you for that Mr Taylor. Tell me did you notice or hear anything unusual yourself that night?'

Taylor shook his head, but seemed to think for a second or two before actually replying. 'No, it had been a quiet night until Fred Olson came and told us something was wrong and that he was going to investigate. After that, everything seemed to happen and there was a lot of coming and going with people rushing about all over the place.'

'So you didn't see or hear anything out of the ordinary?'

Again there was that strange hesitation. 'No nothing. It had been a quiet night.'

Wilkins smiled, making a mental note to tax the man on that aspect in another interview, before standing up to leave. 'Ok Mr Taylor thank you sir, that'll be all for now. I'll let you get on with your shift, but I may be in touch again.'

As he walked back down the ward towards the door, the policeman could feel the eyes of a dozen patients, along with Taylor's boring into his back. He was quite happy within himself because he felt he'd learned a lot, both about Taylor and the dead man as well as about their relationship.

Clearly Billy Taylor was a man who lived on the edge of his nerves but what he'd said about Johnson had been revelatory, giving him two more possible motives and possibly justifying the Tilly Masters situation. The man had been a bully and a womaniser and both aspects could be the kind that provoke strong feelings of hostility, but could they be strong enough reasons for murder? The policeman in him still wasn't quite so sure about that. Nor had he stopped wondering about the hesitations in some of Taylor's answers, but given the nervousness of the man perhaps that was understandable.

He was still thoughtful as he walked down the corridor to Ward 2. Walking into it he was surprised to find two men on duty there. He looked down at his list as he walked towards the desk.

'Mr Alfred Rice?' he asked. The smaller of the two men stood up to hold out his hand in greeting.

'Yes, that's me. This is Mr Race who is a nursing attendant here and works on this ward during the day. He's just popped in to see if everything was ok because it's been a bit hectic in here today. I was told to expect a visit from you tonight – I understand you're from the police' Rice said.

Wilkins nodded and introduced himself. 'Yes that's right, sir. I'm making some enquiries about the death of Mr Fred Johnson and I understand you were on duty that night.'

'Yes! Bit of a shock all round. Johnson was not a nice man but the last thing you'd expect would be for him to top himself.' The nursing attendant sitting at the table with him nodded his agreement, but Wilkins raised his eyes at the remark.

'Who said he did?'

'Well, that's what is being said around the hospital. Are you saying he didn't?

The policeman shook his head. 'I haven't said anything

of the sort and until we know more about the circumstances surrounding his death we are keeping an open mind,' he said. 'Tell me about that night Mr Rice. Did anything unusual happen? I mean did you hear any odd or unusual sounds or see anything out of the ordinary? I'm told that Mr Johnson never carried out his usual rounds after midnight – did he visit you?'

'No sir. It was a quiet night all round. It was only after his body was discovered in the morning and Fred Olson came and told us about it that things began to happen.' As he spoke Wilkins noticed that his companion was still nodding, so switched his attention towards him.

'I see. Tell me Mr Race – I noticed you seemed to be agreeing with Mr Rice. Does that mean you were here that night as well, even in the small hours?' The nursing attendant reddened at the suggestion.

'Well yes, as it happens I was. I live in the nurse's home here and couldn't sleep because I was worried about one of my patients on this ward. I decided to pop back to check all was well with him and then Alfie and me got talking and before we realised it, it was morning.'

'Is that something you do often – come back to the wards at night when you are off duty?' Wilkins asked.

'Well, no not every night, but I do sometimes. I'm working for my Intermediate Certificate in psychiatric nursing, so the chance of being able to study the patients at night helps me a great deal. A lot of them get particularly deeply disturbed during those hours and Alfie lets me come in sometimes to observe and help out where I can. It's all very unofficial of course, and I would appreciate it if it never went any further' Race told him.

The policeman brushed the plea aside. 'Saturday night was one of those nights, was it? You were both together here on the ward that night and neither of you noticed or heard anything odd?'

'That's right, nothing!' There was a touch of impatience, perhaps even irritation, in Race's voice now though Wilkins made a mental note that Rice maintained his silence. He stood up to go. 'By the way what sort of man was Mr Johnson? Did you get on well with him?'

Almost in unison the two men shook their heads. 'No, he was a pig and a bully to anyone he felt he could pick on and neither of us got on with him,' Race told him.

'Right, thank you both and I do appreciate what you say. I have to tell you however that when it comes to the inquest you will probably both be required to give evidence, because I cannot conceal the fact that you were both here. However, I'm sure your explanation is quite logical Mr Race and will cause you no problems with the hospital authorities.'

As he walked out of the ward Wilkins again had that feeling of being watched at every step until he'd closed the door behind him. He had also sensed an atmosphere in the ward that he'd not felt when talking either to Fred Olson or Billy Taylor. He couldn't put his finger on any reason for the feeling but it was definitely there.

Glancing down at his list he saw that a Mr James Lacey, who had also been on duty that fateful night, was on duty in Ward 4 so made his way up the corridor. As he walked into the ward all was quiet with most of the patients sleeping. At the far end of the room the night attendant looked up and watched as he approached.

'Mr Lacey?' Wilkins asked the question in a hushed level of voice so as not to disturb sleeping patients. The man at the desk nodded.

'Yes, that's me – and you are?'

Reaching it Wilkins sat on the chair opposite him. 'My name's Detective Sergeant Wilkins and I'm looking into the death of your night supervisor, Mr Fred Johnson. My purpose here tonight is to talk to people like yourself who were on duty that night, to see if they can throw any light on how he died and to find out a bit more about Mr Johnson.'

'Right, yes well of course I will help in any way I can. A lot of people here never liked him but Fred was a pal as far as I'm concerned. Who have you spoken to so far?'

'Well, apart from Mr Olsen of course, I've also seen Mr Taylor and Mr Rice.'

A look of contempt seemed to pass over Lacey's face at the mention of Rice's name. 'You've spoken to Alfie Rice. Well, I bet he wasn't too complimentary about Fred. Was his boy friend there as well?' he sneered.

Not for the first time that night Wilkins was taken by surprise. 'Boy friend?'

'Yeah, his boyfriend - Tommy Race! Didn't anyone tell you?' They're poofs!

HE WAS A PIG

'...he and Alfie had planned to kill Fred'

It had been a totally unexpected remark and it took a few seconds for Wilkins to fully take it in. Lacey, clearly pleased to have provided the policeman with information he hadn't been aware of, waited for him to react.

'What?' Even as he gasped out the word Wilkins knew what had been worrying him, without being able to put his finger on it, since his visit to Ward 2 a few moments ago.

Lacey nodded to emphasise the point. 'Yeah, I bet that was something they never told you. Was Tommy there then? He usually turns up on the nights Alfie's on duty.'

'Mr Lacey, what you are suggesting is that a criminal offence is being committed. It's one that people can go to prison for so it's a very serious allegation. Are you sure about that?' Wilkins asked.

Lacey nodded his head and grinned. 'Course I am, everyone here knows about it, and I'm only surprised someone didn't tell you before now. No one's ever reported them, probably because most people here like Alfie who is a good mate; but believe me, it's true. Personally, as long as I am not affected, I believe in live and let live and even Fred Johnson never actually did anything about it. He knew about it and always made it clear how much he despised them, but he never turned them in.'

Wilkins took a deep breath. Clearly this put another new and totally unexpected aspect on the whole case and was giving him a lot more to think about. To win some time as he collected his thoughts he reverted to his normal line of questioning by going back to basics.

'Mr Lacey, on the night Mr Johnson died did you see or hear anything unusual?'

Lacey thought for a second, clearly enjoying his moment. 'Well, this ward is a long way down the corridor from the office so it wouldn't be unusual not to hear anything. There was one odd moment, though.' Again the ward attendant paused for effect before slowly adding, 'Some time around 1 o-clock in the morning I thought I did hear somebody shout something out, but nights in this place can play funny tricks on the mind,'

'Can you remember what that shouting was about?' the policeman asked.

This time Lacey thought much harder before answering. 'Well, at first I thought I heard someone shout '*you dirty bastards*', but to be fair I couldn't be certain it was that. It could have just as easily come from a disturbed patient on another ward. You do get a lot of them shouting during the night when they are having bad dreams so no, I could not swear to the exact words,' he admitted.

Wilkins stared hard at Lacey for a moment himself this time before asking his next question. 'About that voice - you mentioned that Mr Johnson despised Mr Race and Mr Rice because of what you say they are. What were their feelings about him, and could it have been his voice you heard?'

'Well, Fred was ex-army and very much a man's man. He had no time for weak blokes and especially not for poofs. Why he never reported them I'll never know but he never hid his feelings about them to us and I know for a fact that they hated him. Race once told me that Fred had tried to get him the sack, and at one time there was a story that they plotted to kill him, but I think it was just a rumour started up by another member of staff at the time.'

'What, who was that?' Wilkins interrupted.

'Well, I got that from Jack Masters who used to work here,' Lacey said. 'He left to go and work in that big motor factory over in Dagenham and he never had a lot of time for the queers either, or for Fred come to that. To be honest I think it was probably just wishful thinking because Fred disciplined him a few times for not keeping his night log up to date. Anyway, Jack reckoned that Tommy Race once told him that he and Alfie had planned to kill Fred and make it look like suicide but I think it was just talk.'

The mention of Jack Masters had rung an immediate bell with the policeman who remembered Cyril Hart's experience with that young girl with the same surname. It was too much of a coincidence to ignore, but he pressed on.

'I see, but apart from that, what did most people here think of Mr Johnson?' he asked.

'To be honest, he wasn't exactly popular with everyone but I guess he did his job and was always on hand whenever any of us needed help with a restless patient. He liked his drink though and he fancied himself with the women. I think he'd been a sergeant in the army and sometimes he tried to treat us like squaddies he could bully. If he thought he could get away with it he'd try it on, but if you stood up to him he respected you for it. People like Silly Billy, another one of the night staff, suffered because Fred saw him as a weak man and bullied him unmercifully, but like I said if you stood up to him he respected that,and left you alone.'

The mention of Jack Masters name a minute or so earlier was still buzzing around in Wilkins brain even as Lacey was been speaking. It was yet another element of what had become a tangled web of riddles, a maze becoming more labyrinthine by the hour, but one that he needed to find a way through to find his answers. He needed more time to think now, so he stood up and held out his hand.

'Thank you so much Mr Lacey, you've been very helpful, and I would appreciate it if you kept what we have discussed to yourself,' he said.

'Yes of course. If you need any more help please feel free to ask', the night attendant replied. He grinned as he watched the policeman turn to make his way up the ward and disappear back out into the corridor. Though he'd implied otherwise he had no love for the poofs himself and was privately hoping he'd caused them some problems.

Outside the ward Wilkins paused for a moment or two, thinking about what he'd been told that night by all the people he'd questioned so far. He glanced up the corridor towards the night supervisor's office, mentally calculating the distance and wondering whether anyone shouting from their bed could be heard in other wards. He had learned much more than he'd expected, but now he had to work out how all that information fitted together.

He could go back to Ward 2 to confront Race and Rice

about their relationship and question them about the allegation that they'd threatened to kill Johnson. His instincts as a copper however told him that would be counter-productive and put them on their guard at this stage. No, he needed time to think over his tactics now and he also knew he had to go to Dagenham as well.

• • • • • •

Wednesday morning, press day, was always fairly quiet in the newsroom and as usual on this one the editor was busy downstairs in the composing room, putting the paper to bed. Still having a great deal to think about, Hart was idling the time away looking over local flower show and cricket match reports, when his phone rang. He picked it up to hear the switchboard girl tell the caller he was through to the news desk.

'Cyril, is that you?' He recognised the voice immediately. He'd only known Albert Wilkins for a few days but already it felt as though they'd been friends for years.

'Yes. Good morning, Albert. I was going to give you a call myself later,' he replied.

The policeman interrupted the small talk to get straight down to business. 'Can we talk over the phone?'

Hart hesitated for a moment. He had been about to reassure his caller but there was always the chance that the switchboard girl was eavesdropping so decided against it. 'I would rather not actually, but I do need to talk to you now rather that at lunchtime. Suppose I say I'm coming down to the station for police calls? I can be with you in five minutes', he said.

'Yes, that's fine Cyril. I'll put the kettle on,' Wilkins promised.

The reporter stood up and looked out of the window. Just for a change that week it was a nice sunny morning and with Hamilton out of the way for a few hours, there was no pressure on the newsroom. Rather than torture himself on the bike again, he decided to take a stroll down to the police station. Picking up his notebook and thrusting it into his pocket, he walked down the stairs and telling the girl on the switchboard he wouldn't be long, walked out.

True to his word Wilkins had the tea ready and waiting as the desk sergeant showed Hart into his office. Smiling a welcome he got up to shake Hart's hand, gesturing him to sit down.

'First of all Cyril, did you get an address for Tilly Masters?' he asked.

'Well, no not a full one. Only that she lived in a road called Becontree Avenue, but there can't be that many families called Masters in that road so she shouldn't be hard to find,' Hart replied. 'Why do you ask?' he queried.

'Well I spoke to some of the night staff in the hospital last night, and a couple of interesting points came up. It does seem that you could be right about her father's anger but it also seems that he may have had a grudge against Johnson before that. Obviously in view of what you found out, it's clear his girl getting pregnant gives him an additional motive, but I need to find out if he also had opportunity' Wilkins told him.

Hart nodded thoughtfully. 'Yes, it does seem that Johnson was a bit of a Romeo who would chase anything in a skirt. There's a rumour he even tried it on with the wife of the Deputy Director, Susan Abbott. I do happen to know Susan quite well and I am certain she would have rejected him but it could show what sort of man he was,' he commented. 'What else did you find out?' He added

The copper grinned as he sipped his tea. 'Yes Cyril, quite a lot actually so hold on to your hat. It appears that two of the men working in the hospital that night are poofs. One, Alfred Rice was actually on duty while the other man, called Thomas Race who is a nursing attendant was also in his ward. The suggestion is that they are a couple of queers, so a man like Johnson would certainly have been disgusted by them. It does seem that there was no love lost between him and them, in fact it's even been alleged they plotted to do him in. That's another reason I need to talk to Jack Masters because it's said that he knows something about that.'

'Blimey!' The reporter was totally stunned by what he'd just heard, and it took him a few moments for it all to sink in. Thoughts of great national newspaper stories and now even a book, once again began to excite his mind.

'Albert, this whole thing is getting very out of control. Murder, perhaps even two murders, suicide, conspiracy to murder, adultery and now homosexuality. Jesus Christ, this is a plotline that that Agatha Christie woman could come up with for one of her books.' He thought for a few moments more before continuing.

'Anyway, like you asked I did read through our Gillespie story files yesterday and you could well be right. Dr Byron was very quick at that time to suggest that Gillespie had committed suicide, just like he is saying about Johnson now. It also seems to be a remarkable coincidence that Johnson was on the scene as well that Christmas morning. Do you think he was involved too?'

Wilkins shook his head. 'No, I don't think so, although

it's possible and at this stage we can't rule anything out. If Byron did shoot Gillespie why would he have wanted to involve a member of the night staff in the actual shooting? No, I think Johnson's presence there that morning was pure chance but perhaps he did seize the opportunity to get involved. It's just possible you could add blackmail to your Agatha Christie list,' he grinned before continuing.

'For the moment Cyril I think the best thing to do is to keep all this to ourselves because we don't want to alert the killer or killers, or your editor either come to that. I don't want Scotland Yard's glory boys coming down here to take over, which they might if they get a whiff of something this big, any more than you or your editor want Fleet Street to come here in strength. For the moment see if you can dig up anything more about Fred Johnson - what sort of person he really was, did he have money troubles and that sort of thing,' he suggested.

Hart was still trying to take in everything they had discussed as he tried to form some kind of pattern in his mind. He nodded his agreement and took his pocket watch out to give him more time to think. 'Look I have to be getting back to the office. It's press day and I'm on my own in the newsroom', he muttered. He looked up at Wilkins again.

'Albert, something is bothering me a great deal, even more so now you've mentioned the two queers. You said the post mortem found that Johnson had died because of drinking that Lysol stuff. Well, if it was forced down his throat surely one man on his own could not have done that? It would have taken at least one person to hold him down while the other poured it into his mouth. Even then it would have been a great struggle given the agony Johnson must have been going through – agony which must have given him added strength. Do you think Race and Rice could have done that between them?' he asked.

The policeman stared back for a second or two before answering.

'Yes Cyril, you're quite right again and it's a point that's has been bothering me ever since the body was found and now for the first time we have a 'pair' of potential suspects rather than one. Not only would Johnson have had to be restrained but also silenced to prevent him screaming in agony at the same time. I am certain that would certainly have taken more than one killer. Whoever did it must have had an accomplice, but I do know how he could have been restrained.'

Hart waited as his friend made full use of the drama of the moment before continuing. 'Tell me Cyril, what do they use in mental hospitals and lunatic asylums to restrain violent or disturbed patients?' The journalist shook his head and the policeman smiled, got up and walked over to a filing cabinet on the other side of the office to pull something from the top, which he plopped onto the desk.

'They use straight jackets, like this one of the type escapologists like Houdini use in their acts. Once forced into one the patient is totally unable to move a single limb, and there is no shortage of that sort of equipment in the hospital. In fact I bet every ward has at least one. I even spotted one in Johnson's office – this one in fact - so I guess he could well have been killed while being restrained wearing one of them – perhaps even this one, which I am waiting for our forensic people to collect and examine.

'It would still have taken two men to put one on him of course, because he was still a very powerful man; but if he had been knocked out first then by the time he came round he would have been at their mercy. He would have been unable to stop the Lysol being poured into his mouth'.

Hart nodded his admiration of the detective's logic. 'Yes, that would explain it of course, but there would still be the problem of keeping him quiet as his stomach burned before he died. He would have been screaming out in agony. I suppose they could have gagged him, but that would not have been possible while they were pouring the stuff down his throat. How did they do that?' he stood up to go.

Wilkins stood up to show him out. 'Well, you're quite right mate, and I haven't figured that bit out yet, but I will' he growled.

• • • • • •

Later that afternoon Wilkins found himself standing outside the house in Becontree Avenue where the Masters family lived. He'd got there more by luck than judgement, because when he'd found the road it was to find that it was almost three miles long and a dual carriageway - hardly the small street where everyone knew everyone else, as Hart had thought.

He'd struck lucky simply because as he drove along it he'd happened to find a uniformed 'Bobby' cycling towards him and had stopped to ask if he had any idea where the Masters lived. As it happened the copper not only also lived in the avenue but only a few doors away from the very man he was looking for.

'Oh yes sir I know Jack Masters quite well, he's one of my neighbours, though they've not lived there long. To be honest not many of us have, because it's a very new estate and they're still building it. Most people round here are Ford workers like Jack, and seem to be pretty decent hardworking sort of folk. I am the local bobby but I don't get a lot of trouble from them, well other than with a few drunks outside the pubs on St Patrick's night. You see sir, a lot of them round here are Paddys who've come over here to work in Ford's but generally speaking they are pretty good people.' *From Ford's factory in Cork*

Wilkins interrupted the policeman's chatter to ask exactly where the Masters family lived, and he pointed to a man hard at work in a front garden about a hundred yards further down the road.

'That's him down there sir. That's Jack Masters down there doing his garden – very fond of his garden is Jack'.

Thanking him for his help Wilkins got back into his car and gently motored the hundred yards along the dual carriageway, through which ran a central reservation full of bushes, trees and shrubs. It was a finger of woodland which he idly thought, as he drew up by the house where the man was digging, must have been a wonderful paradise for all the kids arriving onto the new estate.

As he got out of his car the gardener looked up from his work, stretched his back to relieve it and stared, questioningly. The policeman noted that he was a tall and very powerfully built man, perhaps in his mid-fifties.

'Mr Jack Masters?' Wilkins introduced himself. I am Detective Sergeant Wilkins from Brentwood police, and I wondered if I could talk to you for a few minutes.'

'What about? The gardener's eyes narrowed suspiciously.

'Well, it's in connection with the death of a man I believe you once knew and worked with at the Brentwood

Mental Hospital - Mr Frederick Johnson. Is there somewhere less public that we can talk?'

'Yes. I heard the bastard was dead and good riddance to bad rubbish as far as I'm concerned, but what's it got to with me?'

'Well, perhaps we can talk inside,' Wilkins persisted, his hand on the front gate defying Masters' obvious reluctance to welcome him by showing his determination to push it open anyway. The gardener made up his mind, straightened up and stuck the garden fork he'd been using into the ground, before beckoning his visitor to come into the house.

Inside Jessie Masters was peeling potatoes in the scullery and she looked up when the two men came through the front door. 'It's alright love. This is Sergeant Wilkins from the police in Brentwood and he wants to talk about Fred Johnson,' her husband told her as he showed the policeman into the back room.

'Tea?' She asked.

Wilkins nodded his thanks and sat down at the dining table his host had indicated. 'You already knew about his death. How did you know, Mr Masters?' he asked.

'Got a letter yesterday from an old mate who still works at the hospital,' Masters said, getting up and moving over to the fireplace where an envelope was stuck behind the clock. Picking it up he took out a letter, which proved to be from Jimmy Lacey telling him about Johnson being found dead that weekend. 'It came yesterday,' his host explained, as the policeman scanned through it.

'Thank you,' he said, handing it back. 'OK, so now what can you tell me about Fred Johnson?' he asked.

Jack Masters hesitated and before he could reply, Jessie came in with a tray with two cups of tea and a plate with some biscuits on it. She had heard the question too and glanced at her husband. 'Tell him Jack and tell him all of it because if you don't I will,' she urged.

Her man needed no further encouragement, and nodded his thanks to his wife who sat down with them before turning to Wilkins. 'You probably heard that Johnson and me never got on and if I am to be honest, if he was still alive right now I would be strongly tempted to go over there and do him myself,' he told Wilkins.

'Any reason in particular?' Wilkins had to ask. Even though he knew the probable reason he was still slightly surprised at the vehemence in Masters' voice as he replied.

'Yes, the bastard got my daughter in the family way and she's only a kid herself,' he said bitterly. Wilkins decided not to reveal that he already knew of Tilly's situation, but now Jessie Masters chimed in to have her say as well, joining the attack on Johnson over the kind of issue that was usually kept within the privacy of the family.

'If Jack hadn't killed him I would have,' she said. 'That man ruined my girl's life, I'm glad he's dead and I hope he rots in hell,' Jessie added, her fury adding to the anger in her voice.

'Yes, well I can understand that now. So tell me, Mr Masters, did you kill him? Where exactly were you last Saturday night?'

The full import of the visit and the interrogation suddenly appeared to hit Masters. For the first time he realised that there may have been more to Johnson's death than he'd been told and that he was under suspicion. A relieved and confident smile crept across his face.

'I was at work. I am on nights in Fords this month and a lot of people can vouch for me being there, as well as my clocking-in card which would verify it on Saturday night.

That's why I am not at work today – I don't start until 9 o-clock tonight and it's too nice a day to spend all of it in bed,' he grinned. 'No Sergeant, it wasn't me but if someone did kill him then I'd certainly like to shake his hand,' he added.

'Thank you for that sir. Tell me, would that gratitude also apply to Mr Race and Mr Rice?' The policeman hoped his surprise question would throw Masters off balance, but it didn't. He grinned back at the questioner.

'What, the poofs – do you think they might have done it? I doubt if they had the bottle to be honest' he laughed.

'Well, I understand they once told you they were going to kill him,' Wilkins persisted.

'Yes they did, but I think they were just shooting their mouths off. Fred picked on them a lot because he had no time for queers, but to be fair I can't see them really topping him. They told me they'd once lain in wait for him because they were going to knock him out, hang him and make it look like he'd done it himself. This was not long after we had a patient hang himself in the hospital and I think they were just using that as an idea. I never liked either of them much and like Fred I had no time for them but to be fair, I don't think they'd really go that far. I could be wrong of course but I think they were all talk,' he ended.

'Thanks for that. I do appreciate what you say and accept that you physically could not have done it yourself because you were at work, but what sort of man was Fred Johnson?'

Before he could reply Jessie interrupted again. 'He was an arrogant foul-mouthed bully who treated his wife like dirt and tried to chat up any women he thought he could get into bed. He wasn't too fussy about how young they were either and our Till wasn't the first by a long way,' she snapped bitterly.

Her husband laid his hand on her arm to calm her down. 'Yes, alright Jess, alright love, but she's quite right Mr Wilkins.' He looked at the policeman with a look of great contempt about the man they were discussing on his face.

'Fred Johnson was all of that and more. Like a lot of us in the hospital he was ex-army and never left any of us in any doubt about who was boss. By and large, apart from being a bit fussy about night time procedures and ward logs, he left me alone but he treated some of the team like dirt. Anyone who he thought was a weakling, youngsters like poor little Billy Taylor for example, who suffered at Johnson's hands and often felt the lash of his tongue.

'There were times when some of us even wondered whether Billy would finish up as a patient in the hospital because of Johnson's bullying. Billy is a bit highly strung but wouldn't hurt a soul. He is a very caring sort of bloke but Johnson bullied him unmercifully. Some nights, especially when he had a few beers in him, which was often - Johnson just wouldn't leave poor Billy alone. The man was an out and out pig and while I'm sorry for his wife and children, they're probably better off without him,' Masters was getting more and more vehement as he poured out this torrent of words.

Wilkins picked up his teacup again and drained it before standing up to leave. 'Thank you both for your help and thank you for the tea, Mrs Masters - it was very welcome', he said.

Back in the car outside he acknowledged Masters' wave of goodbye before picking up his garden fork again. In the short time he'd known them he'd been quite favourably impressed with the honesty and decency of this family both of whom had confirmed his growing feeling about Johnson's character. He hadn't seen Tilly, but there didn't seem to be any real point because he was investigating Johnson's death and clearly she'd had nothing to do with that. In any case she probably had enough to deal with without further hassle from him.

Giving Jack Masters one last farewell wave, Wilkins started up his motor and drove off in the direction of Brentwood. He was quite happy that the trip had been worth the effort.

• • • • • •

By the time John Hamilton got back to the office with the first copies of that week's Brentwood's Time, he found Cyril Hart pounding away on his typewriter churning out copy for next week's paper. Unusually the editor appeared to be in a good mood and as he made his way to his own desk he tossed a copy of the new edition onto Hart's desk.

'Good story that Cyril and well written, so well done. Let's keep an eye on it to see how it develops,' he said. He would not have been so happy had he known the full extent of what his reporter knew.

Hart picked the paper up and scanned his eye across it. Hamilton had not only used the story he'd written, with hardly any editing and the same headline he'd suggested, but had even given him the by-line for the story. That's the kind of editorial gesture that makes any journalist feel like Kipling and compels him to read the words he'd written over and over. His self indulgence was interrupted as he became aware that Hamilton was watching him with mild amusement etched across his face.

'You like it, eh?' he said. 'Well so you should because it's a good story and you have handled it just right. Keep it up and stay with it because I have a feeling there's more to come', he added.

Hart smiled his thanks for the praise. 'You just don't know the half of it, matey,' he muttered to himself as he put the paper down and turned back to his typing. The phone on his desk rang, and picking it up he heard Wilkins' voice in his ear.

'Hello Cyril – can you talk?'

'Not really,' he replied glancing over at the editor.

'Ok I get the message, but you can listen. Look, I have been speaking to Jack Masters and I'm satisfied that he's in the clear. He was on the night shift in Fords that night and the company has corroborated his alibi, so he couldn't have been in Brentwood. I've also spoken to the coroner and he's arranged for a jury inquest in two weeks time, so find out what more you discover can about Johnson. Talk to his missus again and see if she knew he was a womaniser'.

'Right thank you. Leave it with me,' Hart said loudly enough for his editor hear before putting the instrument back onto its cradle. He looked over at Hamilton who was staring enquiringly in his direction.

'That was the police sir. Sergeant Wilkins says a full inquest into Mr Johnson will be held in two weeks time,' Hart explained.

'Great. It's nice to see the coppers have enough confidence in you to give you that information. Keep building bridges there Cyril and don't write anything else about the story until after the inquest. We still don't need Fleet Street poking its nose in until we're ready and in full control of the story' Hamilton said, the rare use of Hart's first name being a good indicator of his mood.

The reporter grinned back, happy that he'd managed to conceal most of what Wilkins had told him from the editor. 'Yes sir, I will do that and I think I'll also pop in on my way home to see how Mrs Johnson is,' he said. 'Is it alright if I take her a copy of the paper?' he asked.

'Yes, of course! She might not know about the inquest yet, so you can tell her and see if you get some kind of reaction from her for a follow up story.'

An hour later Hamilton stood up to go. Once the editor had said his goodbyes and left the newsroom, Hart picked up the phone and asked to be put through to the police station again. Within a few minutes he was talking to Wilkins again, and apologising that he wasn't able to be too forthcoming during the previous phone call.

'Don't worry about that. I guessed as much. Have you made any progress today?' the policeman asked.

'Well, not really Albert. Press day is always a bit hectic because we're busy setting up the early copy for next week's paper, but I did tell the editor about the inquest. I suggested that I popped into see Mrs Johnson on my way home to tell her about it and he welcomed the idea. Actually I thought I could also use it as an excuse to ask her neighbours about 'dead Fred' as well'. Hart grinned at his own unfunny pun.

'Good idea Cyril. I'll leave you to it and perhaps we can talk tomorrow' Wilkins said as he hung up.

Hart stood up and put his jacket on before picking up a few copies of the paper and making his way out of the office again. Downstairs his trusty bike was waiting and, swinging his leg over it, he began to pedal away in the direction of Gresham Road.

It was a warm evening and just as he had hoped a few women were gossiping at a gate close to Emma Johnson's house. Propping the bike onto the kerb he walked over to them and introduced himself as a local reporter.

'Ladies, I wondered if I could have a few words,' he said. The women looked at each other.

'What about?' said one warily.

'Well you've heard about poor Mr Johnson of course. I'm just going back to see Mrs Johnson, but I wondered if you could tell me anything about him – strictly off the record, of course. You know, what sort of man, what sort of neighbour etc, was he?'

'Freddy? Oh yeah we all know about Fred, and no one round here is going to miss him' they laughed cynically. 'The man was a drunken beast who treated Emma like a dog and most other women as fair game,' one of them said.

'What, you mean he was a bit of a ladies' man?' Hart queried. They all nodded in unison.

'Yes, he really fancied himself, especially if they were young women. Never stopped boasting, even to us, about all the girls he'd had. He was good to his kids though and, despite how he treated her, Emma probably won't hear a word against him but if he'd been my old man I would have poisoned him long ago,' the lady who'd spoken first told him. Her companions nodded their agreement at the assessment as he thanked them and prepared to move on.

'Well, thank you ladies. I do appreciate that.' Hart said as he left the group to carry on with their gossiping and made his way to Emma's front gate. Knocking at the door he had to wait a few moments before she opened it to greet him.

'Oh, hello Mr Hart, come in', she said opening it

wider. He followed her down the hallway into the tiny kitchen where she was cooking tea for her and the children. 'Cup of tea?' she offered.

'No, not for me thanks Mrs Johnson. I'm on my way home but thought I'd drop a copy of the paper in for you,' he said handing her the newspaper. He watched her closely as she quickly read the story on the front page. Then, as she finished and put the paper down, he spoke again.

'Well, is it alright?'

She smiled wanly and nodded. 'Yes, that's fair enough. Have you heard any more about the inquest?' she asked.

'Oh, yes. That was the other thing I came to tell you. The police tell me it will be take place in the hospital in two weeks time. It does appear that the post mortem concluded that it was the Lysol that killed him. The only question seems to be whether he took it himself, deliberately or by accident, or if someone poured it into his mouth somehow.'

The expression on her face didn't change at the idea. 'That still puzzles me, to be honest Mr Hart,' she said. 'Fred enjoyed life and never seemed to get upset enough or be the sort of person who would want to kill himself. In any case I still can't understand how anyone could hold him down long enough to pour acid into his mouth; he was a very strong man you know. Look Mr Hart, I know Fred wasn't the most popular man around here, but he was good to us and I would not like my children to think that anyone would want to murder him,' she lied.

'Well, yes I understand that and hopefully that's what the inquest will find out. Look, in the meantime, my earlier offer to you still goes and if there is anything at the paper we can do to help, please let us know,' he told her, standing up to leave.

'Thank you Mr Hart. You've been ever so kind', she said as she watched him get back onto his bike and pedal away. She stood at the door, much as she had a few nights earlier when she'd watched her husband leave for the last time, but now with far different emotions causing her to rub her tongue against the inside of her cheek. She knew that in a couple of weeks, with any luck, it would all be behind her and she and the children would finally be able to get on with the rest of their lives.

Thinking about the children brought her back to the reality of the moment. Closing the door she moved back into the house and out to the back door into the garden where they were playing in the evening sunshine.

'Sarah, Freddy – come on in. It's teatime!'

HE WAS MY HUSBAND

'I'd thought the bastard was dead long ago'

By the following morning, when he sat down at his desk, Wilkins' mind was still turning over what he'd heard about Johnson and other members of the hospital's night staff. The suggestion by Jimmy Lacey that two of the people involved in the hospital during that fateful night were homosexual, had been firmed up by what Jack Masters had told him about their alleged murder attempt.

He'd lain awake most of the night, tossing and turning so much that a sleep-frustrated Marie had finally threatened him with the spare room. He was convinced, by what he'd seen as much as what he'd been told, that the allegation was true. It was also very obvious that any relationship of that kind between the two men would have disgusted the very macho ex-soldier. That being the case, then the suggestion that they'd tried to murder him was also very credible. So had they succeeded this time?

It had added yet another strand to what was already becoming an impenetrable web of innuendos, speculation and half truths. He grinned as he remembered Hart's casual reference to the famous crime novelist, cynically thinking to himself that perhaps he really ought to invite her to come to Brentwood to solve the mystery.

He reached across the desk for the phone, and asked the station operator to get him Cyril Hart at Brentwood's Time instead. After a minute or so it rang and he picked it up to hear the reporter's voice.

'Hello Cyril, it's me – Albert. Look, are you coming along to police calls this morning?' This was a regular part of the day when local reporters went to the police station to be briefed on what the police had been doing and what mischief some of the town's local rascals had been up to over the previous last twenty-four hours.

'Yes I was actually, why? Do you have any more news?' Hart asked.

'Well yes, I do think we need to talk again so when you've finished with the duty officer pop in and see me,' Wilkins told him.

An hour later he looked up and smiled a welcome as his friend walked into his office. 'How's things back at the ranch?' he grinned as Hart sat down on the proffered chair.

'Yes, pretty good really. Hamilton is still pleased that we've managed to keep a bit of a lid on the Johnson story because he doesn't want to alert Fleet Street any more than you want the Yard to be aware, but he doesn't know the half of it. I gathered from the tone of your voice on the phone that something else was up.'

The policeman nodded. 'Yes there is. Tell me, what have you heard about a couple of the people working at the hospital called Alfred Rice and Thomas Race?'

Hart shook his head. 'Nothing, never heard of them. Why do you ask?'

Wilkins told him what he'd been told about the sexual relationship between the two men and also the allegation about their plan to murder Johnson. The reporter, genuinely stunned at the new direction the story had suddenly taken, sat listening while at the same time wondering how he could write it all up and still control things.

'Bloody hell Albert! Now what? Are you going to arrest them, or pull them in for questioning, or what?'

The policeman shook his head. 'No, I've been thinking long and hard about that all night. Trouble is that at this stage it's all hearsay. If I did that and asked them about it they will simply deny everything and I can prove nothing either on that or whether they had any involvement in Johnson's death. No, I need to lull them into a false sense of security and having them questioned under oath at the inquest offers the best chance of that.

'It will also give us more time to look at the possibility of anybody else's involvement in this along, with any links to the alleged suicide of Dr Gillespie because there lies another issue I am now even more curious about' he added.

Mention of the death of the previous hospital Director jerked Hart's thoughts back to his own investigations the previous evening. 'I had a chat with some of the Johnsons neighbours yesterday. I know they're all local gossips, but those women all had a very dim view of him. They told me he was a bit of a bully and skirt-chaser, more or less confirming what Tilly Masters had told me about that side of him. They were all in sympathy with Mrs Johnson over the way she'd been treated and said they wouldn't be shedding any tears for him.

'I also spoke with Emma Johnson, who remains very loyal to him again and she is still mystified about how anyone could have killed Fred. She pointed out that he was a very strong man well able to defend himself, and can't see how anyone could pour acid into him or, come to that, even get him into a straight jacket to restrain him without a struggle.'

Wilkins face showed he was still puzzled about that part of his own theory too. 'Yes, that is a bit of a problem but if Race and Rice were both involved that might have been possible. Let's not forget that they must both be used to having to restrain patients who are out of control. Look Cyril, if you can make any discreet enquiries about our poofs without alerting them, it would help. Perhaps your Deputy Director pal might know something, but don't tell him too much.

'Incidentally I went over to Dagenham and spoke to Jack Masters and his missus yesterday. They confirmed that they were furious about what Johnson had done to their daughter, but his alibi is rock solid and I checked it out. He was definitely at work in Fords on Saturday night. In fact both he and his wife came across as pretty decent people and I tend to believe them. '

The telephone on his desk rang again and as he picked it up to answer it Hart stood up to leave. Wilkins waved him a friendly but silent goodbye and carried on talking to his caller. Deep in thought the reporter walked away from the police station as confused and excited as Wilkins had been the previous day. It was clearly going to be another interesting week, and it was shaping up into one hell of a great story that could really make his career as a journalist, perhaps even an author.

• • • • • •

Since its beginnings in the Middle Ages, Romford's market day had been a bustling and noisy affair and that

Wednesday was no exception. To a backdrop of lowing cattle, cackling geese, frightened lambs and squealing pigs, the frenzied calling of the auctioneers and shouts of stallholders bragging about their fruit and vegetables added to the din. Throughout the market and in odd corners, the persuasive yelling of the 'fly-pitchers' brandishing their bargains and noisily haggling with their prey added to the general clamour of excitement and expectation.

For centuries its ancient cobblestones had resounded to the clatter of the boots and carts of the farmers and the shrill voices of the wives who'd come with them for the day to sell their home produced cheese and butter. In ancient days it had even been known for some farmers, fed up with their marital situations, to bring their wives to 'sell' them on to new husbands.

Despite the rise and popularity of the department stores around it, nothing much had changed in the ancient marketplace over all those years. Between the stalls and barrows, hordes of bargain hunters jostled each other, fingering and pressing the fruit, haggling and being lured ever closer by the inviting chatter of the fly pitchers and barrow-boys on the fringes of the market. In the many pubs surrounding the market square farmers and dealers were noisily celebrating with best ale, gossiping, telling rude jokes or trying to seduce the barmaids, just as they had done for centuries.

For Jane, one of the barmaids in the Golden Lion, it had been just another market-day. One of six girls working the public bar that day, she'd been hard at it since the place opened, pumping up foaming jugs of ale and handing out pies and cheese rolls so by lunchtime her feet were killing her. She wasn't young any more, though even at forty-plus it wasn't hard to see that she'd been a very attractive woman in her day. These days the bar-room banter with her was jocular humour rather than seriously seductive but it was always respectful.

'Jane, clear up some of the glasses, clean the ashtrays and go for a quick smoke yourself.' The landlord's voice broke into the cheerful banter and nodding her relief and thanks for the respite, she moved out from behind the bar to do his bidding. Collecting the glasses and stacking them onto the bar for collection by other barmaids, she mopped up tables, wiped ashtrays and piled up the empty plates on the bar with the glasses. At one table she found an old newspaper and having passed over the plates and lit a cigarette, she sat down with it to relax for a few minutes.

It proved to be a week-old copy of another town's newspaper, Brentwood's Time and as she relaxed with her cigarette her eye idly began to scan the front page. Suddenly she sat bolt upright at the mention of a name and, in order to hold the newspaper more firmly to read it, balanced her cigarette onto the ashtray. The chatter and laughter in the bar melted into the background of her consciousness and her hands shook as she took in the full significance of the story.

'Good God!' she breathed. 'I'd thought the bastard was dead long ago, and now he really has snuffed it.'

Her mind went back over twenty years, to another time and another place: to a young man, proud in his new uniform and every inch the soldier about to march off to war. She remembered a baby, dead from pneumonia within weeks of being born, and the months with no official news before the reluctant acceptance that her man had been one of the thousands of unknown or unidentified victims of the Great War.

Even worse, when she'd contacted the authorities it was to find that he had never registered their marriage with the army, so she'd never received any money from his pay, or a pension.

They'd met a year before the world had gone mad. Two young people, part of the last generation of 'young Victorians' born only a few years before the great old lady had joined her predecessors leaving a great empire as her legacy.

Victoria had inspired explorers, adventurers, engineers and entrepreneurs leaving behind her a nation ruling half the world, and drunk with its own importance. A rich country, with many of her subjects still living in dire poverty. At the start of the new century the social divisions between rich and poor were as deep in the mother country as they were in the many colonies and possessions of the empire. As a result politically the socialists were gaining ground as the dream of a new world emerging from the 'dark satanic mills' was taking root.

Young Jane Thomas hadn't had much schooling – few working class girls did, because most of them were destined to go 'into service'. At almost fourteen and as the eldest in a large family of nine kids none of whom could barely read or write, she'd found work as a scullery maid in a new hotel in the Strand. It was a job that offered a pitifully small wage for a working day that began at 6a.m. and never ended until 9p.m., but bed and board went with it and there was always plenty to eat of course. It also meant she could send money home to help feed the family and help keep them out of the workhouse after her father, the main breadwinner, had died from consumption.

She was still working in the kitchen when a young man arrived on the scene, wearing his first uniform. Freddie

Johnson had been taken on by the hotel as a page-boy and looked resplendent in his smart red and black suit. Like other members of staff at that level he was given his meals in the kitchen, rather than in the staff dining room where more senior staff ate theirs.

It didn't take long before the pageboy and the maid began to talk. He had the natural cheery chat of the cockney kid and she was receptive. Soon they were walking out on their days off and taking every opportunity to see each other at work that they could.

These were the halcyon (for some) days before an Austrian arch-duke was murdered and Europe, followed by the rest of the world including the British Empire, tumbled into war. For a young man especially, this was an exciting time promising adventure and the calls from people like Lord Kitchener to join up filled the recruiting offices. It was a call that gripped Freddie too.

With Jane's enthusiastic and proud support he decided to leave his pageboy uniform behind to take up arms for his country. Within weeks of enlisting he was home on leave, standing proud in his new uniform and setting her heart fluttering anew. Now more masculine and assertive he began to press her to take their relationship a stage further and she, so proud of her young soldier was only too willing to do so.

However, like so many young couples in those hurried months, they both felt the need to regularise their relationship before he went off to war. They married, with the agreement of her employer in the hotel chapel and, again courtesy of the management, spent their one night honeymoon in the bridal suite.

Then all too soon he was marching off to war, neither of them knowing at that moment that she was already carrying his child. She had never seen or heard from him again or even received the dreaded telegram announcing his death in action and their child had lived only a few weeks.

So, all those years later, it had been a tremendous shock when he'd walked into the Golden Lion for a drink six weeks earlier. Despite the years that had passed, with both of them now in their early forties, they'd recognised each other instantly and there had been a weird moment between them. Her initial surprise had turned to anger and disgust as it dawned on her that she'd been betrayed all those years earlier by his failure to return to her after the war.

In his turn he'd been horrified and embarrassed at seeing her again so unexpectedly but the moment soon passed, for neither of them were emotional youngsters any more. The moment had soon passed for now they had the maturity and understanding of age. Both of them recognised that each of them had built new lives since their parting. After a brief flurry of shocked, angry and apologetic exchanges on both sides they'd been able to come to terms with each other and talk in a civilised manner.

She'd told him about the lost baby and he'd spoken of his new life in Brentwood but, from what she was now reading it was clear he still hadn't told her everything. He hadn't mentioned Emma and the children for example, or even explained why he'd not come back to her after the war, let alone written to her during it. Nor did he explain why he'd never told the army about their marriage. All he'd told her was that he had a good job now and had made a new life for himself. He'd even hinted about the possibility of a new start together for both of them.

As a result she'd even begun to fantasise, perhaps even secretly hope, for reconciliation and a new beginning for their marriage but just as in 1914 he hadn't come back. Now she was reading about his death – but this time it was for real - and reading also that he'd had a wife and family.

• • • • • •

It had not been the best of weeks for Richard Byron either. He'd realised that his hope for Fred Johnson's death to be accepted as suicide was in danger of not being accepted by the coroner, or indeed the police. That had him worrying about what a more formal and investigative inquest might uncover.

Would it for example, reveal the trail of blackmail that he'd suffered at the hands of the dead man and thus put him under suspicion of murder? Supposing Johnson had boasted about what had happened to a friend, or had written a secret confession to be revealed if he died in any mysterious circumstances. Suddenly this time he wasn't as sure of his ground as he had been the last time and that introduced another very worrying aspect in the web of doom he was weaving in his mind.

He began to worry that Marion, a very intelligent and astute woman, might put the fact of two suspicious deaths – her former husband's, and now that of the man who had been so helpful that day – together. A practical lady she never believed much in coincidence and that could cause her to doubt what happened and look deeper into her first husband's death. He loved his wife very much and could not bear the thought of her despising him, as she undoubtedly would if she knew the truth.

Ever since Johnson had first put the pressure on him Byron had been living on his nerves, fearful that he would be exposed somehow. It wasn't the thought of the hangman's rope around his neck that worried him but how Marion would react for, despite her affair with Byron, she had been genuinely in love with her first husband.

Even before he did it he'd decided that if ever he was in danger of being arrested for Gillespie's murder, rather then risk the gallows he would swallow the cyanide he kept hidden in his desk. That still left Marion, and his love for her would never die, but he could not bear the thought of losing her if she found out what he'd done.

He looked up as the lady herself came into the room with a cup of tea for him in her hand. Putting it down onto his desk she leaned over and kissed him on the cheek before pretending to read his mind. She was a very perceptive woman who had lived with two psychiatrists and she'd learned a great deal from them about people and their responses under pressure. She smiled as she stroked his cheek.

'Oh come on, darling. It was a tragedy but in a few weeks we'll have the inquest and it will all be over and done with so we can get back to normal. I've been to see Mrs Johnson to see if I can help her with any council problems, but actually she seems to be coping very well,' she murmured. 'In fact better than you seem to be doing,' she added reflectively.

'Me?'

'Yes, you sweetheart,' she ruffled his hair affectionately. 'I've noticed you've not been sleeping too well the last few nights. You seem to be somewhere else, as though you've got something on your mind. What's wrong, love? Is there anything I can help you with?'

He smiled back at her. 'Oh, it's nothing Marion. I guess it all came as rather a shock that's all. Like you say, it will all be over in a few weeks.'

She wasn't too convinced by his casual explanation, but

decided not to press him any further. He may have been a leading mind doctor but she was a woman with well honed intuitions that told her that if she continued to press him he would clam up completely. She was as much in love with him as he was with her, feeling herself lucky that she had known such love twice in her life.

Her genuine grief at being widowed in such an unforeseen and tragic way had initially been tinged with a little guilt about her casual affair with Richard. However at the time of the suicide he'd been a rock and the feelings she'd had for him then had got stronger. As a deeply religious and devout woman however she would have been horrified had she known she was one of the prizes – the other being her then husband's job – in a murder plot.

She kissed his cheek and ruffled his hair again before straightening up to go. 'I'm sure that's right darling. Look, I've got another council meeting to go to today but I'll be back in good time for you to take me out for dinner later,' she smiled as she walked back out of the door.

His mind was in even more turmoil as he listened to her footsteps fading away down the hallway. Ever since Johnson had begun to blackmail him he'd been more frightened of her finding out the truth than the police, yet even with Johnson dead he'd never felt as vulnerable as he did now. His acquaintanceship with DS Wilkins had been brief, but he'd already realised that the man was no fool. He was worried that the strange circumstances behind Johnson's death might lead the detective to re-investigate Gillespie's too. Had he known how right he was, he would have been even more concerned.

His hopes of a quick end to the case by suggesting Johnson might have killed himself had evaporated after the policeman had expressed his reservations. He had no worries about the inquest on Johnson because the actual cause of death was forensically incontrovertible and he did the autopsy. What was worrying was that the means of how the Lysol got into his body would have to be decided too and that could blow his hopes of a suicide verdict sky high. He could control the autopsy but the coroner was a different proposition. Wilkins worried him too and he could not shake himself of the thought that the detective might already be tying the two deaths together in some way.

He tried to concentrate on the patient's medical report he was writing, but the same dreadful thoughts kept popping into his mind. What if Johnson had struck from beyond the grave? Suppose he'd left evidence behind implicating the hospital director in his predecessor's death as a kind of insurance? Byron was well used to the concept of paranoia in the people he treated yet was now convincing himself that somewhere or other there was a letter or a confession of some sort that implicated him.

He groaned in frustration as he threw his pen down, got up from the desk and began to roam up and down the office like a caged and desperate tiger. Oh God – would this torment never end?

He tried to force himself to think logically. Where would Johnson have kept such evidence? Certainly not in the hospital where it could easily be found - no the man had been more cunning than that. No, if it was anywhere at all it had to be at home but if it was, did Emma Johnson know about it? Was that why she was being so calm?

Still seeking reassurance he opened his desk drawer and was strangely relieved to find that the little bottle he was looking for was still in its place.

• • • • • •

It was dark when the knock echoed on the door and because she knew who it would be, Emma never turned the light in the hallway on. They had long agreed on the signal – the first four notes of Beethoven's Fifth rapped on the door – but there was no point in advertising the identity of her visitor to the neighbours. She opened it and as he came through she fell into his arms. Concealed in the darkness of the hour and despite the still open door, they embraced with a warm and passionate kiss.

'Hello darling' she breathed, closing the door and turning to fall back into his arms. 'How are you coping?'

He kissed her again. 'I'm fine sweetheart – but more to the point, what about you and the children?'

'We're doing fine – they're in bed' she smiled as she bustled around putting the kettle on for tea. 'I take it you are on your way to work'.

He nodded, and pulled her to him as he sat down. She sat on his lap with her head buried onto his shoulder and his arms around her waist - both of them revelling in the pleasurable warmth of each others body, until the steam hissing from the kettle indicated it was time to make the tea. One more little peck on the cheek and she was up and across the kitchen, spooning tea into the warmed pot before pouring the hot water into it to infuse.

'I had a visitor this afternoon,' she said as she stirred the teapot. He looked up as she continued. 'Dr Byron came to see me'.

'Byron? Why, to check on how you were? Well, I suppose he was doing his job as a concerned boss but all the same it was very nice of him.'

'Yes,' she paused, showing she was also still a little puzzled by the Director's visit. 'The odd thing was that once he'd enquired about me and the children, he started asking whether Fred had any hospital documents in the house.

'He said it was just to tidy things up because some log sheets had been mislaid, but he even insisted I went to look in our bedroom to see if I could find them. There wasn't anything that I could see anyway, but it never seemed to satisfy him and before he left he said that if I came across anything at all to do with the hospital, I was to take it straight to him and nobody else. I said that Fred was my husband and I would have known if he'd hidden anything from me in the house.'

Her lover smiled at the idea that Fred Johnson would have had any hospital documents in the house, because he knew the man hadn't been the sort to take his work home, but it was curious nonetheless.

'Yes, very odd, but as far as you and I are concerned it shows that we're still fine. Look Em, once all this is over we can be together, all of us as a family and a long way away from this town. You've heard about the inquest of course?'

'Yes. I've been asked to give evidence about what sort of man Fred was. I'm not looking forward to it, but I will handle it,' she admitted.

'Yes, actually they seem to be very keen on knowing about Fred. Did you know that all of us on duty that night have been told we will be called to be witnesses? We are to give evidence on what we know happened that night, and I hear that Alfie Rice and Tommy Race have already come under suspicion,' he told her.

'What – the queers? Fred often talked about them. He

had no time for them at all and used to tell me that he was just waiting for the day he could catch them at it so he could report them', she said.

'Well, that's right and that wouldn't surprise me – there was no love lost on either side. In fact a couple of the blokes reckon they tried to kill him once before.'

Her eyes widened at the suggestion, and it had clearly given her some hope. 'Well, that's something Fred never told me, but if it was true and the police did decide they murdered him it could take a lot of attention away from us.'

He grinned and nodded his agreement as he finished his tea. 'Yes, sweetheart, it would. To be honest I wouldn't lose any sleep if they got accused, or even swung for it, because they're not nice people. What they do is a sin against God's law and I would see that as His punishment. Also don't forget Em, if the police thought the two of them were involved it would help them explain how they got the stuff into Fred.'

He stood up to go. 'Stay strong my love. We will get through this and then God willing we can move on to our new life once it's all over.'

She stood with him and again they hugged and kissed before she turned the hall light off so the darkness could protect his identity as he left. One last snatched kiss and he was out of the door and away along Gresham Road heading for the hospital to start his shift.

She watched him until he faded into the night before closing the door and standing for a few moments reflecting on the man she loved. They'd met at one of the hospital social nights when, as usual, Fred had virtually abandoned her so he could circulate and flirt with other women there. He'd taken pity on her standing alone there and had introduced himself.

For her it had been a moment of elation that a young man like him could even show interest in her and they had genuinely enjoyed each other's company and flirting. Fred had eventually reclaimed her, but a spark had been lit and each of them had determined they would see the other again. From such small casual beginnings there had grown a full and passionate love. For him it was a new experience and one that he found exhilarating, while for her the difference between him and the surly beast she was married to, was equally uplifting.

What followed had been an agenda of secret trips (with the children) to the seaside and risky adventures in parks with picnics in the countryside. He had grown increasingly fond, both of her and the children who in turn had come to like him. In a sense that's was where it had all begun to turn more sinister. It had been the fear of the children innocently betraying them, and another beating, that had turned them both to thoughts of a life without Fred Johnson.

Divorce had not been an option because Fred would never have stood for that, and running away together with the children would have meant him hunting them down and finding them, probably with disastrous results. Then one day a badly bruised Emma had turned up in the park to meet him, having clearly been beaten up again by her husband. That's when they'd come to the decision he had to be killed. Now, it was done and at last they could have their new life – but for the moment at least it had to be put on hold.

· · · · · ·

Later that same evening the Warley Parliament met and gave Cyril Hart the chance to talk to Tom Abbott, the hospital's deputy director again. They had been members of the local debating society for the best part of two years, and had become great personal friends. It had been Tom's wife who'd told Jane Hart about the dead man trying to seduce her on one occasion and the reporter hoped to get some sort of indication as to whether Abbott had known about it.

He was reading the agenda for the night's debate when his friend arrived in the community hall. 'Evening Tom – how's things? Susan ok? Here's tonight's motion for discussion' he said, proffering a sheet of paper for Abbott to take and run his eyes over it.

'Hmmm, this house expresses its concern at the rise of Fascism in Europe. Well, I don't know about you Cyril but I am more worried by this Hitler bloke in Germany than the Italian Mussolini or Franco in Spain. Yes, I think I will definitely speak in favour of this motion. Oh, Susan, yes she's fine but tell me, what's the latest on the Fred Johnson story?'

The two men strolled into the hall and sat down in their usual places before Hart replied. 'Well, little more than you already know actually. You know the inquest is being held next week and as I understand it a lot of your people will be giving evidence.'

'So I believe,' Abbott replied. 'Personally I still think someone topped him, though how and why, God knows?'

'Well, I suppose it could have been an angry husband, given that apparently he had a reputation for chasing the girls,' Hart said pointedly, staring hard at his friends face at the same time but seeing no reaction.

'Seriously, I'll tell you something else I did hear though,' he added. 'Did you know a couple of your people are poofters?'

'Who, Tommy and Alfie? Yes, of course we know and yes I also know it's against the law – Oscar Wilde and all that. Fact is it's very hard to get good staff in hospitals like ours and as it happens those two both happen to be very good at their job. So, providing we don't find them at it on hospital property, we take the line that it's none of our business. They are more useful to us on our wards working with our patients than having it away with each other in prison cells, for pity's sake. Why do you ask?'

Hart shook his head. 'No reason – it was just that I heard the talk, that's all' he said. Two minutes later the Parliament's 'speaker' called the meeting to order and the evening's debate got under way.

The following morning Hart walked into the police station and within minutes was in Wilkins' office telling him what he'd found out about the hospital's attitude towards Race and Rice. He explained what the hospital's policy of *hear no evil, see no evil* towards them was and that in fairness it was one that he could not argue with.

'That may well be Cyril, but the law is the law and a place like a hospital should not be seen as conniving with criminality,' Wilkins grunted. 'One day perhaps it may be legal but not in our lifetime. Anyway, for the moment we need just to concentrate on what we know about the death of Fred Johnson and for that I am relying a great deal on the inquest. I am sure we are going to get some real answers there, and also whether or not the poofs were involved in murder,' the policeman assured him.

HE KILLED MY PAL

'He made me help him kill my pal.'

As he waited for the jury to be sworn in Dr John Martin looked down the list of witnesses and glanced over the medical and post mortem reports, knowing that he had a few problems. County Coroner Martin had presided over many inquests but this one seemed a little more complex than usual and, following the discussion he'd just had with Detective Sergeant Wilkins, he was even more aware of its complexities.

Like the policeman he had suspicions that murder, rather than suicide, could well have taken place but he was experienced enough to know the importance of keeping an open mind. The essential purpose of any inquest was to ensure that it got to the truth. That meant a competent jury, so he watched carefully as it was sworn in, weighing each member of it up as they took the oath. By the time the last juryman had taken his place he was satisfied that they would do a good job.

The inquest was taking place in the hospital's own main hall – often used as its theatre but now rearranged to include a jury box as well as another for the witnesses. Apart from a desk for himself and the clerk of the court, it also had a press table occupied by Cyril Hart who was also happy to see that nobody from the national newspapers had turned up to share it with him. Pencil poised and notebook open and ready, the stage was set and the reporter looked up as the Coroner opened the proceedings.

'Ladies and gentlemen,' Martin began looking over at the jury just settling itself in. 'We are here today and I suspect for some days to come, to enquire into the circumstances surrounding the death, here in Warley Mental Hospital in the County of Essex, of Mr Frederick Johnson of 23 Gresham Road Brentwood, on Saturday or Sunday June 14th/15th this year.

'The evidence you will hear will relate directly to that one single event, and you may well hear various allegations from some witnesses about those events, as well as about the character and standing of Mr Johnson himself. I would ask you not to just remember that, but always keep it at the forefront of your mind. I am aware that a great deal of newspaper and other local speculation has already taken place but you cannot speculate. You have to make your mind up based on the evidence you will hear, not gossip and hearsay.

'You will hear that the actual cause of death has been confirmed through a post mortem as having resulted from an ingested identified poison. Your task, after hearing the evidence is to decide how and perhaps why, that poison was ingested. Was it, for example, swallowed voluntarily, by accident or forcibly so. I cannot emphasise enough just how important that conclusion will be for if it was forced then the conclusion would be that he was murdered.

'Mr Johnson was a married man and the father of two young children, so for their sake as well as for the law, it's important that we find out what actually happened on that fateful night. So I want you to put right out of your mind any suggestions or rumours you may have heard about murder or suicide and just concentrate on the facts that you hear during this inquest. Unless you find you have very conclusive evidence pointing to anyone in particular being responsible, that is all we need from you. It is the truth we seek here, not speculation.

'Before you do retire to consider your verdict I will be summing up all the evidence we will have heard. Remember, my previous remarks notwithstanding, it is not part of your remit to apportion blame, guilt or to make any accusations unless you have really incontrovertible evidence pointing to that. If any such allegations are found to have substance they will be decided in another court later on. Please bear all that in mind as you hear the evidence and particularly when you eventually come to weigh it all up'.

Martin looked around the room as though as to ensure his words had been noted. 'Now, please call the first witness,' he ordered.

The inquest clerk got to his feet and looked down his list. 'Dr Richard Byron' he called.

A door opened and the hospital director was shown into the witness box, where he was formally sworn in. Considering he was a man whose work had taken him into many similar inquest situations in the past Byron looked a little nervous, but his voice held steady as he confirmed his name and position in the hospital. A quick glance over to the public area showed Marion smiling her encouragement and that seemed to give him renewed confidence as he turned back to look at the coroner.

'Dr Byron, I believe you carried out the post mortem

on Mr Johnson. Can I ask you to confirm your position on that, and what you found?' Martin asked.

'Yes sir. While I am a qualified psychiatrist with full responsibility for the hospital, I also hold the necessary surgical and forensic qualifications that qualify me to carry out post mortems on patients, or anyone else who dies in the hospital,' Byron assured him.

'The body was that of a 45-year old male in apparent good health. We found that the cause of death was almost certainly a quantity of Lysol which we found in his stomach. Lysol is a very powerful acid-based disinfectant that we use in the hospital for cleaning purposes and it was that that almost certainly killed him. While it had also damaged other internal digestive organs, I could find no other cause. In fact for a man of his age, his heart and lungs proved to be in a good condition.'

The coroner nodded his appreciation of what had been a very concise but thorough report. 'Thank you for that doctor. Now, can we assume the only way that the Lysol could have got into Mr Johnson's stomach was via his mouth and throat?'

'Yes that is correct'.

'Then tell me doctor. Whether he drank it himself voluntarily or had it forced into him by other hands, it would have been a very painful experience, would it not?'

Byron nodded, 'I would say excruciatingly so, sir'.

'Yes, I agree, yet he was found very peacefully sitting at his desk as though he was just taking a nap, rather than looking as though he'd been thrashing around in agony. Tell me something else doctor – would Mr Johnson have had access to any potentially lethal drugs? After all, as the night supervisor he was in a position of trust and great responsibility so I imagine drugs to sedate violent patients would have been very easily at hand,' the coroner pointed out.

Byron nodded his head. 'There are such drugs in the hospital of course sir, but even as a senior member of staff he would not have had access to them. Whenever situations do occur with patients out of control then whatever the hour I, or another medically qualified senior member of staff who was on call, would be summoned to administer any drugs necessary to calm the patient down.'

'I see. Tell me Dr Byron, do you have any personal thoughts on how this substance came to be in Mr Johnson's body?'

Byron stood reflecting for a moment before replying. 'Well sir, when we first discovered his body I have to admit my first thought was that he had committed suicide. In the light of what we've found out about Mr Johnson since his death, and considering the likely effects on anyone taking that particular fluid, that does look more doubtful. Even as a psychiatrist I find it hard to believe that anyone, however disturbed, with his background and knowledge of the acidic nature of Lysol, would have used it to kill himself.'

'And do it so quietly,' Martin murmured to himself, before raising his voice to a more audible level. 'So would it now be your view that Mr Johnson did not die by his own hand?'

'Personally I find it difficult to avoid that conclusion sir, but all I can tell you is the nature of the substance that actually killed Mr Johnson. How and why it came to be in his body is for this inquest to decide, not really for me to speculate.'

The coroner nodded his acceptance of the point. 'Of course Dr Byron and thank you. Unless you think you have any other information you think can help the jury arrive at their conclusion, I think that will be all for the moment. We may need to call on you again later in these proceedings so you will remain on oath, but for the moment you may stand down' he said.

'Please call the next witness' he ordered the clerk, as a clearly relieved Byron left the witness box to take his place next to Marion in the public section.

As he did so Detective Sergeant Wilkins took the oath, but even as he made his pledge he was secretly hoping there would be no need for him to tell the whole truth. At that stage of the proceedings he did not really want to show his hand in full, so he just confirmed his name, rank and the reason for his involvement. He described how he'd been called from home early on the Sunday morning and had arrived at the hospital to be shown the body of Frederick Johnson in that tiny office.

'Was there anything at the scene that day that gave you any immediate cause to think anything other than that Mr Johnson had killed himself?' Martin asked.

'Well sir to be honest I have never felt that he did and investigations are still in progress. There was an empty bottle lying on the floor and as soon as I smelt it I guessed it had contained some kind of acid, which I was told later was cleaning fluid called Lysol and which was used extensively in the hospital. At that early stage I wasn't sure of the actual cause of death of course, but if it had been that fluid it did strike me as being odd that the body seemed to be so relaxed in death. Mr Johnson looked as if he was simply taking a quick nap after working all night and I found that a bit odd.

'If the disinfectant had been the cause, as looked probable, I would have expected the whole office to be in a bit of a mess. A man in extreme pain would have been thrashing about in agony all over the place and I would have thought that any papers or other things lying on his desk for example would have been scattered in all directions over the floor, but they weren't. However, at that pre-post mortem stage, we did not know the exact cause of death, only an assumption of it. That was only confirmed after Dr Byron had completed his forensic examination.'

'Yes, I accept that and I have the same reservations as you do about how easily the body was apparently resting.' Martin told him. 'So now that you do know it was the Lysol, what line have your investigations been taking?'

'Well sir, obviously murder has to be one of the primary options but, apart from that empty bottle, there was no real evidence at the scene to back that up. The only fingerprints we found in that office, including on the bottle, were those of Mr Johnson himself. There were some prints on the door handle but they proved to be those of the member of staff who actually found the body that morning, so I would have expected them to be on that.'

'Yes, I see. That would be Mr Frederick Olson, right?'

'That is correct sir. I have spoken to him and other members of staff on duty that night, while making enquiries about their movements. Many of them will be giving evidence later, but apart from a shout that could have come from a disturbed patient none of them reported seeing or hearing anything unusual that night.

'I have also made enquiries about Mr Johnson's character and background of course. Again up to now I've found nothing that would appear to have any obvious direct connection with his death, though I am still pursuing some of those lines of enquiry,' Wilkins concluded.

'I see. So, what have you established about Mr Johnson so far?'

'Well sir, he seems to have been a happily married man with two young children and a highly responsible job. He was ex-army who fought in Northern France, including on the Somme, during the war where he had reached the rank of sergeant and seems to have had a good record as a soldier.

'Among his friends and colleagues he seems to have been generally regarded as what is usually described as a 'man's man', in the sense of a liking for his beer and good living. There have also been suggestions that he had an eye for the ladies when his wife wasn't about, but I don't think he was a philanderer though of course I could be wrong and as I say investigations are still proceeding into all aspects of this case,' the detective added, not altogether truthfully.

'I see, sergeant. Tell us, is there anything at all that you have found that you could see as a possible motive for murder?'

'No sir, although I repeat, this is still an ongoing investigation.'

'Until, when exactly?'

'Well sir, until I find definite proof that any crime has been committed, or until this jury has heard the evidence and come to its own conclusion. Obviously if this inquest brings in a verdict of suicide or accidental death, then as far as I am concerned that draws a line under any suggestion of murder,' Wilkins pointed out.

'Well, thank you for that Detective Sergeant. Unless there is anything else relevant you would like to add at this stage, I think we can let you stand down now,' Martin told him.

'No sir, that's all I can offer at the moment,' Wilkins replied, moving out of the witness box.

Martin looked down at his notes before looking up again. 'I think that before we hear from Mrs Johnson, it would make sense to hear evidence from the man who found the body, Mr Olson,' he said.

As Olson made his way into the room and walked smartly towards the witness box he glanced over to the public gallery and was reassured to see Mary smiling encouragingly at him. After being sworn in he described in detail how he'd found Johnson's body that Sunday morning. 'It gave me quite a shock sir,' he added.

Martin half-smiled as he noted the comment. 'Yes. I can imagine. Not quite the sort of thing you expect to find early on a quiet summer Sunday morning. 'Tell me, Mr Olson why exactly did you go to the office that morning at that particular time?' he added.

'Well sir, the regular night shift routine is usually for the superintendent to come round all the wards every hour to check all is well and to sign the log.'

Martin interrupted him. 'You say the regular routine is usual – does that mean it doesn't always happen?'

'Yes sir. It's always been generally accepted that after midnight all the patients should be asleep so unless there is a ward disturbance there is no real point so Fred, er Mr Johnson, often never appeared again until about 5a.m. Then he'd check all was well and sign off the log sheets ready for when the day staff came in at 8a.m,' Olsen paused to take a breath before continuing.

'Up to midnight he'd done his rounds ok but that morning he hadn't reappeared and by 6 o-clock I was worried that he might have dozed off. I decided to risk leaving my ward to wake him in case.'

'Had that happened before then?'

'Yes sir, once or twice,' the man in the witness box admitted after hesitating for a second.

'And in such cases what was Mr Johnson's reaction when he was woken up?'

Olson hesitated again before answering the coroner. He'd been on the receiving end of Johnson's foul temper himself when he'd been caught asleep, on several occasions. That experience had been one of the reasons for his reluctance to investigate the supervisor's non-appearance that morning, but he was unsure about how to respond to the unexpected question. For a moment or two he struggled before coming to a decision and took another deep breath before answering.

'Fred Johnson was ex-army sir, where being caught asleep on duty is a very serious matter. In such cases the natural reaction is to verbally attack the person who woke you, saying you were not really asleep but just deep in thought. It puts them on the defensive and if they are a lower rank tends to ensure their silence.'

'So you are telling this inquest that Mr Johnson's reaction to being woken up in such a way would have produced a violent response – well, at least violent in terms of being shouted at?'

'Yes sir, I am saying that has happened before.'

'Mr Olson, that seems to suggest that you were in the army too – I take it during the Great War.' Martin said, a new thought having just occurred to him. 'Tell me, did you know Mr Johnson in those days?'

Again Olson hesitated before responding. 'He was in the Essex Regiment sir, but I was with a unit attached to the Yorkshire Light Infantry,' he said, truthfully if a little evasively.

Martin had presided over a lot of inquests in his time and knew instinctively that this was an answer, but not one to the question that had been asked. Suddenly he had the feeling that there might have been more to the relationship between the two men than simply as work colleagues.

'Yes I accept that, but that wasn't what I asked, was it Mr Olson? I repeat, did you ever know Mr Johnson during the war? Perhaps I should remind you again that you are on oath here,' he added.

Inside Olson was struggling, glancing again over at Mary as his mind raced over how to reply to the coroner's persistence. She was still smiling her support but was now looking a little puzzled by his obvious reluctance to reply. He knew he could not lie in front of this wonderful woman.

'Yes sir. We did meet briefly in France just after the battle of the Somme.'

'How briefly, and under what circumstances?' Martin asked.

Olson straightened up, his voice taking on a firmer tone as he finally made up his mind.

'The fact is, sir - he made me help him kill my pal.'

• • • • • •

As Olson said the words Cyril Hart, his notes forgotten for the moment, froze. He shot a look over at where Wilkins was sitting. The policeman's face told him that he had clearly been taken by surprise at what the man in the witness box had just said as well. The same thought had flashed through both their minds – that here was yet another possible motive for murder and this time even involving the person who'd found the body. It could put a whole new slant on their investigations and on Hart's story.

The reporter thought back to what Hamilton had told him before he'd come to the inquest.

'Look Cyril – there is bound to be a good story here but let me remind you again, we don't want Fleet Street to know about it until we are good and ready. Just write your notes up each day and then we'll decide together how we handle it. It could be the greatest story the Time has ever had and we don't want it pinched by the nationals before we've got our story out,' the editor had reiterated again and again.

Now he sat at the press bench very aware that he not only had another good story but that the potential for a great career in journalism, never mind the book prospect, was dangling in front of him like a carrot on a stick. The problem now was that if Hamilton saw what Olson had just revealed by reading today's notes it could ruin everything. It was a time for instant decision so, flipping his notebook over to a new page at the back of the book, he prepared to write Olson's evidence down separately.

Across the room from him Wilkins' mind was going through the same turmoil. He was mentally cursing himself for not realising when he'd interviewed Olson, that there might be more to his relationship with Fred Johnson. He remembered how the man had explained why he was drinking from an Essex Regiment mug, but had never mentioned having met Johnson during the war.

Mary Olson too, had been staggered at what her husband had now told the court. Some kind of intuition that her husband and the night superintendent had known each other before had always bothered her but, unlike the coroner, she had never pushed the issue. She had always dismissed it from her mind as some kind of female foolishness but now she realised there were things about her man that he'd hidden from her. Her heart went out to him at that moment and she longed to race over and hug him because she knew there would be a reason for his anguish.

From where Martin sat, Olson's admission was reassuring in that it had justified his pushing deeper into the man's mind. Like Hart and Wilkins he too had realised that another reason for murder had suddenly surfaced, but it was his job to get back to business.

'Mr Olson, that's quite a statement to make to this jury. Would you care to elaborate and tell us the whole story, because I fear it could be relevant?'

Olson nodded his head, in a sense relieved that his great secret was now in the open, yet fearful about what it could lead to. He was particularly concerned about how Mary might react. He began to explain about the Bradford Pals, his friend Kenny Thomas and how they had both been wounded on the Somme during that deadly advance.

His voice was choked with emotion as he told how, while he'd still been in hospital, his friend had been accused, court-martialled and judged guilty of cowardice and desertion. By the time he reached the part in the story about how he had been forced to play a part in Kenny's execution, he was as close to tears as a man could get in public; but he forced himself to continue.

'Fred Johnson was the sergeant in charge of that firing squad and even though he knew of my lifetime friendship with Kenny, he made me blindfold him and help tie him to a post before they shot him. I had grown up with Kenny, we'd joined up and had served together but it made no difference. Johnson may have been ordered to lead the execution party, but he was not under orders to make me take part like that and I hated him for it. That was the nasty kind of man he was, a callous and wicked bully, but I swear to God sir, although I thought about it many times, I didn't kill him' he added, his voice choked with emotion.

As he finished speaking he glanced over again at Mary who was openly sobbing. At last she knew and understood the full horror of what her man had been through and why he'd kept it from her. Now her tears were for him and for what he'd suffered and she ached to rush over to the witness box to comfort him.

She was not alone – there was hardly a man or woman in the room who hadn't been emotionally affected to some degree by what Fred Olson had told them. Most of the women were wiping their eyes with their handkerchiefs, and even John Martin's heart had been touched by what his insistence had revealed.

'Thank you Mr Olson,' he said gently'. 'I think that will be enough for now and perhaps this could be a good moment to adjourn for lunch. It's 12.30 now – we will resume at 2pm this afternoon.' he added standing up.

As he did so the silence was broken by a massive buzz of voices as everyone in the public section who'd heard Olson's revelation, began discussing it with each other. Mary took the opportunity to run across to her husband to do what she had been so desperate to do. He fell into her arms and holding tightly on to each other, both wept unrestrainedly finally oblivious to all around them.

It was a defining moment of their love for each other

with it being so publicly consummated, for at last they had no secrets. Together they wept for Kenny Thomas, and for the dreadful secret he'd kept to himself for almost twenty years. It was a tender moment that neither Hart nor Wilkins felt was one they could interfere in, though clearly it was a development they had to discuss. They made their way across the room towards each other.

'Pub?' Wilkins suggested.

'Yes definitely, but not across the road in the Alexandra. Let's pop down to the Essex Arms,' Hart said. 'It was Johnson's local and who knows what we might pick up there' he added.

As the two men walked through the hospital grounds towards the gate nearest to the pub, they discussed what they'd been hearing.

'Did you know about Olson and the army?' Hart asked. The policeman shook his head.

'No I didn't. Believe me Cyril that was as big a surprise to me as it was to everyone else. I did interview him of course but, while he told me that Johnson didn't always follow the book on the night shift, he didn't tell me about knowing him in the army.

Obviously I will need to talk to him again now as a possible murder suspect, though I have a feeling he will be in the clear. He is too obvious a suspect and that always worries me. He also seems to be a thoroughly decent man but I will not be ruling him out altogether,' he said as the two men walked through the doors of the pub and ordered their beer.

'Well, I certainly have to talk to him because, apart from anything else, for a journalist that was the most moving story I've ever heard and one in its own right. But

I need to make sure I'm not treading on your toes Albert,' Hart said.

Wilkins thought about it for a moment as the two men sipped their beer. 'Actually it might be a good idea for you to talk to him first, and then give me your views on the man. He might be a bit too defensive to a copper. Is your editor going to give you any grief on this though?' he asked.

Hart shook his head. 'No - I am not going to tell him yet and I'll risk him hearing about it from anyone else. I took the notes about the firing squad separately, so he won't see them, but what a hell of a great story.'

They spent the next hour enjoying their pies and beer, generally discussing what they'd heard that morning and agreeing that Olson had made the biggest impact. Then, just as they prepared to get up and leave the pub, Wilkins asked about the other issue that had been nagging at him.

'Tell me Cyril, what did you think about Byron's evidence?'

Hart grinned, because he knew the reason for the question. 'Well, he was certainly very careful in how he answered,' he said.

'Yeah, that's what I thought too,' the policeman said, with a degree of satisfaction in his voice. He was happy that his friend had had the same reservations and made a mental note to continue looking into the Gillespie death.

· · · · · ·

Precisely at two-o-clock coroner Dr John Martin came back into the room, noting that the jury seats were full and that most of the public seats had been taken again as well. Making himself comfortable he decided to address the jury again.

'Ladies and gentlemen. Before we adjourned for lunch we heard a rather startling and very emotional story about the previous relationship between Mr Johnson and Mr Olson while they were both in the army. I will include my thoughts on that particular aspect in my summing up later in this inquest, but I would urge you not to put all your eggs into that one particular basket, especially at this early stage. It was a sad, indeed a very sad, story but when the time comes, and only then, you will have to decide whether it has any bearing on this inquest. Now I ask the clerk of the court to call the next witness, who I believe is Mrs Johnson.'

Once again a buzz of speculation spread through the room as Emma, dressed conventionally in black, slowly made her way to the witness box. Her face was pale and her thin voice quivered as she took the oath.

'Would you like to sit down, Mrs Johnson?' Martin asked gently, gesturing for chair to be brought forward for her.

'Thank you sir,' she smiled gratefully, sitting down on it.

'Mrs Johnson, first let me tell you how sorry we all are for your loss. I think we all appreciate this is not easy for you and we will do our best to make it as painless as we can, but there are procedures we have to go through.'

Emma smiled her gratitude. 'Thank you sir, yes I know that. Everyone has been so kind to us since it happened and I would like to say now just how grateful my children and I are for all those kindnesses.'

'Ok, thank you Mrs Johnson. Now do you think you

can take us through that night up to the moment your husband left for work?'

Emma, speaking in that small timid, yet firm, voice, told how her husband had left for work that evening and that nothing out of the ordinary had taken place. She'd made his sandwiches as usual and after kissing her and the children goodnight he'd left for work at the usual time.

'Did he seem to have anything on his mind, Mrs Johnson?' Martin asked gently.

'No sir - not then, or before. Look sir, I know that some people have been saying things about my husband and what sort of man he was, but I would like to say here that he was a good man. He was very kind to us and was a good father to our children, who loved him,' Emma's voice had got stronger as she loyally defended her husband's name. As she spoke there was hardly a person in the court, including Coroner Martin, whose heart at that moment did not go out to the tragic young widow loyally defending a brutish husband.

'I'm sure that is so, Mrs Johnson. I don't believe you can help this inquest with anything further, so I think that will be all for now,' he told her gently. Having given their evidence, most of the witnesses had found seats in the public section but Emma, with her head held high, left the room altogether to go home.

As the door closed behind her the Clerk of the Court stood up and turned to speak to Martin in a very low and confidential voice.

'Are you sure?' everyone heard the coroner ask. The Clerk nodded his head.

'Well, it's a little unorthodox but you'd better bring her in,' Martin told him.

The Clerk nodded to the usher standing by the door of

the witness's room and he opened it to admit another witness. A tall dark haired middle-aged woman walked in and was guided towards the witness box. Everyone in the room watched in puzzled silence as she picked up the bible to take the oath before giving evidence.

'Can we have your name, please' the clerk asked.

'Yes, sir. My name is Mrs Jane Johnson'

'And what was your relationship with the late Mr Frederick Johnson?'

'I was his wife, sir!' she said.

I SAW THEM KILL HIM

'He never did come back and then our baby died'

For the second time within hours Hart, still scribbling into his notebook, froze and he looked up around him. It was immediately clear that he wasn't the only one taken by surprise at what the new witness had said. Once again his hands moved to flip the back of his notepad to another fresh page so he could take 'unofficial' notes on this new aspect. He could see Albert Wilkins looking just as stunned by what the new witness had said as he was. How many more twists and turns will this story take? he thought to himself. The silence was broken by Coroner Martin.

'What do you mean, you're Mrs Johnson?' he asked. 'We've already heard from Mr Johnson's widow – did you mean you are his ex-wife? Were you divorced?'

The new witness shook her head and grimaced. 'Well sir, if we were it would be news to me, and not something he mentioned when I saw him a few weeks ago. I suppose you could say I am the deserted or abandoned wife – but as far as I am aware I am still his legal and only one.'

'Mrs Johnson, I have to remind you that you have just

taken an oath to tell the truth here. Are you sure you want to pursue the claim you have just made?'

'Yes sir I do know that and yes I'm telling the truth, but I am not here as the grieving widow or even to cause her any problems. Fred and I were married and I still have the marriage licence to prove it, though until a few weeks ago I thought he was dead' she replied.

She rummaged through her voluminous handbag to produce a familiar-looking official document, which she handed to the Clerk. He quickly scanned it and looked up at the coroner, nodding his confirmation that it did seem genuine. Martin shook his head in frustrated resignation.

'Well, Mrs Johnson, I won't pretend that this hasn't taken us all a little by surprise, which doesn't seem to be an unusual turn of events in this case. Would you kindly tell us the circumstances of how you say you came to marry the deceased, Mr Frederick Johnson and when you last saw him? You may sit down if you wish,' he invited.

Jane smiled her thanks and sat in the offered chair before speaking again. When she did it was in a tone vastly different from the distressed one used by Emma, the other 'Mrs Johnson'. This was a very confident woman of the world, who these days spent most of her working days shouting 'Last orders please!' in the pubs and clubs of Romford.

'Well sir, I met Fred Johnson over twenty years ago when we both worked in a West End hotel. He joined up in 1914 and was posted to Warley Barracks not far from where we are now to do his training. He was a young soldier about to go off to war, we were both young and I was very proud of him. We had a very brief and passionate romance and had a quick civil wedding in the hotel.

'Neither of us knew that I was already pregnant at the

time, but then he went off to France and I never heard from him again. There were so many young men killed or just went missing in that awful war and after some months with no word I began to fear he'd been one of them. He never did come back and then our baby died very young.

'I made enquiries with the army of course sir, but they were not very helpful. In fact it turned out that he'd never registered our marriage with the army so I couldn't even claim a widow's pension but I was still young and had a good job in the hotel by then so it never really mattered. The months and years went by and gradually I got used to the idea that he had been one of those unknown warriors that people used to talk about. I developed new friendships and built a new life for myself gradually forgetting all about Fred. Then six weeks ago he walked back into my life.'

Coroner Martin, along with everybody else in the hushed room, had been listening intently. 'How did that come about?' he asked.

Jane explained how Fred had walked into the Romford pub she was working in by chance and, after the initial shock of recognition and recrimination on both sides, the two had talked at length. She even told the inquest that some of her old feelings for him had begun to resurface during that brief reunion.

'Did he mention having another wife and family?' Martin asked.

'No sir, he didn't. He told me he had a good job in Brentwood and said he would be in touch with me again, but he never mentioned another wife or any children. He said he'd suffered from shell-shock during the war and had been very ill, even losing his memory for a long time. He said that it had been so long that by the time he had recovered, although he remembered me, he felt it was best not to try to make contact in case I had built a new life.

'Well sir by that time I was starting to feel sorry for him with all that he'd suffered but now I realise he was just trying to keep me from finding out he was a bigamist. He never mentioned having another wife and children. Then, the next thing I knew was that a few weeks later I was reading about his death. I saw a report about it in a local paper I happened to find in the pub I work in,' she finished.

As a buzz of whispered chatter swept through the public gallery, Dr Martin rapped his gavel on the desk calling for quiet. Then he looked back at Jane.

'Mrs Johnson what you have told us today is quite astounding and of course totally unexpected. I think I need to give the jury, and indeed myself, time to absorb what you have told us and for the police to make further enquiries about that and other issues because this could change a lot of things, so I will adjourn this hearing for two days.

'Before I do that, is there anything else you can tell us that you think might be helpful to this inquiry? For example, when you met him in Romford that day did Mr Johnson show any signs of stress that might have led him to commit suicide?' Martin asked.

She shook her head vigorously and smiled knowingly. 'Oh no sir, the Freddie Johnson I knew in the old days was a man with a zest for living and not the sort to top himself. I hadn't seen him in years of course but I didn't get the impression he'd changed at all in that sense. To be honest he still seemed to fancy himself and once we got over our initial reactions he proved to be quite chirpy,' Jane told him firmly.

'Right! Well, thank you Mrs Johnson, perhaps you can leave a contact address with the clerk.' Martin looked up to speak to the inquest. 'Ladies and gentlemen, as I have just said I need to adjourn this hearing for two days. I will ask the police to make further enquiries about Mr Johnson's marital situation and undertake any further investigations they feel might be appropriate in the light of anything else we've heard so far in this room today.'

He stood up and gathered his papers before sweeping from the room. Behind him he left small groups of stunned gossipers, all contributing to a buzz of high-pitched and excited chatter. On the press bench Cyril Hart sat for a moment wondering just how much he could keep from his editor now. What with Olson's revelations and now another Mrs Johnson on the scene he knew the back pages of his notebook contained some journalistic dynamite, but first he had to get back to Emma Johnson to find out whether or not she'd known about Jane. He hardly noticed Wilkins threading his way through the crowd towards him until the policeman appeared in front of him.

'Cyril! What do you think about that, then? Johnson was a bloody bigamist,' the copper muttered, so that nobody around them could hear.

Hart shook his head. 'I am as confused as you are Albert. Hells bells mate – this puts yet another new twist into this bloody story. How many more can there be? Look, I'm off to go and see Emma Johnson, to find out if she knew about this and of the possibility that she wasn't his real wife. Do you want to come?'

'No, but while you're doing that I'll catch up with the latest Mrs Johnson and question her, but let's keep in touch tomorrow with what we find out about these two ladies,' Wilkins told him, before dashing out of the door in the direction Jane had taken.

• • • • • •

Twenty minutes later Cyril Hart was banging on Emma Johnson's door. When she opened it she seemed slightly surprised to see him there, but stood back to let him into the house. Without saying a word she led him through to the tiny kitchen and gestured for him to sit down, while she put the inevitable kettle on for tea.

'The inquest finished, is it Mr Hart?' she asked with a smile that invited him to tell her the result and with an ease she wasn't feeling inside. Despite her lover's confident assurances she was still worried about a verdict that could lead to her arrest, conviction and the gallows.

He shook his head. 'No it hasn't. Tell me Mrs Johnson, why didn't you stay after giving evidence?'

'I had to get home for the children and I guessed somebody would tell me how it went,' she said, still clearly unaware of what had happened.

'I think you'd better sit down love,' he said. The kettle had begun to hiss on the gas stove but she seemed to be suddenly aware, probably by his manner, of something serious and obeyed. His mind was in turmoil, deciding how to break the news to this rather nice little woman who he liked a lot, while for her part she still feared what he was going to tell her.

'Tell me – did your late husband ever mention a woman called Jane? He asked.

She looked puzzled for a second or two before shaking her head. 'Jane? No not that I can remember. Why do you ask? She said hesitating as though afraid of what he might be about to tell her. The memory of Tilly Masters still rankled and instinctively she feared a similar revelation and that this Jane would be another pregnant woman laying claim to her husband.

'Well, after you left a lady calling herself Mrs Jane Johnson turned up and she claimed to be your husband's legal wife,' Hart told her, staring intently into her eyes to see if he could gauge a reaction from them. What he did see in them was shock and disbelief and he put his hand out protectively towards her.

In the background the impatient kettle spurted its angry jet of steam into the kitchen as she struggled to understand what he'd told her. It seemed an age before she could actually find the words and the breath to speak them. 'That's an absolute nonsense, Mr Hart. Who was this woman and why should she say something like that?'

Hart did his best to calm her and, sitting her down before making the tea himself, he explained what had happened. 'I'm sorry to say Mrs Johnson, that her claim does seem to be genuine and that your late husband was a bigamist.'

'That would make my children illegitimate, wouldn't it?' Emma interrupted – a confused and almost frightened edge to her voice.

Hart spread his hands wide and nodded. 'I am so dreadfully sorry Emma, I really am, but yes that might well be the case, though at least he had no children with this other Mrs Johnson' he confirmed compassionately preferring to ignore that Jane had spoken of a lost baby. As he spoke he was a little puzzled to see that her obvious anguish was not accompanied by any tears. Though she was physically trembling in shock her eyes were dry.

'But I have my marriage lines' she protested

desperately. 'Fred and I were married here in Brentwood six years ago. Perhaps he was divorced, though he never mentioned even being married once before.' She moved as though to get her own documents to prove her point but he stopped her.

'Look Emma, I am sure you do have them and that you believe they are genuine, but she has some too and hers, which also seem genuine, date back to 1914. The fact is that it does seem that your husband lied to you and the registrar, in fact to everybody. He married you when he already had a wife,' he said gently. 'Look, it's very clear that you are the wronged wife here and I will have to write up this story that way. Is there anything you want to be quoted on about all this?' he asked.

She thought for a moment or two before responding, and then the loyalty to her dead husband that she'd already demonstrated in good measure before, seemed to click in again.

'Yes, as I said in court today he was good to me and a good father to our children. I am sure there must have been a good reason why he never told us about this other woman. That dreadful war affected a lot of men who'd served in the army and I can only assume that something happened during that time to make him want to build a new life and forget his old one. I will continue to bring our children up to be proud of him,' she maintained, with a hint of defiance in her voice. Now, surprising even herself with her acting ability, she began to relax a little and turned back to him.

'Mr Hart, thank you for coming to tell me about this yourself. I really do appreciate it,' she added, touching his arm gratefully. 'But will you leave now and give me time to think,' she said.

'Of course Mrs Johnson,' he said standing up, 'but will you be alright?' he asked.

'I'll be fine. Thank you so much for coming to tell me about this, and clearly I now have a lot more to think about,' she reassured him as she led him to the front door to show him out.

As she closed it behind him she stood in the small hallway for a moment or two, digesting what she'd just been told. Her face was a mix of emotions and that tongue was violently massaging inside her cheek as her mind desperately tried to come to terms with the tangled mess of shock, amazement, relief and anger this latest turn of events had provoked. If only she'd known... impatiently she dismissed the speculation from her mind, or at least she tried.

At the end of the day Fred had still been the husband who had brutalised and humiliated her and this latest revelation only strengthened her disgust of the man she'd married, or up to now at least thought she'd married, in haste. Had she known, she wondered, would she and the man she really loved have needed to murder him?

For his part Cyril Hart, cycling back up the hill towards the office, was as confused and worried as Emma was, but for different reasons. He knew he had to report this particular new development to the editor and write it up, so he'd decided to keep the Olson revelation up his sleeve at least for the moment. The question was, could he do so?

Hamilton glanced up at him as he walked into the office. 'The inquest finished already?' he asked.

'No sir. It's been adjourned for a couple of days, but there has been a development.' Hart began to explain what had happened, or at least some of what had happened. The editor sat, listening open-mouthed, as he was told about the story of the other Mrs Johnson. Even as his reporter gave him the details, the journalist in Hamilton was working overtime in his mind.

'And she does seem kosher?' he asked.

Cyril nodded. 'Yes, there doesn't seem to be any doubt about it. Fred Johnson was a bigamist who fooled everyone – especially Emma Johnson, who I popped in to see on my way back to the office. I broke the news to her and she was totally devastated. She really had no idea that her husband had another wife tucked away somewhere in his past,' he added.

'Poor woman. Right Cyril – look let's play it down this week until we get the whole story. We can't ignore this development, but let's not make it headline stuff and just do a few paragraphs on it downpaper because I still don't want Fleet Street sniffing round yet,' Hamilton ordered.

It was what exactly what Hart had been planning to do anyway and for the same reason, so he was relieved to hear his editor actually tell him to do it. 'Yes sir, of course. I also need to go and see Sergeant Wilkins down at the police station and see what he thinks,' he added, sitting down to type up his notes.

As he did so the phone on his desk rang and pure instinct told him it would be the policeman on the other end. 'Cyril, in the pub tomorrow morning' the voice in his ear said before hanging up without giving him a chance to respond. He glanced over at Hamilton who was actually smiling, comfortable in the fact he would have another good story going into the paper that week at a level he could control.

When he got home that evening Cyril told his Jane about what had happened in court, and about the unexpected appearance of the other Jane. She was incredulous but not wholly surprised.

'I told you, love, that he fancied himself with the ladies and that just goes to show he always did. It's his poor wife and children I feel sorry for,' she said as she put their dinner on the table and sat down opposite him. They could not know that even as they sat eating their food, Emma Johnson was opening her door to another visitor. Her eyes lit up when she saw who it was.

'Come in, darling. I hoped you'd come,' she said.

He grinned. 'Couldn't do otherwise bearing in mind what we heard in the inquest today. I take you heard what happened?' he said, taking her tightly into his arms and kissing her.

'What, that my dear husband was a bloody bigamist? Yes, I had the local press here a few hours ago telling me all about the other Mrs Johnson. It's ironic, isn't it – there we were worried about how he would react if I left him, when he had no real legal claim on me anyway.'

He smiled reassuringly. 'Well yes darling, but I think he would have caused us trouble anyway and he wouldn't have let us take the children if we'd left. No, at the end of the day I still think we did what we had to do. The point is that everyone is more confused than ever now about whether he was murdered or killed himself and that's good. It's a bit like that Hampton Court maze I told you about and I think we'll try and keep it that way,' he laughed.

'Ok, but be careful my darling. We are too close now to risk any suspicion falling on us,' she murmured.

'Don't worry about that Em. In any case there will be so many people feeling sorry for you now this other Mrs Johnson has come out of the woodwork that no one will ever suspect us,' he said ruffling her hair. 'Look, sweetheart, I have to go to work now. Keep your chin up and don't worry about a thing. We'll soon be together, all of us, and we can start that new life' he told her.

• • • • • •

Wilkins was already in the Grey Goose the next day when Hart arrived, to find the policeman had already bought the beers and ordered the pies. He sat down and gratefully swallowed a few mouthfuls before speaking.

'Gosh, I needed that Albert, thanks. It's been a busy morning with the bloody flower shows. I haven't even touched the Fred Johnson story yet,' he said.

The policeman smiled laconically, 'Yes, this must be turning into quite a story for you, what with Olson and the other Mrs Johnson that no-one knew about until yesterday. Don't forget either that we still need to explore Byron's involvement with his predecessor's suicide as well. Have you made any progress there?'

The reporter shook his head. 'Not had a chance to even think about it, to be honest Albert. The fact is that this case already seems to have more twists and turns than a corkscrew, let alone that one as well. Do you really think there is a connection?'

Wilkins nodded. 'Yes Cyril, you're right about all the angles this investigation is taking, and my problem is that I still have nothing but suspicion to go on. Actually I wondered if you would like to go and rattle his cage before the inquest reopens. You never know what falls out of the tree when you give it a good shaking,' he said thoughtfully, mixing his metaphors.

'Ok, I'll try. How did you get on with the new Mrs

Johnson? I popped in to see our local one and she was very upset to hear about her husband's matrimonial track record. Not surprising really but I was a bit surprised that she took it so well and even still defended him,' Hart said.

'Yes, well I couldn't catch up with Jane Johnson before she left the court but I am hoping to see her later today. I have a feeling her story will be genuine though, because I can't see that she has anything to gain, apart perhaps from some insurance money, by deception. If there's any justice that ought to go to the Mrs Johnson we already know of anyway, but still we'll see,' Wilkins grinned.

The two men enjoyed the rest of their lunch hour making small talk - their friendship developing through growing mutual respect and similar views on life in general. Then having set the world, communism versus fascism and the career of tennis player Fred Perry, to rights over a few pints they left the pub to go their separate ways. Hart went back to Brentwood's Time to write up his 'wronged wife' story and Wilkins walked back to the police station where a car was waiting to take him to Romford. He was going there to find a market pub called the Golden Lion, where hopefully a barmaid called Jane would still be working that day.

It was late afternoon before he got back to the police station. He'd had a long conversation with Jane Johnson, and was convinced that her story was right and that she had only found out about Fred's death by accident. He was also satisfied that she hadn't put him under any pressure sufficient enough to make him suicidal.

'We just caught up with old times, that's all Mr Wilkins. I was angry at first about the way he had forgotten about me when he was sent overseas, but he was always a charmer and it's been a long time. Mind you, I might not have been so understanding if I'd known about his other wife and his kids though,' she'd laughed.

'Are you planning to make any claim on his money?' Wilkins had asked and she'd shaken her head at the thought.

'No, what would be the point. They may not be my kids, but they were his and I am not about to hurt them or his new missus come to that. None of this is her fault and to be honest I feel a bit sorry for her. No, I've already built a new life for myself and only turned up at the inquest out of curiosity and to let people know what a bastard he really was. All my sympathies are with her and the children, not with him now I know more about him' she'd reassured him.

After writing up his notes about the 'new' Mrs Johnson twist in the story, careful to ensure it wasn't sensationalised, Hart made his way to the hospital and asked to speak with Dr Byron again. As he was shown into the Director's office Byron looked at him quizzically.

'The inquest resumes the day after tomorrow Mr Hart and you know I cannot talk about that,' he said pointing the reporter towards a chair.

'Yes, well it wasn't that inquest I came to talk about really, Dr Byron,' Hart explained. 'I came here to talk about Dr Gillespie's suicide.'

The effect the sudden mention of his predecessor's name had on the hospital director's face startled even Hart, a reporter well used to asking questions for effect. Byron sat bolt upright and began fidgeting with his hands, fiddling with a pen that was actually lifeless in his fingers at that moment.

'What? Why? Good grief man, we are in the middle of an inquest about a man who died in this hospital only a few weeks ago. Why are you dragging up Dr Gillespie's suicide?' he stuttered.

'Well it's not me actually, sir. It was Detective Sergeant Wilkins who mentioned he was looking at the coincidence of Mr Johnson's being there at the time and it set me wondering. He's asked me to dig out all the old newspaper files relating to the story. Between ourselves I got the impression he thinks Johnson may have actually murdered Dr Gillespie. ' Hart told him, watching Byron's face for reaction.

On the other side of the desk the hospital director was struggling with a host of long-buried fears that had suddenly resurfaced in his imagination. He knew the truth of what had happened, but was suddenly scared that he had overlooked a clue or anything that Wilkins, who was clearly more thorough than the detective who'd investigated Gillespie's death, might turn up now. It seemed ironic that the blackmailer he had thought had died with his secret, could now come back to haunt him. His recent fears that the blackmailer might have left evidence behind suddenly seemed less paranoid.

In his rising panic he thought of Marion, dear darling Marion, fearing how she might react to the revelation that he had made her a widow before marrying her. Although they'd had an affair at the time, as far as she'd had been concerned it had only been a casual one and she had genuinely loved Gillespie. Her love for Byron had only grown deeper after his death and losing it now by being exposed as his murderer was the one thing Byron couldn't bear to even think about.

The one hopeful feature as he considered what Cyril had told him seemed to be that Wilkins apparently suspected Johnson, rather than him, of being the murderer. It was clearly important to encourage that suspicion and even as Hart watched closely he pulled himself together and began to respond to the reporter's bombshell.

'Well, it's a theory that has never come up before of course but I suppose it could make some sense. If it was true it would mean that Johnson would have fooled us all and not just about his being a bigamist either. It would have meant he was already in the house that day without our knowledge and thinking about it he did appear up those stairs very quickly' Byron said, with as much conviction as he could muster.

The reporter nodded his agreement. 'Well that's certainly true, but is there anything, anything at all doctor, that you can think of about Dr Gillespie's death that has not come up before. I mean, I understand there was a suicide note, but does anyone know what became of it after the inquest?

'Yes. I think I can answer that. When my wife and I married I know she burned a lot of photos and other stuff connected to her former marriage and I assume that was probably among it. I do know she was very bitter because his suicide put her in a position that left her penniless because the life insurance was invalid of course and they didn't have a lot of savings. She could also have been made homeless but the hospital governors said she could stay as long as she needed to then of course we fell in love and she married me.' He paused for a moment before continuing.

'My wife is also a deeply religious woman and of course, apart from attempted suicide being against the law of the land, the taking of your own life is very much against God's law so she was very angry about that too,' he pointed out.

Hart smiled his thanks and rose to leave. 'Thank you doctor, you have been very helpful.' He paused as he turned to go, as another thought struck him. 'Oh, yes one other thing - did you know before he told the inquest about Mr Olson and Johnson having met during the war?'

'No I didn't, but really I suppose there was no real reason for me to know about what went on before people came here if they had good references. Clearly Fred Olson has carried quite a grudge for many years but he's a good worker, who I am actually going to confirm as the new night superintendent once all this is over' he added, making it clear that the interview was over.

Cyril smiled his thanks, and left the office. His inter-rogation techniques might not have been as direct and official as those of the policeman, but they were just as probing. He was now convinced that Wilkins could well be right in his suspicions that something about the Gillespie death wasn't right.

Like the detective he couldn't put his finger on anything specific, but he was now just as sure as Wilkins had been that there was more to the previous director's death than had been realised at the time. His bluff to Byron about Johnson being a murder suspect had been rewarded with answers that had clearly indicated relief rather than shock.

As he walked down the corridor towards the main entrance to the hospital, he bumped into Tom Abbott coming out of his office and stopped to pass the time of day with his friend.

'What are you doing here, Cyril,' Abbott asked.

'I've been to see your boss again.'

'What, about Fred Johnson? I'm surprised he'd say

anything to the press before the inquest has reached a verdict,' his friend commented.

Hart shook his head. 'Well no actually. I was asking him about another death – that of his predecessor,' he said.

'What, Gillespie?' Why?'

'Oh, it was just something that came up. Tom, I know you weren't here then, but did you ever hear Johnson and your guvnor talking about it?'

It was Abbott's turn to shake his head and look mystified. 'No, I know that they were both witnesses at the inquest but that's about all. There was a rumour in the hospital that Johnson got the night superintendent's job because he knew more than he was letting on about something, but that was just hospital gossip nothing more. Look, Cyril, what's going on? Why are you asking about that anyway?'

'Honest Tom - no particular reason other than it was something I overheard at the inquest and then picked up down at the nick. Probably the same gossip with no foundation that you heard. Look, I have to go. Give my love to Susan - bye,' Hart said as he carried on walking down the corridor. Behind him the hospital's deputy director stood bemused, and even a touch irritated by his friend's lack of communication.

· · · · · ·

As he made his way back to the hospital to reopen the inquest Coroner John Martin was suffering the same sort of level of bewilderment and confusion as Abbott had been when he'd spoken to Cyril Hart in the hospital a day or so earlier. He'd presided over many inquests in his time but never one as complex as this one. As he prepared to re-open it he couldn't help wondering what new twists and turns it would take.

He was looking over his notes in the room he'd been allocated when there was a knock on the door and he called for whoever it was to come in. It opened to reveal the burly figure of Detective Sergeant Albert Wilkins standing in the doorway. 'Can I have a word Dr Martin?' the policeman asked.

'Yes, of course, Sergeant, come in and sit down for a moment. I'm glad you came actually. Tell me – is there anything we can do to help each other get to the truth here because, to be honest I am finding this one very hard going?' he asked.

'Actually sir, yes there is but it might seem a little unorthodox, possibly even bordering on the illegal. I want you to direct the jury towards an open verdict.'

Martin looked up with a start at the request. 'That might be a little difficult Sergeant to say the least. I think you'd better explain that one,' he said.

An hour later Martin made his way into the inquest room and glanced around to see that everyone was in their place before speaking.

'Good morning, ladies and gentlemen. I have to tell you first that I have spoken with the police investigating the death of Frederick Johnson. I am told their investigations are proceeding and will not hamper the continuation of this hearing so we will proceed.' He leaned over to hand the Clerk a sheet of paper. 'This is the order of witnesses I want to be giving evidence at this stage,' he told him. The Clerk looked at the list, looked up and called, 'Mr William Taylor!'

The door to the witness room opened and Billy Taylor

nervously entered the room. Slowly, even reluctantly, he made his way over to the witness box and visibly shook as he swore to tell the truth.

'Thank you Mr Taylor,' Martin said. 'Now I understand you were one of the night staff on duty the night Mr Johnson died. You originally made a statement to the police that you noticed nothing unusual happening that night, so for the record I have to ask you to formally confirm that.'

Taylor fidgeted from foot to foot, his hands clenching and unclenching as he struggled to reply to the question. It seemed an age before he managed to stammer out his words and it was clear they were not coming easily.

'Er, no sir, I can't do that. Please can I change my statement?' He said, his voice quavering and very thin.

'What?' Martin's surprise was shared, as a clearly audible intake of breath from everyone in the room showed. Wilkins' jaw dropped open while on the press bench Hart's pencil hand froze over his notepad yet again. Around him a quiet murmur very quickly grew in volume to a buzz of chatter. The coroner was the first to recover, and banged his gavel onto his desk.

'Silence, silence, please!' He glared at poor Billy who was now trembling even more violently than before. The thought passed through Martin's mind that he was reminded of a frightened rabbit caught in headlights, but it was not his job to be sympathetic.

'Mr Taylor, did I hear you right? You want to change the statement that you originally gave to the police about what you saw or heard that night? Why on earth would you want to do that?'

The vehemence and impatience in the coroner's voice did little to help Billy's nerves. 'Well sir, I was always unhappy about it and when my brother, whose house I live in, heard about it he was furious. You see, he is a policeman in Southend and when I admitted to him that I'd given the police a false statement about that night, he told me to tell the truth or get out of his house. I'd have nowhere else to go if had to do that because after I came out of hospital a few years ago he and his wife took me in and gave me a home.'

'Yes, yes, very commendable and we fully appreciate and acknowledge your brother's instruction that you tell the truth. So are you now saying that you did see something that night that could have a bearing on this inquest? You are aware that this is a very serious matter and giving false evidence could itself lead to a prison sentence?' Martin warned the sad figure who was now the focus of everyone's attention.

'Yes sir and I'm really sorry, but I was so scared. I will be glad to tell the truth now and get this off my chest,' Billy said in that timid 'frightened rabbit' voice.

'Well, I will decide what to do about that later, but what do you have to say now?' Martin asked. 'Come on, get on with it man – did you hear or see anything that night and if so what was it?' he added impatiently.

'Well sir. Not long after midnight I heard Mr Johnson shouting in the corridor.' The poor man was close to tears as he spoke but Martin ignored his show of emotion.

'You heard Mr Johnson shouting. What was he shouting and how do you know it was him?' The coroner said impatiently

Taylor looked fearfully around the court, before replying.

'I heard him shout something like *'you dirty bastards'*

and I know it was his voice because I looked out into the corridor and saw him.'

'What, you actually saw Mr Johnson in the corridor? What was he doing and why was he shouting?'

'He was struggling with two people, sir.'

'What do you mean? Who with and why?'

'He was struggling very hard sir, because I think they were trying to kill him,'

Cyril Hart could hardly believe his ears, though his detective 'partner' Albert Wilkins certainly could. From the very beginning he'd never been comfortable with Billy Taylor, or the two people he guessed Taylor was about to name. Sure enough, as soon as Coroner Martin demanded it he confirmed the policeman's very thoughts.

'It was Alfie Rice and Tommy Race, sir. I think they done him in and I saw them doing it.

WE'RE MATES AND THAT'S ALL

'It looks like what the crime-writers would call a perfect murder'

If there had been a buzz of excitement earlier when Billy Taylor had asked to change his original statement, it was nothing compared with the uproar his words provoked now. It was as if a cork had been popped from a bottle of expensive fizzy wine, bursting with uncontrolled energy as the full meaning of what he'd said struck home.

Suddenly people were shouting at each other and screaming invective at the pathetic and frightened figure in the witness box. 'You bloody liar! Why are you saying this? You never saw anything.' From all sides the packed room shook as horrified onlookers, even some members of the jury, forgot themselves and where they were to join in the chaos, all of them shouting at poor Billy.

He cowered in the witness box, his lean body visibly shaking at the response he'd provoked. Above the din Martin was frantically banging his gavel trying to make himself heard, while Wilkins hurried across to the press bench to have an animated conversation with Cyril Hart.

Finally the gavel began to win the day and the noise subsided sufficiently enough for Martin to get his way and make himself heard. 'Ladies and gentlemen – please. Settle down. Remember where you are and what we're here for.'

Wilkins sat down at the press bench alongside Hart and the coroner turned his attention back to the frightened figure in the witness box.

'Mr Taylor, I take it you are aware of the implications of what you have just said? You do know what you said, don't you? You have accused two of your colleagues of murdering Mr Johnson and claim you saw them doing it, but you have never mentioned this before. Why not?'

'I was too scared sir. They threatened that I'd be the next one they'd do in if I told anyone what I'd seen.'

'So, as well as accusing Mr Race and Mr Rice of murder, you are now also saying they threatened you to make you give a false statement?'

Billy, pathetically anxious to please, nodded. 'Yes sir. I was so frightened of what they might do to me that for over a week afterwards I kept the door to my ward locked every night I was on duty.'

'I see. Well before I ask you to explain further I will adjourn again for ten minutes while I consult with the investigating officer. Please sit down, remain where you are and do not move from there or talk to anyone else until I come back,' Martin ordered. Then, gesturing towards Wilkins to follow, he left the room.

Back in his private room he turned to the policeman in fury. 'Sergeant, what the hell is going on here? Are you going to tell me you had no indication at all about what Taylor was going to say? Surely to God, you must have had some suspicions when you questioned him? You must have recognised what kind of an unstable character he is.'

Wilkins shook his head slowly – he was still trying to collect his own thoughts about what had happened. 'No doctor. Believe me this has taken me as much by surprise as anyone else, though I must admit *that* as soon as he said so I guessed the names he was about to come up with. Yes, I did have Taylor down as a bag of nerves whose statement might be a little fishy, but never for a moment did I suspect it might be because he was being threatened and certainly not for the reason he's just given.'

'If indeed he did see anything of course,' Martin grunted sarcastically. He stopped to think for a moment before speaking again. 'Look here Wilkins, you are an experienced policeman who must have interviewed hundreds of suspects in your time. Just how much credibility do you place on this man's claims?'

'Well sir, if I'm to be honest, at this moment none at all. Clearly he hates Race and Rice and seems to have picked up on the stories about them planning to kill Johnson'.

Martin looked up sharply and he told the coroner about the rumours of the two men having plotted to murder Johnson and how they had been generally discounted in the hospital as idle chit-chat. He also told him more about the two men at the centre of the rumours and Martin was appalled.

'Now you're telling me that Race and Rice are a pair of queers. For God's sake Wilkins, what else is this bloody case going to turn up? Given Johnson's probable attitude as an ex-soldier towards queers, there would almost certainly have been some friction. That might well give them a motive for murder I suppose, but do you think they'd really go that far?'

'I'm not sure sir. I don't think so but that possibility did come up during my original investigation because I always felt Johnson might have been murdered. How, or by whom, I still just don't know for sure and to be honest, even after I learned about their illegal sexual activities, my suspicions never really included those two other than as just a possibility.'

'You do have a suspect, then?'

'Yes sir I think I do, but I'd rather not say who right now because I still can't be sure. At the moment it looks like what the crime-writers would call a perfect murder and as a policeman I cannot accept that. That's why I need this inquest to come up with an open verdict, because it's the only one that will give me the reason, time and opportunity to dig further.'

'Alright yes I understand that, but as I told you before I cannot guarantee it and especially after what we've heard today. We will continue for the moment, but only long enough for Taylor to make his statement while he's still under oath. Then I will have to adjourn yet again to give you a chance to investigate both him and the poofs to get at the truth,' Martin concluded.

Making it clear their talking was over he picked up his papers and made his way back into the inquest room with Wilkins following close behind. A lively buzz of chatter was still echoing round the room, but it was silenced as the coroner and the copper came back and resumed their positions. As Wilkins rejoined Hart on the press table the coroner looked at Billy, still noticeably shaking on his chair and scowled.

'Mr Taylor. I have to remind you again that you are still under oath to tell the whole truth. Clearly what you have just said puts a whole new light on this business and on your evidence. Every word you say from now on will be very carefully and fully noted and I have to warn you that there may well be repercussions over the veracity of your original statement. Now I propose to let you tell the whole story as you claim it happened, in full and without interruption. Do you understand all that and now you have had time to reflect, do you stand by what you have told us today?'

Billy, still shaking with nerves, nodded his head. 'Yes sir, I understand and what I have to say now is the truth and the whole truth, so help me God,' he stammered.

'Well, then, get on with it,' Martin ordered curtly.

Billy took a deep breath to summon up his courage and began to speak in that quavering timidly thin voice again.

'It had started out as a normal Saturday night and Mr Johnson had done his early rounds as usual. He did seem to be a bit drunk at the time but not more so than normal and whatever his condition he always knew what he was doing. He could hold his drink sir, and I never saw him incapable of doing his job.

'Just after midnight he made his usual rounds again and signed the log sheet, we chatted for a few minutes and he left to go back to his office at the end of the corridor. It was all very normal. The whole hospital was quiet, although a few of the patients were restless though that's fairly normal too. Then around 2-o clock in the morning I heard Mr Johnson's voice outside along the corridor. He was shouting and I am very certain he was saying '*you dirty bastards*'.'

Martin looked up and glowered at the public gallery, to halt another murmur in its tracks before Billy continued. 'I cracked my door open and peered out into the corridor where I saw Mr Johnson being held by Mr Race who was pinioning his arms from behind. Mr Rice was there too and he appeared to be pouring something into Mr Johnson's mouth. He was struggling and gurgling like mad, but they were holding him tight and gradually his struggles began to get less until there was silence. I was terrified, my legs were like jelly and I was so confused I could not think straight.

'Suddenly I realised Mr Rice was staring in my direction and that frightened me more than ever, so I closed the door and went back to my desk. About half an hour later he came into my ward and accused me of spying on him and Mr Race. He warned me to forget anything I'd seen, or they would kill me. Believe me sir he meant it, he was so angry that for a moment I thought he'd do it there and then.

'An hour later Mr Race came into my ward to make the same threat. I am not a strong man sir and I was scared stiff. I told him I hadn't seen anything, then, on the Sunday night after Mr Johnson's body was found, they stopped me as I was coming into work. They threatened me again and said that if I said anything that implicated them they would claim I was part of it and that I would be accused along with them. That is why I didn't tell the police what I'd really seen, sir.'

Billy seemed close to tears as he finished his story, by when the whole room had been shocked into silence by what he'd said. It took Martin a few moments to respond but when he did he was very angry.

'Mr Taylor, in the first place I am still extremely puzzled why you never gave this somewhat incredible version of events to the police when you were first asked about that night. Leaving that aside for a moment, if it was true then you're not only admitting that you witnessed a murder but that you did nothing whatsoever to help Mr Johnson.

'This does implicate you very seriously and makes you

an accessory to whatever you say happened. You're telling us that having seen what you claim you saw, you scuttled back to your ward locked the door and acted as if nothing was wrong. For God's sake, what sort of man are you? A coward or a liar?' He was almost shouting at the wretched man in the witness box who seemed to be shrinking with every word hurled at him.

Billy looked up again, his tearstained face a mix of fear and remorse. 'Sir, I have no excuse and I have cursed myself over and over again for not being able to help Mr Johnson that night. Yes I am a coward and I've had to live with that even before the war, but I swear to you that I am telling the truth now,' he sobbed, the tears streaming down his cheeks.

'Oh stand down man and get out of my sight, but do not leave the building until the police have spoken to you,' Martin said impatiently brushing him away in disgust.

Taylor stood and almost fled from the room looking neither right nor left in his anxiety to get out of it as quickly as possible. The coroner turned back to the matter in hand and stared at the jury before speaking.

'Ladies and gentlemen, what you have just heard is one of the most extraordinary depositions I think I have ever heard in an inquest. I have my own views on Mr Taylor's credibility which I will talk about at a later stage, but for now I am duty bound to urge you not to come to any hasty and possibly rash conclusions based on what he has said. This does of course throw yet another whole new light on this extraordinary affair and that now has to be looked at again, in order to help you form a real verdict at the end.

'So I am very sorry to impose on you yet again but in view

of the seriousness of what we have just heard you will understand that once again I have to adjourn this inquest. I need to give the police more time to investigate these allegations but as before, you will of course not talk about or discuss in any way what you have heard here today even with each other.'

He turned back towards Wilkins. 'Sergeant, how much time do you think you will need to investigate these allegations?' he asked.

Wilkins, hoping his face was expressionless enough to be convincingly professional and more confident than he felt, stood up. 'I don't see it taking too much time sir, I would hope that 24 hours will be sufficient.'

'I hope so, but I think I may need a little more time for reflection myself, so I will adjourn this inquest for another 48 hours.' Martin stood and swept out of the room, leaving a rising crescendo of noise behind him. Wilkins beckoned to the police constable guarding the door of the witness room.

'Roberts, I want you to go in there, take Mr Rice and Mr Race to a room and keep them from talking to each other, or anyone, until I get there. I will be with you in a few minutes but do not tell them anything yourself other than that they are to wait for me,' he ordered.

Roberts nodded and hurried into the room to carry out his instructions. Wilkins turned to Cyril Hart who was now fully aware that he could no longer keep a lid on the story as far as Hamilton was concerned and wondering how to approach it.

'What a turn-up. Tell me, when do you go to press, Cyril?' the policeman asked

'Day after tomorrow, Albert, though God only knows what I can write now. Hamilton's going to go berserk because we won't be able to keep it local now,' the reporter grinned wryly.

Wilkins looked a bit relieved. 'Good - that still gives us time. Look Cyril I am going to interview our queers now but can you get hold of Taylor and get his story. I want you to tell me whether you think he is a credible witness and see if you believe this extraordinary story he's come up with,' he asked.

'I take it from that that you didn't believe him,' Hart observed.

'To be honest mate, I just don't know. This came right out of the blue. We knew that   Taylor came back from the war as a basket case with his nerves shot to pieces even though he was on non-combatant duties. He spent a long time in a hospital just like this somewhere in Norfolk so, for God's sake how the hell did he get a job looking after patients here?'

. . . . . .

Hart nodded and slipped his notepad into his pocket as he stood up. 'OK, I'll go and check him out,' he said. The two men parted company, with Wilkins going out to talk to the two men who had been accused of murder minutes before. He found them together and puzzled by what the constable guarding them had told them about not discussing the inquest, though he hadn't gone into details about the statements made by Billy Taylor.

'Right, thank you Roberts, please stay here with Mr Race. Mr Rice, would you like to come with me please sir?' He led Alfie back into the now deserted inquest room and gestured for the mystified man to sit down.

'Mr Rice, before I go any further I have to warn you

officially that you are not obliged to say anything but anything you do say may be taken down and given in evidence. Do you understand? At this stage I am not charging you with anything, but I do have to ask you some very pertinent questions relating to the death of Mr Frederick Johnson.'

Alfie, thunderstruck at having just been cautioned and with his face rapidly draining of colour, nodded. 'Yes Mr Wilkins, I understand what you have just said –but not why you are saying it', he seemed genuinely shocked.

Wilkins smiled his reassurance. 'Can you remember what it was that you told me about the night Mr Johnson died sir?' he asked.

Rice nodded. 'Yes, of course. It was a quiet night with nothing out of the ordinary happening until the early hours when they discovered his body.'

'And how long was Mr Race with you that night?'

Rice shrugged his shoulders. 'Oh, an hour or so I suppose. As we told you at the time, he is studying for his qualifications and often comes into the wards at night to study the way patients react when they are disturbed during the night hours,' he said.

'I see, now did you at any time that night see Mr Billy Taylor?'

Rice smirked as he replied. 'What, you mean 'Silly Billy? Christ, no! Why do you ask?'

'Silly Billy?' the policeman's response, as though he'd never heard it before gave the phrase the status of a question. The other man grinned back, relaxing for the first time since he'd been brought into the room.

'Yeah – that's what all the night staff call him, because he is a bit weak in the mind, sometimes as bad as some of the patients. I suppose we are being a bit cruel because that's the way he is, but it's not said with any real malice. I understand he had a bad time during the war and that could have affected any of us. But he's harmless and does his job but to get back to your question, no. Once the shift started that night I did not see him.

There was something about the manner of the answer that came across as pretty sincere. His instincts were reluctantly telling the policeman he was listening to the truth, but there was still another issue though.

'Well, thank you for that Mr Rice. Now I am going to ask you another, very personal, question that I need you to think about very carefully before answering.' Wilkins paused for effect before continuing. 'Are you and Mr Race in a homosexual relationship?' he asked.

The response was an answer in itself. Alfie's eyes widened in horror, and a look of blind panic spread across his face. He was well aware of what exposure would mean – certainly the loss of his and Tommy's jobs and probably prison sentences too. For the first time he began to stammer as he denied the suggestion.

'No, no definitely not! How dare you ask such a thing? It's true that Tommy and I are very good mates but what you are suggesting is against the law for God's sake. We're mates and that's all. We are not woofters.'

The vehemence of his protestations told Wilkins that the suggestion had validity. Experience had taught him that most innocent men would have scoffed at and ridiculed it, rather than reacting the way Rice had done; but he also knew that guessing something was right was not proof and he had none. In any case murder was a much more serious allegation and now he decided on a full frontal attack on that alone.

'Ok Mr Rice, let's leave that to one side for the

moment. A much more serious charge has been made about you and Mr Race.' Once again he paused to let the implications of that suggestion sink in before continuing.

'Tell me about your personal relationship with Mr Taylor?'

'Why? Am I supposed to having an affair with him as well? He's just a workmate that's all and I've already told you what we all think about him.'

'I see. So you and Mr Race have never threatened him?'

'Threatened him? What about? No, why would we ever want to do that? The poor sod is to be pitied rather than bullied, though it is true that as far as Billy was concerned Fred Johnson was a bully. Why do you ask?'

Wilkins half smiled. 'Well because he has just told the inquest under oath that he saw you and Mr Race murdering Mr Johnson and that afterwards you threatened to implicate him if he told anyone.'

If the suggestion about his and Tommy Race's sexual orientation had shaken Alfie, what the policeman had just said had had an astonishing effect. The man's mouth fell open and had he not been sitting he would have staggered back with the shock.

'He said what?' he gasped, unable to get his breath back. Wilkins, watching him closely as he did so, let him calm down a little before explaining what Billy Taylor had actually told the inquest. Rice was appalled at the allegation.

'That's a bloody lie. It's bad enough that he talks about me and Tommy being queers but to say this is sheer bloody wicked nonsense. He's accused us of being murderers and blackmailers as well and that's absolute rubbish Mr Wilkins, you have to believe me.' Oddly enough, although his impassive face never betrayed it, at that moment the policeman did start to believe him.

'Actually I never said it was h : who accused you and Mr Race of homosexuality. I only said he claimed to have seen the two of you murdering Mr Johnson. Please stay there for a few minutes until I come back, please sir.'

He stood up and motioned for Rice to stay where he was, before leaving the room to go back to the room where Tommy Race was still being watched over by the silent constable.

'Thanks Roberts. Will you go back into the other room now and wait with Mr Rice while I have a quick word with Mr Race?' The constable nodded and left, leaving a frustrated and very worried nursing attendant behind.

Wilkins sat opposite him silently for a few minutes, squeezing out every moment of tension he could to make his new victim more nervous. Then, having cautioned Tommy in the same way he'd done with Alfie Rice he went through exactly the same routine. He wasn't too surprised to get exactly the same kind of reaction to every question and statement that he'd got from the other man. Fury mixed with obvious fear of the possible consequences at the suggestion of homosexuality, total denial at any suggestion of murder or of threatening Billy Taylor whom he also ridiculed. Like his friend he was in absolute shock at what Taylor had claimed he'd seen that night.

'This is ridiculous. Why should me and Alfie want to do Fred Johnson any harm, let alone do him in? I hardly knew the guy, for Christ's sake. No, no sergeant – there is nothing in this and for the life of me I can't think why Billy should be saying such things.'

'But did you not once brag to other members of the night staff about plotting to ambush Mr Johnson, kill him and make it look like suicide?' Wilkins said calmly.

Race stared at him, uncertain of just how much the detective knew and then deciding to come clean. 'Well yes, but that was just a joke. It was in poor taste I will grant you, but just a joke. It happened after Johnson had discovered Alfie and me together on the ward one night and had threatened to expose us as homosexuals. In fact he demanded money from us for his silence, and we paid him a lot of money over the months,' he admitted.

'So Johnson was blackmailing you? But you said you were not homosexuals so what could he blackmail you about?'

'Yes he was because a lot of people know that me and Alfie are close friends and he said he would say we were lovers too. That would have been difficult to repudiate because he had possession of a silly note I'd sent Alfie that, while innocent, could easily be misconstrued. Alfie had done me a great favour with a patient and I send him the note saying I could kiss him in thanks. It was entirely innocent but he'd found it under one of Alfie's log sheets when he'd been nosing around and put the squeeze on us, but I swear we did not kill him. Why would we when all we had to do was keep paying him?'

There is a great difference about the prospect of a prison sentence for homosexual activities and the possibility of a hemp rope around your neck for murder of course. However somehow Wilkins was convinced that Race and Rice, though poofs, were not killers. He stood up, thanked Tommy for his help and told him he could go before going back into the inquest room to tell Alfie Rice he could leave too.

'Look, as you well know homosexual acts are against the law but at the moment I am not interested in anything else other than the death of Frederick Johnson. Just watch yourselves and don't tempt providence because I may be back,' he told Rice before he left.

Both men left separately but Wilkins was pretty sure they would be meeting   outside to compare notes. In fact he hoped they would because he still wanted to stir things up a bit more in order to get at the truth and not just about Johnson's death. He still had the death of Harold Gillespie nagging at him, along with a growing determination to get at the truth about that one as well. Now he also had a further suggestion that Johnson was a blackmailer and the two men he'd just seen may not have been his only victims.

Still deep in thought he made his way through the long and grimy corridors of the hospital until one of the doors opened suddenly. It proved to be Dr Byron's office and as the policeman made his way towards it, the hospital director himself emerged and spotted who was approaching.

'Oh Sergeant, I'm glad you're here, do you mind if I have a word, please? He said, holding the door open invitingly. Wilkins nodded and went in to sit down opposite the hospital director at his desk.

'The point is, Mr Wilkins, I am in something of a quandary. After hearing what we heard today during the inquest I have no idea what I am supposed to do about some of my staff. Do I sack or suspend them or do I let them carry on for now? Are they murderers, queers or what? Just what am I supposed to do?' Wilkins held up his hand to stop Byron speaking.

'Dr Byron all those things have to be your decision of course but personally I think that for the moment you should carry on as normal. It might just complicate my investigation if you didn't and at this time anyway the inquest is still valid and so the allegations are sub judice. Since I am here though, what can you tell me about Taylor, Race and Rice?'

'Well, only what I know from their personnel records really. On the face of it they all seem to be pretty decent chaps. In fact Taylor had been a patient in a very similar hospital to this one up in East Anglia before he came to us looking for work. He had been very psychologically damaged during the war but had made a complete recovery and was keen to work in a mental hospital. Such people are not always easy to find.

'In any case putting his experiences as a patient to good use here seemed rather a good idea. If I am to be frank having him work here also gave me a chance to study the progress of a man who had been so damaged. He's always been a bit neurotic but very good at doing his job and is very popular with the patients.'

Wilkins nodded his appreciation for the information. 'And what about Race and Rice, sir?'

'Well I certainly don't believe they are murderers, but we have all had our suspicions about the real nature of their relationship. Still, as long as they do their job Sergeant and that particular issue doesn't become public knowledge as far as I'm concerned that's all that matters. As I just said it is not easy to recruit workers for this type of work'

'Yes, well we'll see, thank you for that. Tell me doctor, off the record. On the day your predecessor shot himself, Mr Johnson was one of the first on the scene, wasn't he?'

Byron was taken aback at the sudden and unexpected mention of Gillespie by the detective even though Cyril Hart had tipped him off that he was looking at it. 'Well yes, he was as it happens. Why do you ask?'

'Oh, I suppose the copper in me is just curious. Tell me, do you think it's possible that Johnson shot Dr Gillespie?'

The question had been very specific, deliberately timed and targeted. The reaction it provoked from Byron was almost as revealing as when he'd told Race and Rice about the murder allegations against them. Perhaps not at the same strength and certainly more controlled. The hospital director never batted an eyelid but had stiffened sufficiently for the policeman to notice. Wilkins' instincts and experience told him that that was not a natural physical reaction to such a question and inwardly he celebrated.

'You don't seem surprised, doctor?' he observed dryly. 'Surely, even at that time you must have considered the possibility that Dr Gillespie had been murdered?'

Byron shook his head. His voice remained calm and steady as he replied. 'Not for a moment. In fact it is a ludicrous suggestion and I am at a loss to know why you've made it. The inquest at the time was quite clear about its verdict'

'Yes sir I know that but, well just put it down to my copper's nose. I wasn't here at the time of course so I have had to draw conclusions from the police and newspaper records of the time. I have nothing really specific to point to, but had to look at it again now because of the possibility it could be linked with Mr Johnson's death, that's all.

'As I said he was one of the first people on the scene and from what I've been told now he was involved in blackmail too, so the suggestion of being a murderer too may not be so far-fetched. Do you think it was possible that he actually got to Dr Gillespie's room before you did that day and shot him?' Wilkins asked, standing up to go clearly indicating he wasn't expecting a lengthy answer.

Byron stood to shake his hand. 'Yes, I see your point sergeant and yes it would have been possible but to be honest I really cannot believe that of Fred Johnson. I was only along the corridor in my own room so he would have had to move very fast indeed'

As he left the room the policeman was well aware of the silent and immovable figure, brooding on what he'd just heard, still sitting at his desk. The fact that Byron had not even offered to show him out told him a great deal about the chaos he guessed was now swirling around the hospital director's mind at that moment. He was still smiling with satisfaction as he left the building.

• • • • • •

As Wilkins made his way back to the police station Cyril Hart was doing his best to explain to John Hamilton what had occurred at the inquest. He had already kept some details back from the editor but he knew he couldn't do that now, so he told him about Billy Taylor's performance in the witness box, but still not about the Olson angle.

Hamilton sat back, thinking hard. He was a journalist with many years experience so he knew they could no longer keep Fleet Street out of the story, but he was still reluctant to be pushed into headlining it too soon.

'How do you rate this man's evidence?' he asked. 'Is he reliable, or is he just a publicity seeker?'

'Well sir, the same thought had occurred to me and to be honest I think both the Coroner and Det. Sergeant Wilkins have the same doubts. What he said, and the way he said it, really bordered on the hysterical and was the total opposite of his original statement. He said he'd had pressure from his brother, who is a copper in Southend, to change his statement and tell the truth; that never really rang true either.'

'So did he change to telling the truth or from it, do you think?' Hamilton speculated. 'Look Cyril this does give us a chance to sit on the story for a little bit longer, at least until the inquest resumes, while you track this guy down and try to get some truth out of him. In the meantime write up another down-paper piece about some of the less dramatic events of the inquest so far'.

Hart didn't need any more encouragement – indeed he was almost out of the door as the editor spoke. It was only when he was halfway down the stairs that he realised that he had no real idea of where Billy Taylor was at that moment because, despite the Coroner's instructions, he had left the hospital after the inquest.

All Hart knew was that he lived somewhere in Southend and that he may, or may not, be working in the hospital that night. He decided to look into 'the asylum' himself later that evening.

Half an hour later he was at home taking his cycle clips off and appreciatively sniffing the smell of something provocative happening in the kitchen. He took his jacket off and hung it up before walking in to kiss Jane on the cheek as she stirred a saucepan bubbling away on the stove.

'Hello darling', she smiled. 'Dinner will be ready in about ten minutes, so go and wash your hands. The table's already laid,' she added pointedly. 'How did the inquest go?' she called, as he made his way over to the sink.

'Sweetheart, you would not believe what happened today. I have never heard or seen anything like it,' he said, washing and drying his hands in the sink. She listened open-mouthed with her spoon frozen in mid-stir, as he told her what had happened.

'That's incredible,' she said, suddenly remembering what she had been doing and whipping the spoon back into feverish movement again. 'What are you going to do about it all?' she asked.

'Well, Hamilton wants me to talk to Billy Taylor and Sergeant Wilkins wants me to do that as well. So later on this evening I will go to the hospital where he is scheduled to be working tonight, and try to talk to him,' he said.

'Have you spoken to Tom about all this?' she asked, referring to their mutual friend, the hospital's Deputy Director Tom Abbott.

'No, I haven't but once I have spoken to Taylor I'll be off to a Warley Parliament meeting where he is listed as a speaker tonight. I'll invite him out for a pint afterwards,' Cyril told her, his face brightening up as she put their steak pie, hot and steaming from the oven, onto the table.

'Sounds like a good idea love,' she said as she prepared to cut into the pie. 'Tell him to give my best to Susan. We're supposed to be going shopping on Saturday but I don't think she was too well yesterday.'

'Yes, of course. My goodness Jane, this smells absolutely delicious,' her husband said, gently changing the subject.

Two hours later he left the house to make his way back to the hospital, still fairly unsure of how he would interview Billy Taylor. He found the duty officer's office where Fred Olson, the temporary head of night staff, was already preparing to start his rounds. Introducing himself Hart asked whether it would be possible to speak to Billy Taylor, assuming he was on duty of course.

'Well, yes he's here tonight and is working his usual ward but I'm not sure he should be talking to the press after what he said in the inquest,' a reluctant Olson told him. 'I think I had better check with the Director first,' he added, picking up the internal telephone.

Dr Byron, still in shock from his chat that afternoon with Sergeant Wilkins, was taken by surprise at the journalist's visit and by his request to talk to Billy Taylor. But like everyone else he'd been stunned by what Taylor had said in the inquest that day and could see no harm in a professional journalist trying to get the truth, so he gave the go-ahead.

Thanking Olson, who pointed him in the direction of ward 3 where Taylor was listed as being on duty again he made his way towards it, his footsteps echoing along the corridor. Reaching it he turned the handle and walked in. Heads, most of them belonging to patients in the beds on each side of the ward, turned to look at him as he entered. At a desk at the far end sat 'Silly' Billy Taylor, but it wasn't his head that turned to see who it was because he was already facing him.

The ones that did turn to see who was coming in belonged to the two men standing by the desk talking to him – Alfie Rice and Tommy Race.

HE NEEDED KILLING, BELIEVE ME

'Fred Johnson was a bloody evil bully'

As he considered what he'd just been told, Wilkins was very thoughtful, shaking his head slowly from side to side as he put the phone down. He hadn't actually been too surprised by the information he'd just been given but he still remained a little puzzled by what Constable Peter Taylor had told him.

He'd rung Southend police station because it was where Billy Taylor's brother worked and he needed to talk to him on a copper to copper basis. Since the night attendant had said it had been pressure from his brother that had provoked his change of evidence in the witness box it was a lead he had to follow up.

PC Taylor had confirmed that his younger brother had been lodging with him and his wife since coming out of a psychiatric hospital five years earlier. He had told Wilkins that it was true that he'd urged Billy to tell the truth about what he'd seen that fateful night, but only after his brother had told him what he'd told the inquest a few days earlier. He'd not been aware what he'd actually been planning to tell the inquest.

He'd been shocked and furious when Billy had told him what he'd said and had then admitted to him that he'd actually told the truth in his original statement about nothing unusual having happened that night. He assured his Brentwood colleague that when the inquest resumed his brother would now tell the truth and revert back to his original statement. He tried to explain about his brother's problems.

'To tell the truth Sarge even as a kid Billy was always a bit of a fantasist and after what he'd seen and experienced in the Dardenelles had become even more so. He was a real head case when he was invalided home, and it took years in a hospital in Norfolk before he recovered enough to work again.

'Mary, my wife, and I took him in and gave him a home and he really did seem to be finally on the road to recovery, though slowly. Then he got the job in the Brentwood Asylum and suddenly his whole world seemed to change for the better. Having been a psychiatric patient himself he knew how the ones he was caring for felt, so he was able to respond and empathise with them. I think he was good at it and, though he still lives on his nerves, it certainly seemed to do him a lot of good too.'

Wilkins had thanked him for his information and asked why he thought his brother had made the allegations about Rice and Race in the first place.

'What do you know about paranoia, Sarge?' Taylor had asked. Wilkins had to admit he knew very little other than that some insecure people often feel they were being picked on even when they weren't.

'Yes, that's right Sarge, they do. That's what we learned from the shrinks in Norfolk who treated Billy. Often they also tend to develop paranoid hysteria about anyone around them who they hate or fear, building it all up in their minds even if it's not real. They dealt with it in

Norfolk by encouraging patients to go to drama classes to help them differentiate between reality and paranoia. I'm afraid that in that sense Billy never really recovered fully. There were three people, including the two he mentioned at the inquest in particular, that he told me about in that sense,' Taylor had explained.

'I believe he will do anything if he believed it would let him escape from what he said, or imagined, was the threat they made towards him. Billy told me he'd found out they were queers who threatened to kill him if he told anyone and got them sent to prison. Whether that was true or not I don't know, but he believed it and told me he'd created that fantasy and lied to the inquest about them because he was so frightened of them and saw a way of getting them out of his life.

'I told him he had to come clean and retract that ridiculous inquest statement and that if he didn't then I would, for his own sake if nobody else's. It was important that he faced up to reality and to his fears, imagined or otherwise and I think you will find he will do that,' the older Taylor brother had pointed out.

Wilkins had listened patiently and to a large extent sympathetically. 'Yes, well thanks a lot for that constable. To be frank I never really accepted what he told the inquest anyway and I know it worried the coroner too but I felt I had to talk to you before interviewing him again. What you are telling me now fits in with what I suspected - that your brother is still a little sick in the head. But tell me – you mentioned three people that Billy hates. Who is the other one?'

'No question about that,' Peter Taylor had said. 'It was Fred Johnson who I'm told was little short of being a bloody bully to anyone who he saw as being a weak link and my brother fitted the bill. Billy feared and hated Johnson with equal passion. As a copper myself perhaps I shouldn't say this, but if just half of what Billy told me about him was true he needed killing, believe me. But having said that I am also very sure that he never saw anyone actually doing it.'

'Tell me more!' Wilkins had pressed.

Taylor had paused before replying. 'To be blunt Mr Wilkins, the man was a thug who terrorised my brother at every opportunity. I did my own bit in France during the war too, so I do know a bit about NCOs who get carried away with their little bit of power. They're barrack-room bullies who can't handle power like proper officers are trained to. Too often they abuse it and heaven help the most vulnerable members of their squad when they do.

'Poor Billy is such – even as a kid he was never big on self-confidence and when he came back from the Dardanelles where he'd been a stretcher-bearer he was a broken man entirely. Don't get me wrong Sarge, Billy is highly strung and a little paranoid but he is no coward. Johnson was a nasty ruthless and uncaring swine who never had sympathy for people unable to stand up to him.

'In fact there was one occasion when Billy had to talk me out of coming down to the hospital and warning him off myself. Billy, and my wife, pointed out that that could have made things worse and they were probably right. No, sergeant – Fred Johnson was a bloody evil bully, pure and simple, and while I am sorry for his family, I am glad he is no longer around to make my little brother's life a misery', Taylor finished.

At the other end of the telephone line, Wilkins had smiled and thanked Peter Taylor for talking to him and putting him in the picture. Then he put the phone down and sat back in his chair to think over what he'd been told. Clearly his instincts had been right. The murder allegations about Rice and Race had been a giant red herring conceived in a confused mind, but the chat had confirmed the kind of character Johnson had been. He was a known bully and an alleged blackmailer, but was he also a killer?

PC Taylor had described him as being 'ruthless' with his team at work, but had the night supervisor been ruthless enough to kill too? Had he killed his old boss, Dr Harold Gillespie, and if so why? He'd been promoted after Gillespie's death, but only after Byron had been appointed to the position of Hospital Director himself. Wilkins had begun to suspect Johnson's involvement, now he was becoming surer of it.

Suddenly a new scenario swam into his mind. Obviously it would be ridiculous to think that Byron himself had murdered Gillespie, but had he paid Johnson to do so? He'd hinted to Byron about his suspicions on the possibility that Johnson had killed Gillespie, but up to that point had never seriously imagined that the director himself had been involved.

Mentally he began to weigh up the benefits to each of the two men that had resulted from Gillespie's death and suddenly Byron began to emerge as having been the person who had benefited most. He had not only been handed his predecessor's job on a plate, but had married his widow too.

Suddenly the director's early eagerness to establish Johnson's death as a suicide, assumed a new and rather sinister significance. Had Johnson been, not just a blackmailer, but also a contract killer who knew a secret? Just how desperate had Byron been to get Johnson's death wrapped up so neatly and so quickly? If that had been the case, then surely there could only be one reason – that he'd killed the night supervisor himself.

Was it possible that in the dead of night and perhaps after drugging him somehow, Byron himself had poured that deadly poison down Johnson's throat? Had he been driven to remove the constant threat of exposure by killing the man who was blackmailing him over Gillespie's murder?

Wilkins shook his head, trying to convince himself that his copper's instinct was playing him tricks and not really succeeding...but were they?

· · · · · ·

When Cyril Hart walked into ward 3, it was hard to guess who was the most surprised at his entrance. Was it Billy Taylor the man on duty, or was it Alfie Rice and Tommy Race who clearly had no business being there? The one thing the reporter was very sure about was that there was a very heavy atmosphere in the room, very evident even from the moment he walked through the door.

It was Billy who broke the stunned silence first. 'Hello, Mr Hart isn't it? Where did you come from? I don't think you are supposed to be here? Can I help you?' he added, somewhat lamely.

'Well, yes I hope you can and yes I do have permission to talk to you,' the reporter grinned, ignoring the questions about his right to be there as he advanced towards the group. 'But I never expected to find you two here as well,' he said, nodding towards the other two men. They should not have been there of course, but were ready with their response.

'We're here for the same reason you probably are, Mr Reporter,' Rice told him, a bitter note of defiance in his voice. 'We want to know why he accused us of killing Freddie Johnson because we never done it,' he added. Next to him Tommy Race vigorously nodded his agreement.

Hart stared back at them, his mind racing before shrugging his shoulders recognising that they probably had more right to be in the hospital that night than he did. 'To be honest, yes that is why I'm here too, but I repeat should you be?' he asked.

'Look,' a still fearful Billy Taylor interrupted. 'I will be going to the police tomorrow to tell them that I lied in the witness box, so will you all please go away and leave me in peace. You are disturbing my patients,' he added gesturing towards the beds containing some very curious and still wide awake men.

Hart looked around, gesturing the other two to be quiet as well. 'OK Billy, we will go but just tell us why you lied,' he whispered.

'I had my reasons,' Billy muttered, staring pointedly as his two colleagues, 'and I will tell them to the police and only the police,' he insisted.

Clearly there was little more to be gained in prolonging the interview so Hart, gently shepherding Rice and Race in front of him, left the ward. Outside in the passage, the three men stood together to discuss what Taylor had told them.

'Look, here Mr Hart. You heard what he said and you can bear witness to that if he changes his mind again,' Alfie said.

'Yes, of course I will if it's necessary, but more to the point – why did he say it in the first place?' the reporter queried. Both men shrugged their shoulders as if mystified and the ward attendant was just about to speak when another, more authoritive, voice broke into the conversation.

'What are you two doing here tonight?' They looked around to see the hospital director walking along the corridor towards them. Clearly Dr Byron was not a happy man.

'Mr Rice, are you on duty here tonight?' Alfie shook his head but before he could reply Byron turned to the other man. 'What about you Mr Race? You are not even supposed to be on nights in the hospital anyway. What the hell are you doing here?'

Tommy was less hesitant than his friend. 'Well doctor, as you well know allegations were made against me and Alfie – some untrue and very damaging allegations – and we came here tonight to find out why Billy said the things he did. He accused us of murder and that's why we're here and Mr Hart here will verify that a few minutes ago, in front of all of us, Billy agreed he'd lied to the inquest. He said he was going to put the record straight with the police tomorrow.'

Byron glanced at the reporter, who nodded his verification. He remained very angry however and before Cyril could say more he swung back to face the two hospital employees.

'Right you two get out and I want to see you both in my office in the morning. I warn you both now that I am in the mood to dispense with your services and that has nothing to do with the death of Mr Johnson. Unless you both have satisfactory explanations about your relationship with each other and why you, Mr Race, are apparently here some nights when you are not on duty, dismissal could well be the case. Taylor may, or may not, clear you of murder but you still need to explain why you were both here in the hospital that night and why you're both here now. Now get out, both of you', he snapped.

As the two friends turned and scurried away down the corridor towards the main door, Byron turned back to the journalist. 'Mr Hart, I was told you were here and I agreed but I don't understand why. You are not the police and while I have opened up the hospital for the purposes of the official investigation into Mr Johnson's death that did not include the right for you to come here and concoct stories for your newspaper. I will have to ask you to leave as well, if you don't mind.'

Hart began to apologise, but his words were brushed aside. He had got what he'd come for anyway, so it was time to go. 'Ok doctor, point taken and I will leave. Goodnight sir!' he said, before turning and following the other two visitors back towards the main door. When he reached it he found that Tommy Race and Alfie Rice had already disappeared into the night and it was still early so, rather than go to the Warley Parliament as he'd intended, he decided to go home.

Meanwhile outside the door of ward 3, Dr Richard Byron stood and thought for a moment. Then he turned the door handle and walked into the ward himself. Billy Taylor looked up, a worried frown on his face as he recognised that his latest visitor was his boss. The director walked up to the desk and sat down facing him, with a reassuring smile on his face.

'Don't worry Billy,' he said gently. 'I've sent them all away and they won't be bothering you again tonight.'

The ward attendant relaxed, and smiled his relief. 'Thank you sir, I am very grateful.'

'That's fine son. They have also just told me that you have retracted the allegations you made against them. Is that true, and if so why did you make them in the first place?'

Billy Taylor was clearly very embarrassed by the whole thing and was reluctant to explain further, but Byron gently insisted.

'Billy, considering you are still recovering from your own problems I have a lot of respect for the work you do here. You are a decent man son and a good conscientious worker with a great feeling for your patients; but why did you even think about making those allegations if they were not true? Did you really see or hear anything at all that night that is relevant to Mr Johnson's death?' he pressed.

Suddenly Billy began to tremble again, his face showing a mix of dismay and desperation at the unexpected question. He fidgeted with his desk papers, as he struggled to find the words.

'Well, yes sir I did, but I don't think you will want to know and I'd rather not say either, because it probably meant nothing. I made up the story about those two in the witness box because I didn't want to say, under oath, who I really saw in the corridor that night.' he murmured.

Byron put a steadying hand on the trembling ward attendant's arm to reassure him. 'Billy, anything you tell me stays with me and will go no further unless you want it to but if I am to help you, then you must tell me son. Come on – who or what was it you saw that night?'

'Dr Byron, it wasn't so much   what I saw, but who I saw coming out of Mr Johnson's office about 2 o'clock in the morning,' he said, still having to have the details dragged out of him inch by inch.

'Who, Billy? Who did you see, son?'

'Look sir – like I said, I made up all that stuff about Tommy and Alfie to give me time to think and to divert attention from the person I really did see because I was so confused. Mr Johnson often entertained women visitors during the night, and he was very popular with the ladies,'

'Yes, yes Billy, so I've heard. So who was it you saw that night? Byron pressed him testily.

The ward attendant looked across the desk, inner turmoil written all over his face as he struggled to decide whether or not to reveal the identity of who had been Fred's mystery visitor that night. Finally he appeared to make up his mind and took a deep breath before responding.

'I am sorry sir, believe me I am, but please remember you have forced this out of me. It was your wife sir, Mrs Byron,' he said.

$$\bullet \quad \bullet \quad \bullet \quad \bullet \quad \bullet \quad \bullet$$

Albert Wilkins wasn't surprised when the desk sergeant announced he had a visitor that morning. He'd already had a brief telephone conversation with Cyril Hart about what had happened in the hospital the previous night, so when Billy Taylor was shown in he knew what it would be about. He gestured Billy towards a chair and offered him a cup of tea.

'No, no thank you Mr Wilkins – I won't stay long. I need to go home and get some sleep, it's been a long night,' he explained. 'The fact is sir, I have a confession to make.'

'Well, police stations are the place for confessions Mr Taylor,' the detective smiled cynically. 'Are you going to tell me your evidence at the inquest, in which you implicated two men in a serious allegation, was just a pack of lies?' he added.

He noted that Billy's hands were shaking as he waited for the ward night attendant to respond. 'Yes, sir! That is exactly what I was going to say and I am so so sorry. I have already apologised to Mr Race and Mr Rice and I am here to formally retract that allegation,' the man's voice was quavering as he made his confession.

Wilkins sat and stared hard at him for a long time before he spoke. 'Why did you lie, Billy?' he asked.

'Personal reasons,' Taylor said hesitantly, fidgeting on his chair.

'Not good enough, son. Why did you make that allegation, and did you really see anything at all unusual that night?'

'I will be honest Mr Wilkins. Rice and Race are bullies who have been threatening to kill me if I exposed them for what they are. What I said at the inquest was just a spur of the moment thing that I thought might get them off my back, but it was a silly thing to say and I am so sorry. I told my brother and he was furious with me' Billy said.

The policeman had decided to be relentless. 'Exposed them for what they are? What do you mean by that?' He stared meaningfully at the uncomfortable man squirming in front of his desk.

'Everyone at the hospital knows they are queers and that Tommy Race is always visiting Alfie's ward at night. I saw them cuddling and kissing each other one night last year by accident and they've been threatening me ever since,' Billy said.

Wilkins, now feeling desperately sorry for the forlorn figure facing him, sat back in his chair

'Alright Mr Taylor, you can go. I will inform the coroner that you have retracted your evidence and why. It will be up to him if he wants to take it further,' Wilkins dismissed his visitor with a wave of the hand.

After he'd gone the policeman sat and thought hard. He remembered his conversation that morning with Cyril Hart, who'd told him how the hospital director himself had arrived on the scene the previous night when he'd been talking to Race and Rice. Something in him was telling him that Byron's arrival at that moment had been significant; but for the moment he couldn't think why.

In fact at that very moment the object of his thought was sitting a mile away across town at his own desk in the hospital, wrestling with his emotions. It was bad enough having to deal with the possibility of Marion being Johnson's lover but it also meant that if Billy Taylor's words had been true she'd been the last person to see him alive. Surely to God, Marion could not have administered the fatal dose of poison but if she had, how and why?

He loved his wife passionately. After all he'd even murdered her first husband so he could win her – and the thought of her betraying him with the likes of Fred Johnson turned his stomach. He'd known the man to be a blackmailer and was aware of his reputation with the women but he'd never remotely considered the possibility that he was being cuckolded by the ex-soldier with a reputation as a ladies man.

Quite suddenly he had another flash of inspiration. Supposing Marion had discovered somehow that Gillespie had been murdered, but thought it had been Johnson who had pulled the trigger that Christmas morning?

She was a highly intelligent and a very strong person, more than capable of having worked that out. If she had, and then felt that the murderer of her first husband, a man she had genuinely loved, had got away with it she could be very likely to take matters into her own hands. Had she pretended to fall for Johnson's charms in order to get close enough to him to lull him into a false sense of security before killing him?

His mind went back to what Billy Taylor had told him – how he'd seen her leaving Johnson's office wiping her hands on a towel. Had she been wiping her hands free of the Lysol that she'd just poured down Johnson's throat? But how would she have immobilised him? Even as he worried about it, he knew the answer. He himself had prescribed some sleeping tablets for Marion after she'd complained about some insomnia. He remembered having slept very well himself that fateful night so had she drugged his bedtime cocoa too so that her absence from their bed wouldn't be noticed?

He was convincing himself more and more. My God! It was all becoming clear now. Marion had put some into Johnson's mug of tea while under the pretext of letting him seduce her. Then, once he was in a deeply drugged state she'd gone into the hospital to get her revenge on the killer of her first husband. Byron sat with his head in his hands as he realised that the woman he loved so deeply now stood a good chance of going to the gallows and all because he had killed her first husband.

He had sworn Billy Taylor to secrecy about seeing Marion Byron that night, but he knew he would never be able to depend on the silence of a man who was almost a basket case himself. He would never challenge Marion himself but he also knew that he could not let her hang and on the face of it there was only one way to prevent that. He looked at his watch. The inquest was due to resume in an hour and he had much to do before that. He reached out for his telephone and made a call.

• • • • • •

John Martin was not in the best of moods when he walked back into the inquest later that morning to re-open it after having spoken to Albert Wilkins. Impatience and frustration showed in his voice as he addressed the jury.

'Ladies and gentlemen. I know that you must be feeling as angry as I am that so much time and energy has been spent and wasted on this enquiry. I have now been told that Mr William Taylor has now withdrawn the extraordinary allegations he made about two other members of staff killing Mr Johnson. Why he made them in the first place is still unclear but I do understand that his judgement may have been impaired because his own mental stability is not of the strongest.

'I will be advising the police to take no further action as far as Mr Taylor is concerned because I suspect he is as much in need of psychiatric help as many of the patients in this hospital. I do not see any purpose in pursuing him further. He may find his situation in the hospital changed from worker to patient, but that will be up to the hospital authorities.

'However I am also now told that I need to recall Dr Richard Byron to the witness stand so that he can make a further statement. Once again ladies and gentlemen I apologise to you for the circus that this hearing has become and believe me I am as angry and frustrated as you must be. I trust it will not need to be extended much further. Clerk of the court, please recall Dr Richard Byron.'

As Martin finished his remarks, the clerk rose to carry out the instruction and in a few moments the Hospital Director made his way back to the witness box.

'Dr Byron, you do know you are still on oath?' the coroner asked. Byron nodded his agreement. 'I understand you want to give more evidence and also want to change a previous statement.' Martin continued.

'Yes sir, I do. The fact is that Frederick Johnson was already dead when the Lysol was poured down his throat. I know that because I poured it' As Byron spoke the words Martin hammered down his gavel again and again to stop the gasps and shouts from the public gallery.

'Dr Byron, I think you had better explain,' he glowered at the witness as he spoke.

'Thank you sir, I will. The fact is that shortly after 2am on the night in question I had an internal phone call from Mr Johnson telling me he was feeling unwell. By the time I got to his office he'd collapsed in his chair. I examined him and found that he was already dead from what looked to me like a heart attack.

'I admit that that was the moment of course I should have called the police even at that hour, but I was confused and bitter. The man was already dead from natural causes yet he'd left a suicide note, so it was clear he had intended to take his own life – probably by drinking the Lysol I found near his body but had suffered his heart attack before doing so.

'It was purely a spur of the moment thing to do and I regret it to this day, but when I read the note I opened his mouth and poured the stuff down his throat. It was a stupid thing to do and I knew it, but by the time I'd done it I was past caring.'

'Why? What does the note say and where is it?'

If he was already dead he could not have swallowed anything.

Coroner Martin interrupted. The suddenness of the question appeared to throw Byron off track for a second or two and he hesitated before replying.

'Sir, I had a moment of pure hatred for that man and I have the note here. I took it and hid it in my office' he said taking a sheet of paper from his pocket and handing it to the clerk. 'In it he confesses to the murder of my predecessor and very good friend, Dr Harold Gillespie. The thought of him having a natural death when he should have hung, sent me momentarily insane with rage. As for the rest of the note, all it says was goodbye to his wife and kids but not why he was going to kill himself.'

Martin banged his hand down onto his desk again, as much to stop the hospital director in his tracks as to stifle the rising murmurings of shock at what he'd said.

'Dr Byron, for God's sake man, do you know what you are saying? Are you well sir? This is something quite new even in this already very complex and extraordinary case. You, the director of this hospital and a professional man of medicine are confessing to interfering with a sudden death from natural causes. To make matters worse you are making an accusation about the dead man that has never been raised before. Doctor, would you like to take a few minutes to reconsider what you have just said?'

Byron had made his mind up and shook his head. 'No sir!' He said, before going on to explain about the morning Gillespie had died.

Conveniently leaving out his own role in the murder he said he had always been suspicious about the speed with which Johnson had arrived upstairs that fateful morning, almost as if he was already there. He claimed he'd always had the suspicion that it had been Johnson who had pulled the trigger that day, but was unable to prove it. Then, shortly after he'd been appointed to the job of Hospital Director, Johnson had come to him to demand promotion as well.

'He said that if I didn't give him the top job he would implicate me in Dr Gillespie's death somehow. He knew that even a hint of such a thing could destroy my career so I went along with his demands, though in fairness he always did a good job as supervisor and in fact would probably have been promoted sooner or later anyway. I know that what I did the night he died was a silly and spiteful thing to do but it was spontaneous revenge on behalf of my poor friend.

'After I'd done it I decided to leave things as they were until the morning. I arranged his body to look as though he was asleep, took the suicide note and went back to bed. It was wrong sir, I knew that even at the time, but it is what happened,' he said.

He glanced across the room to where Marion was sitting, and saw that her face had gone as white as a sheet and she was staring wide-eyed at him. At that moment he knew that he'd been right – she really had murdered Johnson in revenge, thinking he'd killed her first husband. Now he was sure that he had to protect her at all costs, which was why only an hour or so before he had typed out the alleged suicide note and signed it with a reasonable copy of Johnson's signature that he'd found on some old worksheets.

'Dr Byron', the coroner's angry voice dragged him back to reality. 'You sir, are a medical practitioner and what you have told us here today is a disgrace to the profession and the oath you took. Your conduct has been reprehensible and will be reported to the BMA as well as to the police. Now kindly get out of my sight,' he snapped.

As Byron stood up and, without a glance in any direction, walked out of the door John Martin turned back to the Clerk of the court and asked him whether any other witnesses were scheduled to speak.

'Any more little surprises?' he asked cynically. On being assured there were none he turned his attention back to the jury.

'Ladies and gentlemen. I daresay that, like me, you are confused and angry about the way this inquest has developed. We have seen a previously unknown wife emerge from the woodwork and heard the most lurid allegations about unnatural sexual relationships between witnesses, as well as many other accusations that clearly need more investigation by the police. We will also need a new autopsy on Mr Johnson's body to establish the truth about his death, for this morning we have heard the most terrible admission of all.

'The director of this hospital no less, one of the most important psychiatrists in the land and who carried out the original autopsy, has told us that he has been lying from the start and that he interfered with evidence. By any standards this makes the accusations made by one of the other people working here, look quite mild. This whole matter will now be placed into the hands of the police for further investigation and I do not believe that I can, in fairness, ask for your tolerance any longer.

'You have been patient and attentive and I have no doubt that had this been a normal inquest you would have arrived at a fair and reasonable conclusion. But it has not been normal by any means and it is my intention now to direct you towards a verdict that will, I believe, eventually open the way for this whole macabre tale to be cleared up once and for all.

'So I ask you to formally return an Open Verdict on the death of Mr Frederick Johnson – a verdict which will allow a more thorough investigation to take place. Do you want to have more time to consider that?' he asked.

There was a brief moment of hushed conversation between the jury members before one of them stood up. 'Sir, the general consensus here is that we do not need time to consider this any further. In general we agree with you and as you suggest, we would like to declare an Open Verdict on the death of Mr Johnson,' he announced, before sitting down again.

'Thank you all for that, ladies and gentlemen and also for your attendance and amazing patience here today and on previous days. I will now register your decision and enter it into the record,' Martin said, standing up to go.

As he left the room the buzz of chatter rose again. Wilkins walked over to the press bench where Cyril Hart, head in hands, was once again puzzling about how to report this latest twist in the story. He looked up at the policeman approached.

'Albert, did you know what Dr Byron was going to say?' the reporter asked.

Wilkins nodded his head. 'Yes, he phoned me this morning. What did you make of his story Cyril?'

'Bloody ridiculous, to be honest,' Hart replied. 'He's hiding something for sure.'

'That's what I think too, but now I can at least arrest and question him further to get at the truth of both deaths, though I suspect the Gillespie case will be a dead issue now because one of our potential suspects is dead and the other under suspicion of killing him' the policeman grinned. He glanced over to where Marion Byron had been sitting, but there was just an empty chair.

In fact the lady was in her husband's office, furiously demanding to know what was going on. 'Richard, what is this nonsense? You have wrecked your career for God's sake. Why? You never killed Mr Johnson so why make up that ludicrous story about him having a heart attack and then doing what you said you did? Whatever has possessed you darling?'

He looked up at her. 'I think you know why darling. I did it to protect you because I love you so very much,' he said, tears streaming down his face.

'Protect me? Are you mad? What is that supposed to mean? Richard, for God's sake tell me what's going on in that sick mind of yours,' she was angrily shouting at him as she banged her fist on the desk.

He stood up and tried to take her in his arms. 'Marion look, the police will be here to arrest me shortly. I know you killed him and I know how and why you did it. You drugged him and then poured the Lysol into him while he was unconscious; but don't worry sweetheart, I will protect you, even if it means going to prison myself,' he said.

She could hardly believe her ears. 'What? I killed him? Richard, what the hell are you talking about?'

He looked up at her standing over him and realised it was time for him to tell her that he had guessed her ghastly secret.

'Marion, I think you found out that Johnson had shot Harold and plotted your revenge, because I know how much you loved him. You let him get close enough to you to think he was about to seduce you and somehow you slipped him the sleeping tablets I prescribed for you. Then, once he was unconscious you poured the Lysol into his throat.' As he spoke he found himself gripping her arms staring up at her horrified and speechless face.

'Darling, please don't worry,' he confided. 'I will stick to my story about finding him dead in the office and no one will be able to prove otherwise. It will cost me my job and perhaps I might even have to go to prison for a couple of years but after that we can make a fresh start somewhere else, on the continent or in Canada perhaps.'

He suddenly became aware that she was looking at him with a strange new expression, one of disbelief and contempt, on her face. 'Richard, what are you talking about? Are you totally insane, man? You are telling me that Harold was murdered by Johnson and that you think I killed him in revenge? You really are crazy, if you think that.'

The vehemence of her reaction and emphatic denial suddenly began to raise doubts in Byron's mind. He suddenly remembered that it had been Billy Taylor's fanciful imagination that had planted the suggestion of Marion's involvement in Johnson's death into his brain. Even as the realisation of his own stupidity sank in, there was a knock on the door and Detective Sergeant Albert Wilkins walked into the room.

At that moment Richard Byron knew he had to confess – but to what?

WE DIDN'T NEED TO KILL HIM

'He was my Uriah Heep'

Byron stared up at the detective as Marion stormed out. The psychiatrist in him enabled him to do so without showing any emotion but he was thinking hard, desperately looking for a way out of the allegation about to be put to him. At all costs he had to prevent Marion from knowing his role in her first husband's death. Finally he came to a decision.

'Mr Wilkins. I know you have been suspicious about the death of my predecessor and you are right to be so, but it was not by my hand. He was killed by Frederick Johnson and I feel very guilty about it because in a sense he did it for me.'

He paused for a moment or two, his mind still trying to put together a cohesive and credible story. 'Johnson and I got to know each other when he was just a member of the night staff and I was deputy director. As you know he was an old soldier but although our paths did cross at one time in France it wasn't until he came here to work that we really met. We had many memories of those dreadful days to share and gradually I became aware that his feelings towards me were much different from mine   to him. For some reason he began to – well, for want of a better word – crawl round me. Have you ever read David Copperfield, Mr Wilkins?' The policeman nodded.

'Well there's a character called Uriah Heep, whose creepy subservience covered an evil determination to succeed at any cost. Frederick Johnson, without my intending it, became my Uriah - always anxious to please and I believe that led to the death of Dr Gillespie.'

The look on Wilkins' face by now was one to behold. On the one hand he was delighted that a different truth was coming out, but puzzled over the line it was taking. Without speaking, he waited for Byron to continue.

'Over the course of months Johnson and I had several casual discussions about the philosophy of the hospital and somehow he picked up that if I was in charge things might change. He had some differences with the Director about the treatment of patients - Johnson was an old soldier and had a less sympathetic way of treating them. Dr Gillespie had caught him manhandling a patient and threatened him with instant dismissal if he did it again.

'Oh, please don't get me wrong Mr Wilkins – I don't believe Johnson killed him simply because of that. No, I think it was just one of the thoughts festering in his mind that, allied to his misplaced loyalties to me, led to it.'

Wilkins was getting a little impatient. 'I hear what you are saying doctor, but exactly what did happen on the day Dr Gillespie died?'

'I'm coming to that.' What he'd said so far had been reasonably close to the truth, but now Byron had to venture further into the riskier world of fiction. So, taking a deep breath, he launched into his explanation of what happened that Christmas day.

He said he'd been in his room shaving when he'd heard the shot and by the time he'd wiped his face clean and put his dressing gown on, a few seconds had elapsed. As he'd raced along the corridor he'd fancied he'd seen a figure leaving Gillespie's room, but it had all happened so fast he wasn't sure. By the time he'd reached it Marion was already screaming and Johnson was already at the top of the stairs apparently on his way up.

'Later I realised that what he'd done was quickly turn on the stairs and come back because he'd heard me running along the corridor. We went into Gillespie's room together and found his body and a suicide note. I assumed he'd killed himself, and believed that for a few months.

'Then, after I became hospital director the position of head night supervisor became vacant and Johnson came to me brazenly admitting he'd shot the director. He had the shotgun because, from time to time, Gillespie used to get him to clean the weapon. He told me he'd killed Gillespie and planted the suicide note, which had been forged, because I'd asked him to.

'I was staggered. It became clear that he'd totally mis-understood our relationship and was convinced I wanted Gillespie dead so I could take over the hospital. I was horrified and threatened to call the police; but he pointed out that while he had no apparent motive, I did. Apart from the job he also knew that Mrs Gillespie and I had had an affair, so any investigation would inevitably point at me.

'Johnson was a nasty and evil blackmailer, Mr Wilkins. He said that unless I gave him the supervisor's job, some occasional money and turned a blind eye if he brought a woman into the hospital at night, he would see to it that the Gillespie death investigation was reopened, with me as the main suspect.

'Think about it. I now have Gillespie's job and am

married to his wife, so you can imagine how that would have looked. I love Marion, and I could not bear it if the slightest suspicion, however unfounded, fell on me and hurt her so I went along with his demands. That is how it all happened and in a way I'm glad it's all out in the open now,' he finished.

Wilkins sat watching him, wondering about the story he'd just been told and how much truth there was in it. At least it had confirmed his suspicions that the previous hospital director's death had not been suicide, but whether it had happened in the way Byron had described was another matter. The policeman in him kept nagging that it wasn't, but for the moment he couldn't see what else he could accomplish.

'Thank you Dr Byron. So now can you tell me how Frederick Johnson died?' he asked.

• • • • • •

The intensity of the morning sunshine streamed through the open window, playing on her face and making her blink as she began to open her eyes. Through the window the persistent calls of the seagulls and the shouts of the native fishermen mingling with the thunder of the surf sweeping up onto the beach below their veranda, woke her.

For a moment or two she just lay there, the cooling draft of an offshore breeze teasing her nostrils with the faint aromas of spices she would never have enjoyed in her earlier life. She opened her eyes fully and turned her head to find those of her husband staring at her from the other pillow.

'Good morning, darling.' She leaned across to kiss him,

revelling in the touch of his hand and arm pulling her towards him until their lips met.

'Morning Em, I take it you slept well,' he smiled and they kissed again with a passion neither had ever experienced before.

'Very well thank you darling. This may be my second marriage, well my first one really because of Fred turning out to be a bigamist, but it's definitely my first honeymoon and I love it. I feel like a young bride should feel,' she said, turning over onto her back invitingly as he cuddled and caressed her willing body.

'Well sweetheart, I'm so happy that you're happy,' he whispered. 'It makes everything worthwhile, though there were a few moments when I thought we'd never make it? It was such a strain, especially during the inquest. It seems a long time ago now but it seemed to go on and on so much I was starting to think it would never end, and certainly never thought it would end the way it did.'

'Yes,' she murmured, 'I was thinking about it all yesterday and especially about poor little Tilly. I was really cruel to her and I regret that because she didn't deserve it. She was as big a victim of Fred's as I was and so very young. Now her little boy will grow up probably never knowing he has a half brother and sister at the other end of the world. I do hope they are both alright.'

His grip around her tightened reassuringly. 'Well, Tilly's parents are bringing the child up as their own now sweetheart, so actually Tilly did alright. Come to that apart from us a lot of other people didn't do badly out of that inquest either. That nosy reporter got a book out of it and a new job with the Daily Sketch in Fleet Street. That copper Wilkins did alright as well. He was promoted and transferred to Scotland Yard's murder squad because he solved the mystery of Fred's death - well at least everybody thinks he did – and Dr Gillespie's,' he grinned.

He lay for a moment or two, his mind still reliving those frantic and sometimes frightening weeks when it could have all gone so wrong, before turning to reassure her again. 'We're in the clear Em and a long long way from Brentwood' her husband told her. Then he grinned as another piece of irony crossed his mind.

'Mind you, if we'd known about Fred's first marriage and him being a bigamist it might have saved his life. It meant he had no real hold on you so we didn't need to do him in' he murmured, pulling her even closer to him and kissing her again.

She laid her head happily on his shoulder with his arm around her, both of them oblivious of everything other than each other and preparing to start a new day in their exciting new world. Neither of them was ever going to let the memory of Fred Johnson and the manner of his end bother them again.

'Darling, it's all worked out for the best,' he told her. We've got a new life, a wonderful new home with servants to wait on us hand and foot with an ayah for the children and I've got a new job here in Singapore. It's a long way from Europe where that German bloke Hitler seems to be causing more problems and with that Spanish civil war stirring everybody up as well.

'We're safe out here with the British navy and army looking after us in the colonies. Even if Europe went to war again it won't affect us out here. Our children will be able to grow up in safety away from all that, so stop worrying sweetheart'. He cupped her face in his hands and stared hard at her.

'Emma, we're on our honeymoon and when I start

managing the rubber plantation next month we'll have that new life we risked everything for. The children will be going to a good English school and I have every intention of making you happy and perhaps even raising our own family too,' he added.

'Oh, darling I am happy, thanks to you', she said snuggling ever closer to him, but she was clearly still puzzled about what had happened and finally she could hold it back no longer.

'I wonder why Dr Byron admitted killing Fred. We know it was us but with most people thinking it was the queers, why do you think he confessed to a murder we did?' she murmured.

He thought back and quietly thanked the drama classes that had not only led to his meeting Emma after a children's pantomime, but then playing the role he did. One that had enabled him to create a maze of mystery with murder at its heart.

'I've no idea Em,' he lied. 'But if it was true that Fred shot Dr Gillespie I suppose it was only justice. As for the poofs they're both doing time and that was nothing to do with us anyway. Look love, Byron told the inquest that he'd found Johnson already dead from a heart attack and that he'd poured the Lysol into him as a kind of weird revenge for seducing his wife; but when they did a second autopsy they found it really had been the Lysol that had killed him.

'Yes, they found him guilty of murder but they did say it was while the balance of his mind was disturbed, so at least they didn't hang him. Instead of running a lunatic asylum he's in Broadmoor now instead, but at least he's alive and we don't have his death on our conscience as well.

'Come on love, you got enough compensation from the hospital for what he said he'd done to Fred to set us up for our new life out here. I mean that was a real bonus we didn't expect, so stop worrying Em.'

She stroked his cheek affectionately. 'Yes, I suppose in a way it's a relief about poor old Dr Byron. I wouldn't have liked it on my conscience if they'd hung him for something we did,' she said.

'No Em, neither would I but if the inquest hadn't got itself so confused with so many different stories coming at it from all angles it might just as easily have been us they focussed on instead of him. Nobody ever asked you about the sandwiches you gave Fred that night, so they could not have suspected the chutney was full of your sleeping powders. I never came under suspicion because nobody knew about us and they never have thought me capable of murder,' he lay back and smiled reflectively again.

'I must admit I was a bit scared when I went into his office that night, because I didn't know whether he'd actually eaten the sandwiches or not, but he was out like a light. He never moved a muscle while I put the straight jacket on him to make it easy to pour the stuff out of his own tea-mug into his mouth with the force-feeding tubes we kept on the wards.'

He didn't mention Johnson's desperate struggle when the pain had woken him to find he was restrained and being force-fed with the Lysol, or how he'd had to gag him to muffle his screams of agony. Nor did he mention the panicky moments afterwards as he took the straight-jacket off Johnson to take back, along with the ex-soldiers mug, to his own ward in the dead of night after rearranging the dead man in the way he was found later that morning.

She stretched and embraced him again. 'You're

absolutely right darling. We must do our best to forget him and what happened - the brute had it coming anyway. Fred Johnson is my past, my children have a new daddy who loves them and I am enjoying my new name and building our new life together.

'Thank you so much my darling for making it possible. We are going to just love it here, it's where we belong and I just love being Mrs Billy Taylor.'

• • • • • •

Note: Five years later, on February 7th 1942 the Japanese invaded Singapore. Its garrison surrendered a week later and western foreigners were interned.

Should the antopsy have found traces of the sleeping powder?

Lightning Source UK Ltd.
Milton Keynes UK
UKOW041757150413

209261UK00001B/5/P